Hush

Hidden Family
Hush Series

BLUE SAFFIRE

Perceptive Illusions Publishing
Bayshore, New York

Blue Saffire/Perceptive Illusions Publishing Inc.
PO BOX 5253
Bayshore, NY 11706
www.BlueSaffire.com

Ordering Information:
Quantity sales. Special discounts are available on quantity purchases by corporations, associations, and others. For details, contact the "Special Sales Department" at the address above.

Hush 3: Hidden Family/ Blue Saffire. -- 1st ed.
ISBN 978-1-941924-33-4

At the end, can you say you gave it your all?
Yes? Then you earned it.

—BLUE SAFFIRE

PREFACE

From the Shadows

Michael

Opening my pocket watch, I step from the shadows. The asshole lying in the bed before me lets out a gasp. It's a familiar sound. One I have grown to expect.

I expect it almost as much as I expect the fear that begins to permeate the room. It's always the same. To them, I'm the man who makes them hush. They don't know that I'm only a carbon copy of him.

My brother has trained me to be just like him. Or at least that was his initial plan. I've become like him, but I'm the subdued version. I bring the sound of peace before I end it all in a hush.

I lift my finger and place it over my lips. It's his only warning of what's to come other than the knowledge of who he believes I am. I then wink at him as a smile comes to my lips.

He deserves this. You don't order a hit on the wife of another man and think it will be as simple as going to bed and having a good night's sleep every night. He chose the wrong man and that has consequences.

"Shh," I hiss quietly.

As "Für Elise" plays, I lift my gun with the silencer on the end and pull the trigger. As soon as his brains are covering the headboard and sheets around him, I turn, close my watch, and take my leave as if I were never here.

I have done what I came here for. I turned off his clock. His time has come to an end.

As I climb into my car, I pull my phone and send a text to my brother to let him know the job has been completed. As I await his reply, I open a picture I was sent earlier this evening. I smile as I run my finger over the screen.

"You're doing so well. I couldn't be prouder of you. It's better this way," I whisper.

My phone buzzes with my brother's reply. I grin and nod. All in a good night's work.

Uri: *Record timing. Well done.*

Me: *I am heading for the plane.*

Uri: *Take some time for yourself. I'm still smoothing things out here for you. You have other problems to solve as well.*

I sigh and lean my head back. He hasn't told a lie. I have many things to think about and fix.

I can't move forward until I deal with the past. However, it's hard to deal with something when you don't know where to begin. I'm a problem solver, but this problem seems to have no solution.

"Not one I can see," I mutter to myself.

Shaking my head, I start the car and head for my flight. I took this job as a way to run from all I had on my plate. I don't know that it's time to take Uri up on his suggestion. I still question so much and still have no answers.

CHAPTER ONE

You're my Brother

Michael

I promised Nico and Annabella that when I turned eighteen, I would find our older brother. I might be the youngest, but I'm skilled at finding people and things when I want. I wasn't sure if it would happen at first.

Then my mother started to act odd during certain times of the month. I decided to follow her to see where she was going and why she would return looking so upset. As if she had lost someone or her heart had been broken.

I never thought she would lead me right to my brother's doorstep. I've known where to find Uri for a month now. I've been working up the courage to meet him face to face.

"You can do this. Just follow him and tell him who you are," I mumble to myself as I follow him up this dark, secluded street.

I'm in awe of Uri. I've been following him since I found my mother with him. Once she returned home, I followed his every move. I have learned a lot about my brother.

His life is very different from ours. He is connected to a lot of dangerous men. I can't help but think about how different my life could have been if I had been raised by whoever raised him.

Anything other than being raised by Roberto Zuko had to be better. I still don't understand why Uri has been kept away from us. Nico and Anna remember him more than I do.

I was only one year old when our father was killed, but I do remember there being one more of us. I remember him playing with me as I learned to walk and then he was just gone.

"Why are you bloody following me?"

The sound of a gun cocking as it's pressed to the back of my head fills my ears seconds before the cold steel placed flush against my head registers in my skull. I close my eyes and freeze. How did he get behind me?

"Don't shoot. I'm your brother, Michael," I plead.

"I know who you are. That's not the question I asked."

I pause to think over the question he did ask me. My heart is racing, and my mind goes blank for a second. If he knows who I am, why does he have a gun to my head?

"I wanted to meet you. We all do. We don't understand why you're being kept from us."

"You have come here on your own? You are either very smart or very stupid," he says.

I note that he has an accent that's much different from mine. It's not Italian like the rest of ours. It has a hint of Italian mixed with a British one.

He removes the gun, allowing me to breathe. I still don't move. I'm fighting with everything in me not to show my fear.

"Turn around," he commands in Italian.

I turn to face him and put my hands up. I suck in a breath as we come face to face. Nico and I look a lot alike, but my brother standing before me now could pass for my twin. Even though there is a five-year age gap, he looks just like me.

The same blond hair, the same blue eyes, we have the same exact face and build. We are almost the same height. Give it a few years and I might catch up to him.

It's like looking into a mirror. However, the scowl on his face is not the same as the expression I have in this moment. I give him a slight smile, wanting to pull him in for an embrace.

"I will ask you this once. If you don't give me the answer I want to hear then I will shoot you and make you disappear."

I nod as I lick my lips and wait for his question. This is not at all how I thought this would go. I wasn't expecting him to be so … cold?

"How did you find me?"

"I followed Mama. She always looks so heartbroken after her visits with you. I noticed and decided to follow her. I didn't know it would lead me to you. I've been searching for you since I turned eighteen."

"You have found me, now what?"

I shrug. "I would like to hug you. After that, maybe we could talk and get to know each other. You are my brother. I want to get to know you. Nico and Annabella miss you. We only want to be a part of your life."

"Have you ever thought that it's safer for you not to be in touch with me?"

"But why? You are my brother. Why wouldn't it be safe to get to know you?"

He furrows his brows as he looks back at me. He's silent for a moment and I don't think he's going to answer me. My shoulders slump. I envisioned this going totally different.

Without a word, he walks by me, leaving me here lost in my own confusion. I don't know what to tell Nico and Anna. I know they will be as disappointed as I am.

"Michael, you're not proving to be smart. You're going to have to do better than this, mate. I move, you move. Let's go," he calls over his shoulder, to my surprise.

I suck in a deep breath and rush after him. I fall in step with him and peek out of the corner of my eye at my brother. Uri wraps his arm around my shoulders and gives it a squeeze.

"It's nice to see you again, Michael. You were just learning to walk the last time I saw you."

I chuckle. "Yes, I remember that."

"You do?"

"I do. We have never forgotten you."

He snorts. "You might wish someday that you did."

"Never."

"We shall see."

CHAPTER TWO

Training

Michael

A year later ...

I lie on my back, looking up at the ceiling as I pant for air. I do believe Uri is trying to make me regret the day I found him. There is training and then there is this.

He is kicking my ass unapologetically. This is what I asked for, so I'm going to suck it up and continue. When I learned what my brother does for our uncle Nic, I wanted to learn.

I wanted to be a part of the side of our family I don't know. I was hurt to know Uri has been connected to our father's family all this time. My mother made it seem like they didn't want anything to do with us.

However, listening to Uri speak of our grandfather, who he was with before our uncle Nic, has made me wonder if he was truly any better off than we were. I couldn't imagine having to live like that. Our grandfather was a monster.

"Get up, Michael. You are a Donati. We don't quit," Uri growls at me.

His words are like fuel. I hate that I've been raised with the last name Zuko. My father was a Donati, and so am I.

I leap to my feet, ready to keep going. Sweat soaks my hair and the back of my T-shirt. I have never been a quitter, and I don't intend to start now.

"That's better, mate. Show me you have some bloody balls," he taunts.

"You say that as if I haven't been holding my own," I say to him in Italian.

"English. You make it too easy to learn the truth about you. English will throw your enemies off," he snaps.

I roll my eyes and keep moving forward, holding my hands up. Uri continues to come at me hard. I fight back, blocking and countering as fast as I can. I have gotten taller, and we are now nearly evenly matched.

With all the training and conditioning, I have more power and stamina than I did when I came to him at eighteen. What a difference a year can make. We have become closer—at least as close as Uri will allow.

"Stop leaving your right open," he bites out.

I grunt and nod. It's all I need to do. He's not asking me for my feedback. He's telling me how to be better.

I appreciate the growth we have. I understand Uri's need to create distance. Given our upbringing, I can't say I blame him. The one thing I respect about my brother most is that he won't allow me to speak ill of our mama.

I can tell he has his issues with her as I do, but he won't allow me or Nico to voice them without knocking us on our ass. Nico and Annabella were eager to reunite with Uri as well.

He was reluctant at first, but my siblings would not be denied. They followed me as I did our mother, much to Uri's annoyance. We didn't understand at first.

Nico had even challenged him. That didn't go as Nico thought it would. Uri ended up kicking his ass.

However, it was after Nico showed up on Uri's doorstep that he told us that our mother believed we were in danger by interacting with him. It's the reason no one is to know he's our brother. He has been training me in secret for almost a year.

"It's a good thing you're better with a gun than you are with your fists," he snorts at me.

"Are you saying I should shoot you?" I taunt back.

"You wouldn't get your finger on the trigger before I took your life instead."

I scoff and continue to circle him. He is right. I've taken well to firearms. Pistol or sniper rifle, I have mastered those. Fighting hand to hand is where I need to get stronger.

I've been on a few jobs with Uri to learn more about the hitter business. He was reluctant even to train me. It took weeks to talk him into it.

If I hadn't been jumped one night while sneaking to see him, he might not have ever agreed. After watching what he did to the guys who jumped me, I wanted to be just like him. My brother is a badass.

However, Uri isn't proud of the cold, calculated man he has become. I picked up on that after the first job. I get it.

Each life taken does leave a stain. Although they all deserve it. Uri only accepts certain types of jobs. He's not going to hush anyone who is innocent. They have to have harmed someone who's defenseless, or they have to be a stain on humanity.

He does his research before taking a job. Uri is smart. I've been studying hard to have a sharp mind like his.

Like my sister Annabella, I have fallen into computers and surveillance—although, for her, that's more of a hobby. Annabella's major in university is medicine.

For me, I thought it wise to get into surveillance with Uri's profession and the fact that there are people out there wanting to harm us. I want to be of use to my family, including our uncle and cousin in America. Uri hasn't told me why he lives here in London while our uncle is in the States.

I know the questions to ask and those not to ask. My brother will shut down and not speak if he's pissed off. I try not to piss him off.

"That's enough for now. Shower. I have a meeting with Don Trovati. You're coming along."

I knit my brows. Uri makes it a habit never to be seen with me. One glance and it isn't hard to see we're related. Uri has made it clear to the three of us that we're not to expose ourselves as his siblings.

That hasn't been hard for Nico, as none of us get to see him often as a professional footballer. Annabella is always busy with her studies. However, I am the one who's always around Uri and I look the most like him.

Which makes me wonder why he's choosing to take me with him this time. My brother has a purpose for every move he makes. Seeming to read my thoughts, he tilts his head at me as he studies me.

"Trovati is an old friend. I have kept his secrets. He will keep mine. Besides, he's a friend you should have in case anything were ever to happen to me."

"This is business?"

"It is. I believe he has a request. I will hear him out."

My chest fills with pride. He's taking me with him. I nod and turn to head to shower and dress.

Uri

I grin as I watch my brother walk away. Michael reminds me of myself when I was his age. He's smart and ambitious.

Sometimes I wonder if I should be doing this, making him so much like me. Although I know he can never be fully like me—not that that's something I want. I wouldn't wish my childhood or the monster I've become on anyone.

I've been training Michael to be a gentler version of myself. I haven't taken him on the jobs where I know beforehand I'm going with the intent to slaughter. I'm not asked to go there often, but at times, a clear message needs to be sent.

It is those jobs that have earned me the name Hush. The times when I released the savage I became when my grandfather tried to break me. I will not break Michael to force him to become that.

However, unlike Nico, Michael has that look in his eyes. I would rather guide him than allow his demons to surface without him knowing what to do. I have been there and wish that on no one.

My phone rings, pulling me from my thoughts. I move to the table I placed it on and grab it. I roll my eyes as I see it's my uncle Nicholas.

At twenty-four, I'm growing increasingly tired of these calls. He wanted me here in London, why not leave me to my own life? He treats me like a lion he wishes to tame.

"Hello, Uncle," I say into the phone.

"Uri, it's good to hear your voice. I have Luca here. He asked me to give you a call for him."

I give a genuine smile. "What can I do for the little brat?"

"His birthday is coming and when I asked him what he wanted, he told me he wants a visit from you or tickets to come join you for a few weeks. I thought I would let you decide which you would prefer."

I chuckle into the phone. "He could get into a lot of trouble here with me. I'm sure that's not what you want."

"I trust you, Uri. You are a busy man. I don't want to burden you with your little cousin if you have work to do."

I note the questions in his tone. I haven't been hitting for the family. I turned down the last two requests, much to his annoyance. I didn't find either situation worthy of my time.

Not liking that he's questioning me, I frown before I answer. Two can play this game. It will take a lot for my uncle to rein me in. I don't believe he's ready for that.

"I will think about it. Tell Luca I will call him soon with my decision. I have to go," I say and end the call before he can say anything further.

My mind turns to Don Alessio Trovati. He took me under his wing when I first arrived here. I had been running with a London street gang when we crossed paths.

He picked me out of the crowd and told me I was a leader, not a follower. It was time I let those losers go. He offered me a place and a job. I also gained my first glimpse into the Mafia world outside of my family through him.

I owe him a lot and I don't say that about many. The connections I've made through him have been invaluable. When he asks to have dinner with me, out of respect, I show up.

I get the sneaking suspicion that is the true reason for my uncle's call, not Luca. I grin and shake my head. Nicholas Donati wouldn't be Nicholas Donati if he didn't know my every move.

"Well, let him watch," I snort and shake my head as I go to shower and dress for my meeting.

CHAPTER THREE

Friend's Request

Uri

I hadn't expected Don Trovati to have guests when I arrived. Otherwise, I wouldn't have brought Michael along with me. However, as we enter the restaurant this meeting is to be held in—after hours—I note the men who I know don't belong to Trovati.

They are Italian, but I've never seen them around Trovati's crew before. I think quickly, I can't compromise Michael's safety. Turning, I place a hand on my brother's shoulder and halt him before we get to the meeting room.

I lean into his ear so he's the only one to hear my words. "I don't know all of these men. I have no idea who Trovati has here with him.

"This was my mistake. Go back the way we came, make a left when you exit the first door. You will find a set of stairs there.

"Wait for me. I will come to get you when I am sure it is safe," I whisper.

Michael nods and quickly follows my orders. Just as he disappears from sight, Don Alfanzo Locatelli steps from the back room with three young guys surrounding him, only two whom I've seen before.

I know of Don Alfanzo and the Locatelli family. If you are Italian and a part of the underworld, you know the name Locatelli very well. However, I'm not expecting him to stop when he sees me.

"Uri," he croons as he embraces me and then kisses both my cheeks. Then he continues in Italian. "This guy. He looks just like his father. God bless the dead. It's good to see you."

"Hello, Don Locatelli."

"Alfanzo, you can call me Alfanzo. Your father was a good friend of mine. I was glad to hear you have connected with my good friend Alessio.

"He's a good man. You know my nephews Marco and D'Angelo. However, I don't think you have met my other nephew." He pauses and turns to the young men with him.

"LaSalle, come. I want you to meet Uri Donati."

The one with the gray eyes and dark hair comes forward. I lift a brow as I come face to face with the owner of the name I've been hearing more of lately. He doesn't look much older than Michael.

I probably have him by four or five years. This is the one making all the trouble in the States. His reputation is beginning to make as much noise as mine and he hasn't seen his first promotion yet.

I can respect how he is choosing to establish himself. It is the smart way to do things. I give him a nod of respect.

"LaSalle, Uri here is a problem solver like you are. You two might find you have some things in common," Don Alfanzo croons, still speaking in Italian.

"Nice to meet you. Don Trovati speaks very highly of you," LaSalle says as he looks me in the eyes.

"I've heard a lot about you."

He nods. "If you accept the request and need anything while you're in the States, you should let me know."

I narrow my eyes at him, wondering what request he's speaking of. My interest is piqued. Don Trovati has definitely called me for something big.

I get the feeling he had to ask permission for whatever it is if Don Locatelli is here. I grin and look LaSalle in his eyes. I also get the feeling he's letting me know his rank or at least trying to establish who he is in the States.

He can relax. I already know everything I need to know about him. Word spreads fast in our world and when you do what I do, there isn't much that gets by without my knowing.

"Let's say I do need something, mate. Who do I call for? LaSalle Locatelli or Sam Mairettie?" I say with a grin.

LaSalle's eyes harden as he seems to realize I'm not going to roll over and bark for anyone. I give respect where respect is earned. It doesn't matter who you are.

Don Locatelli laughs. "This is how your father and I locked horns when we first met. Angelo and I became the best of friends after. Uri, you keep in touch. I would like to see you in Italy.

"Come to my home. We'll drink and eat. I would like to know more about you as a man.

"Not just from the things I hear. We all know everything we hear isn't always the truth," he croons in a mix of Italian and English.

"I will carve out some time to come and visit, Don Locatelli," I say, knowing his words aren't really a request.

This is one of the few men I know it's not wise for me to ignore. The four men nod and file out, with their men following.

I watch as they go before I go to collect Michael. Curiosity is burning through me as I think of what Don Trovati could need from me.

The States?

Michael

I remain silent as I follow Uri into the back room Don Trovati is waiting in for their meeting. The man is a lot smaller than I thought he would be.

However, he has a stern look about him that lets you know he's still not to be tried. I sit next to Uri after we greet the don. I don't miss that he doesn't take his eyes off me.

"Your father would be proud. You two look just like him. Angelo had a presence about him.

"He demanded respect as he entered a room. I see this in the both of you. I respected Angelo and was very sad when we lost him. Men like Angelo and Alfanzo are far and few between," Don Trovati says.

"What is it you want from me?" Uri says, getting to the point.

The don finally pulls his gaze from me to look at Uri. His eyes remain soft with affection as he looks at my brother. I doubt that any other man would get away with that tone and continue to live, let alone speak.

The don sighs and sits back in his chair. "I need you to do me a favor. Someone important to me has been taken. She is in the States outside of my reach," he says.

"If she is in the States, why not have one of the families with roots there handle the favor?" Uri asks.

"This is a delicate matter. I can only ask someone I trust to handle this situation. I trust you more than you know."

"Tell me who she is, who has taken her, and why," Uri says.

"It is my granddaughter," Don Trovati says.

I watch Uri as his face remains expressionless. This is a friend of his, so I wasn't expecting him to remain so cold. I wonder if Uri has ever met this granddaughter.

"How could they have taken your granddaughter? You've told me that your daughter died when she was ten and you never had another child," Uri says.

"My Emma did drown when she was ten. However, Consuela, my housekeeper who drowned trying to save her, had a daughter as well.

"Carmelita and my Emma had been best friends. Carmelita was left without a mother, as I was left without my child. My wife and I took her in as if she were ours. Carmelita was my daughter in every sense of the word.

"I was heartbroken when she decided she wanted to go live in the States. However, she was an adult, and I couldn't keep her here. Two years after she settled there, she met up with some guy.

"I didn't like him. He wouldn't have been my first choice for her. However, she fell in love and became pregnant. The bastard left her and the child. Carmelita returned to me broken and in tears with a swollen belly.

"Of course, I took care of everything like a papa would. My granddaughter was born, and I couldn't remember seeing a more beautiful sight. I was the one to name her.

"She became my pride and joy. I watched her grow and enjoyed her laughter until her mother decided to return to America and take her away with her. To this day, I think my wife died of a broken heart.

"It was like she lost three daughters. Carmelita once again got mixed up with the wrong crowd. I was informed she was involved with some lowlife who was into trafficking young girls.

"I was livid. Why take my little *nipotina* and involve her in that? Three months ago, I got a call in the middle of the night ..." He takes a pause as his eyes begin to mist. He swallows hard and clears his throat before he continues.

"Carmelita was killed. They say she overdosed, but she never touched that stuff. For all her bad decisions, she was still a good girl. Besides, she loved her daughter and wouldn't neglect her for the chase of a high.

"That asshole shot her up with that shit and killed her," he chokes out with rage lacing his words.

"This is who has your granddaughter?"

"Yes, he has my bella. Name your price. I will give you whatever you want. Please, Uri. I need you to go to the States and bring her back to me.

"If you find her with that bastard, I want you to kill him. Make him one of your examples. I want him to suffer."

"Done," Uri says and stands, nodding for me to follow.

CHAPTER FOUR

Finding Symphony

Symphony

I sit in the back of this car wishing my mommy or *nonno* were here. I haven't seen *Nonno* in so long. I miss him.

I want to go to Italy to see him. I want to hear him speak the funny words. Not like the words Mommy sometimes speaks. Nonno's words are a little different, but I can understand him.

He is kind. Not like this man sitting with me—Mommy's friend. I don't like this man. I don't know where he's taking me.

He promised me if I went with him, my mommy would return for me. It's been ninety-six days since I last saw her. Two thousand three hundred and three hours and counting. She has never left me for this long.

"I want my mommy. When will I see her?" I ask while tapping my fingertips together.

The music is playing in my head. Tapping my fingers together helps me to capture the notes and colors that play in my mind.

23

The music has been loud and off-key since Mommy has been gone.

"You're such a pretty girl. Too bad you're a fucking retard," the man says as he places his hand on my thigh.

I look up at him and glare. I hate when he calls me that. He only says it when Mommy isn't around.

I get frustrated and overwhelmed because I don't want to be here with him. I'm starting to think he's lying to me. I don't think I should have left the house with him.

I can't help fidgeting in my seat as I start to chew on my tongue to help me with the anxiety building inside. The strand of music in my head has popped. The next thing I know, I'm rocking and cracking my knuckles.

I want to be far away from here. It's not safe. As I dart my gaze around, I know for sure it's not safe.

"Get all that shit out now. When we get to our friends, you better not start that bullshit in front of them," he hisses at me.

I don't like the feel of his hand on my leg. I begin to slide away from him. However, he tightens his hold to keep me in place.

"Look at me," he snarls as I turn away from him to look out of the window.

I turn my head back in his direction, but I don't look him in the eyes. He reaches to brush his fingers along my hairline. I hate his touch and begin to squirm.

"You have such pretty hair. I'm glad we could cover up those fucking patches. Your mother should have broken you out of that stupid ass habit a long time ago.

"Tearing out your own damn hair. I'm not going to tolerate any of that shit. Clients don't want to hear that bullshit or see you looking unkept. Shut that noise the fuck up, now," he barks.

I knit my brows and try to stifle the urge to chew on my tongue which is making the sound he's so annoyed with. However, by stopping the chewing, I can't help but reach up for my hair to twist and pull a lock of it.

He slaps my hand away from my hair, causing me to hiss at him. Mommy doesn't like when I hiss at people, but I don't like this man. He makes my skin crawl.

"Don't hit me. Abuse. Abuse. Someone help," I call out.

"Shut the fuck up," he growls and grabs my face. "Look at me when I talk to you. I'll show you abuse. No one is coming to save you. I never want to hear those words come from your mouth again. Do you understand me?"

I punch him in the throat, just like in the jujitsu videos I love to watch on my tablet. His eyes grow wide as he releases my face and falls back in his seat. I clap my hand in excitement as I execute the move correctly.

"Yay," I squeal happily.

"You fucking little retarded bitch," he snarls and slaps me across the face. He hits me so hard my ears feel like they're ringing.

My vision is blurred as I fall back against my own seat. The next thing I know, the sound of my dress being ripped fills my ears. He's hovering over me as he leans into my face with his rank breath.

He has halitosis and needs to see a periodontist to treat the gum disease infecting his mouth. It smells like something has died in his gums. He should just cut his tongue out and get a new one.

"I'm going to teach you a little lesson. Fuck saving you for the highest bidder. Your retarded ass is going to fuck it all up anyway," he growls in my ear as he fumbles with trying to tear my panties from my body.

I turn my face and bite him as I shove at his chest. He screams as I keep biting down. I bite through all three layers of skin—the epidermis, dermis, and the hypodermis—until my teeth meet his jaw.

I only release him as he begins to punch me in the head. A metallic taste fills my mouth as I release him. He pulls back and continues to rain blows down on me.

I think the car pulls to a stop, but I am beginning to lose consciousness. My ears are ringing, and my face and head hurt.

However, his weight is no longer on me and he's no longer pounding his fists against me.

Mommy, where are you? Help. Your friend is a bad man.

Michael

Morgan Christoph, that's the name of the asshole who has Don Trovati's granddaughter. The motherfucker intends to auction her off tonight. That's going to happen over my dead body. She's a fourteen-year-old girl.

What kind of sick fuck kills a girl's mother then tries to sell her off to the highest bidder? I can tell my brother is chomping at the bit to torture and hush his ass.

I don't stand a chance to have a hand at this one. I have already been given orders to get her to safety as Uri handles the rest. We don't want to make any waves while we're here.

Uri doesn't want to call in any favors. Hitters are supposed to be resourceful and self-sufficient. Having to call for help is unprofessional.

"Hang back. Don't get too close," Uri murmurs to me, causing me to back off the gas.

When we pulled up to the house—we learned the girl had been staying in—Christoph and a driver had already loaded the younger girl into the car and pulled off to head out. Neither of us could get a look at the girl as Christoph had some type of cape covering her. I could only hope for his sake that wasn't the don's granddaughter.

After confirming the house was empty, I was able to follow them and catch up. We plan to intercept them before they get to the auction. However, something is off.

Our intel placed the auction another ten miles from here. Our rendezvous point is another mile and a half ahead. The car has turned off course. We continue to follow until the car heads into a parking structure. I glance over at Uri. He looks back at me, giving me a nod to get ready.

"Stay with them. This changes nothing," he says.

I lick my lips nervously. This is my first time driving in America. I try my best not to focus on that, sticking to the task at hand.

I pull into the parking garage after the car and follow it as it drives up a few levels to one that's more secluded. I hang back just a bit so we're not detected.

"Pull in over there." Uri points.

I pull into the spot he points out and cut the engine. Uri pulls on his gloves, then pulls his guns and begins to check the clips. I place on my gloves then do the same.

"Remember, your job is to get the girl and get her to safety."

"I've got it."

"Let's go. I don't have a good feeling about this," Uri bites out.

My gut twists as I have the same feeling. We climb from the vehicle and race forward toward the car we've followed here.

I watch as my brother allows his demons to take over. This is when the savage assassin comes to the front. I have learned to notice the different faces and levels of my brother.

This is the darkest version of him. The man they call Hush. It is best for me to allow him to do what he does and stay out of the way.

Uri rushes the car and rips the back door open. In the next breath, he tears Christoph from the car by the back of his hair. The driver jumps out with his arms in the air. His face looks stricken.

"I don't want any part of this. I quit," the driver says.

I move quickly to place a zip tie on his wrists. When I look up, I find Uri with Morgan in his grasp as he squeezes his palm around his neck. With the driver secure and forgotten, I rush to find the girl.

I clench my jaw tightly as I climb into the back seat and find the young girl with her face bruised and battered. However, as my gaze roams for other injuries, my blood begins to boil. Her front is exposed as the dress she had been wearing is now torn down the front.

I breathe a sigh of relief as I note her panties are still covering her lower parts. Giving a silent prayer, I hope that means we got here in time. Quickly, I climb in and cover her little exposed breasts.

Grabbing the cape from the seat, I then wrap it around her. There's blood on her face around her mouth. From the looks of it, she put up a fight.

"Keep fighting for me, *bella*. We're going to get you to your nonno," I whisper as I scoop her up and back out of the vehicle.

I move swiftly back to our car. The sharp sound of a bullet moving through a silencer goes off behind me. I didn't think Uri was going to allow the driver to live.

Instead of turning to look back, I place the girl in the passenger seat and buckle her in. Once she's secure, I rush around to climb into the driver's side and take off for the location where I'm to wait with the girl for Uri to come and collect us.

CHAPTER FIVE

Hushed

Uri

If Don Trovati hadn't asked me to make this piece of shit suffer. I would have put a bullet in his bloody skull when I found him pounding his fists into that child's head. When I pulled him off her and caught a glance of her little exposed body, the only thing that kept me from killing him then and there was the desire to hear him scream in agony.

"Please," he gasps as he chokes on his own blood.

"Did the child beg you to stop?" I tilt my head to the side. "How about her mum? Did she get to beg for her bloody fucking life, you piece of shit."

"I hadn't planned to kill her. Not until I was offered the money. I was told to keep the girl and do as I pleased," he chokes out.

"By who?" I bellow as rage fills me.

Don Trovati is like family to me. He opened his home to me during a time when I was so angry and confused. I never met the woman he called a daughter, but if she was important to him, she's family to me.

That makes the girl equally as important. Seeing her beaten the way she was has fueled me. However, hearing that someone ordered this causes me to see red.

Don Trovati is being targeted. That's the only explanation for all of this. Someone has a death wish.

"It was—"

I turn sharply as a window shatters. Swiftly, I move out of the open and draw my gun. When I look back to Christoph, where I have him chained up, his head is slumped with a hole through his skull that I didn't place there.

I swear and grind my teeth. Clearly, this is over. I need to get back to Michael and the girl.

Making sure the coast is clear, I then grab my torture devices and begin to douse the place in lighter fuel. I torch the place with the vehicle I brought here inside.

My mind is racing with a million thoughts. Don Trovati has a bigger problem going on here. My question now is, does he already know this?

What haven't I been told? Who wanted to silence Christoph and what didn't they want me to find out? I need answers and I want them now.

However, getting to Michael and the girl is my first priority. I need to get them both back to London safely. Then, I'll figure the rest out.

CHAPTER SIX

Safe

Michael

I knew from my research on this assignment that Don Trovati's granddaughter has special needs. However, I don't know what I was expecting. Given the trauma she's been through today, I can't say I'm surprised that she's behaving this way.

I'm a stranger, she's in a strange place, and that asshole tried to violate her. Since waking up, she has bitten me, hissed at me, and kicked me in the balls. I've given up on trying to get too close.

Instead, I'm sitting on the floor a few feet from where she has planted herself as she rocks and hums while alternating between crossing her fingers and pressing the tips together. I remain still as I hold an ice pack in my hand with a sandwich and bottle of juice sitting at my side.

Suddenly, she quiets and tilts her head to the side and begins to study me. Her left eye is swollen and there's a knot on the side

31

of her head. I want to be the one who finishes that bastard off, but I know Uri will take care of him.

"My name is Michael. You are safe here with me. We're going to take you to your nonno. He is waiting for you," I say gently.

"Nonno? In Italy?" she whispers through her busted lips.

"No, he's waiting for us in London."

"With Mommy? Did she go to see Nonno?"

I swallow hard. I don't want to be the one who tells her what happened to her mother. This is all hard enough.

"She's gone. You can say it. My mommy isn't coming back.

"The bad man did something to her. I hate him. He always made Mommy cry and he called me names.

"I am not a retard. I'm just a little different from the other kids. I like different stuff from the kids at school," she says into her lap, not lifting her gaze to me.

Though her speech comes off robotic, there is a deep intelligence to the way she speaks. Almost as if she's put this all together and accepted her loss already, and still, there is an innocence to her at the same time.

"Are you hungry, Symphony?"

"Yes, I would like something to eat, but I don't know if I can trust anything you give me. You might try to poison me."

Finally, she lifts her gaze and blinks at me. Her one good eye stands out. It's large and bright, and her lashes are extremely long. I cleaned her face and placed one of my dress shirts on her when we first arrived before she woke. She looks so small as it swallows her while she sits there.

I release a small chuckle. "I have no reason to poison you. I could take a bite of the sandwich first if you would like."

She makes a little face at me but seems to be in thought. Her stomach growls and she frowns then begins to chew on her tongue. I pick up the sandwich for her to see.

"You look like you have lots of girlfriends. I don't want to be poisoned, but I don't want any STDs you might pass to me by biting my sandwich."

This time, I let out a full laugh as I unwrap the sandwich. I tear off a corner and pop it into my mouth. Her shoulders sag in relief and she holds her small hands out for the sandwich. I lean forward cautiously and hand the sandwich over.

"Thank you, Michael. I am Symphony Isabella Mansilla-Trovati. I'm not supposed to tell anyone I'm a Trovati, but you said you know Nonno, so you know who I am."

"It's nice to meet you, Symphony. Here, you should take this ice pack for your face."

"Is that juice for me?" She points to the bottle beside me.

"Yeah. You want me to test it first too?"

She wrinkles her nose and twists her lips up. "Can you do so without putting your lips on it?"

"*Sì, posso farlo,*" I scoff.

Her eyes light up as I speak in Italian. "Oh, you speak the funny words. I have learned Nonno's funny words and Mommy's. Do you speak both as well?"

I think her words over. Carmelita Mansilla spoke Spanish. Don Trovati is a native Italian speaker. I give her a smile as I realize what she's asking.

"Yes, I speak Italian and Spanish. Do you?"

"Yes, I'm fluent in several languages. I love to learn them. That bad man would try to make me watch cartoons. I would grab my tablet when he would leave to watch my jujitsu and language videos," she says as I open the juice and tip my head back to pour a sip into my mouth.

I swallow and hand the juice over to her. She takes it and sips at it gingerly as she looks anywhere but at me once again. We continue to talk as she becomes more comfortable with me.

This young girl is highly intelligent. After about an hour, she begins to give me eye contact every now and then. I also note that the finger stimming has stopped and she doesn't chew on her tongue unless I ask her something she has to think about for a moment before responding.

With each moment, I grow more protective of her. Like a big brother who wants to make sure she's taken care of. I can't help wondering what will happen to her now.

I know the don cares for her, but will he know how to take care of her. I think of Annabella. She might be my older sister, but I'm protective of her as if she were the younger one.

I couldn't imagine her being out in the world with challenges and no one to help her. Since Uri is good friends with the don, I hope I can check in on this girl every now and then.

Symphony yelps and scurries behind me when Uri returns. She hides behind my back, clinging to my shirt as he moves into the apartment we've been waiting in.

"We need to move. Collect your things. We are to be on the move in five," Uri orders.

I stand to move into action. Symphony climbs to her feet and wraps her arms around me. I can feel her shivering as she holds me tightly.

"Symphony, this is Uri. He's here to help. We need to go," I say soothingly.

"To Nonno? No more abuse, right? I trust you. I don't know him."

"Uri would never hurt you and he won't allow anyone else to hurt you. I promise you, you are safe with us. Think of us like family. We never hurt our family."

"Family," she repeats.

However, she doesn't release me. I have to gather my things while she clings to my side. Especially when she starts to chew on her tongue making a loud sound with the action.

I move as fast as I can with her attached to my side. I don't dare to ask Uri what's happening. I don't want to scare Symphony and Uri's vibe says he isn't in the mood for questions anyway.

Symphony

I am on a plane with the two handsome men. I like Michael. He doesn't make me feel like something is wrong with me like new people usually do.

I feel bad for biting and kicking him when I woke scared and alone with him. I thought he was friends with the bad man. All I knew was that I had to fight to keep him from hurting me.

They both have been kind to me. However, the Uri man is quiet and doesn't speak to me as much as Michael does. Uri has a funny accent.

He spoke to Michael in Italian until Michael told him I understood their words. That's when he stopped speaking. Only speaking in hushed tones every once in a while.

"How is your head feeling?" Michael whispers as I sit curled into the seat beside him.

I turn my gaze to his blue eyes and hurry to look away. He's so pretty. The two men look alike, but Michael has kindness in his eyes.

"It is a little better," I say.

He takes the blanket the lady brings to him and then places it over me. I pull the soft fabric under my chin. It's a weighted blanket.

I can tell because all the noise in my body settles. It's just like the one Mommy has at home for me. Mommy.

I'm not going to see her again. It hurts, but it's the truth. I feel so sad.

The music in my mind is all wrong. The colors have become dark, and the notes seem off. I burrow down further into the blanket and the music dies down some more.

I'm safe. Michael is going to get me to Nonno. I can go to sleep now.

CHAPTER SEVEN

Trovati Family

Michael

Uri wasn't going to take me along to drop Symphony off. However, she broke out into an episode when he tried to leave me behind. She has been through enough.

We both agreed it would be better if I helped him get her to her grandfather since she seemed to have bonded with me. I wrapped her in the blanket I brought along after doing some research before we left for the mission.

I hadn't known all of Symphony's behaviors or symptoms, but I wanted to try to be prepared to help get her back safely. The blanket seemed to work wonders for her. Once I had her wrapped in it after Uri agreed I should accompany them, I was able to climb into the back seat with her.

Symphony nearly crawled into my side and remained there the entire ride to Don Trovati's London residence. Uri still hasn't told me what placed him in such a rush to leave California, where we went to collect the girl.

"Nonno," Symphony squeals as she releases her hold around my waist and takes off into her grandfather's embrace.

His eyes fill with tears as he holds her tightly. I can only imagine what must be going through his head as he takes in her appearance. I thought we would have more time to bring her back to him looking a little more presentable.

The huge honey-brown ponytail on top of her head has become fuzzy around the edges. She's still wearing nothing but my dress shirt and her panties beneath. Her legs are mostly covered by the long fabric, but the bottoms of her brown limbs peek out, revealing her pigeon toes.

The flats on her feet scream that this is a child. The black shoes have flowers embroidered across the front and a strap across the center. I'm once again relieved we got to her before something horrible happened.

Although the beating she took was horrific, it's the bruising and swelling I wish we could've done more about. I guess I should be happy we have gotten her here in one piece.

"I don't think there is anything I can do to repay you both," Don Trovati chokes out.

"You can start by telling me the truth," Uri says tightly.

"Yes, now that she is here, there is more we should discuss."

Symphony releases her grandfather and rushes back to my side, taking my hand. I look down at her curiously. I had assumed she would cling to her grandfather once reunited with him.

However, once she begins to squeeze my hand in hers, I go along with it. I apply a little pressure in return. She seems to relax completely.

"Come with me. There is much to speak of. I have another request," Don Trovati says as he turns and begins to amble forward as he gestures for us to follow.

Uri looks at me and nods for me to follow. However, I can see the storm brewing in his eyes. He's been pissed about something since we left America.

We enter a study with a welcoming gentlemen's feel. The don takes a seat behind the desk. Uri and I take the seats in front of it as Symphony moves to the bookshelves flanking the fireplace.

She picks a book and takes a seat on the floor in front of the fireplace. Don Trovati hasn't taken his eyes off her as his lips hold a wobbly smile.

"Tell me the one who did that to her face is dead," the don says coldly.

"He is, but I wasn't the one who took his life," Uri replies bitterly.

"What do you mean?"

"Michael took Symphony to a safe place. I took the dodgy sod to a warehouse to make him suffer. However, before I could finish the bloke off, someone shot him through one of the windows.

"He was just about to tell me who paid him to ..." Uri looks over at Symphony, then back at the don.

"He was going to tell me who was responsible for your loss and who told him to do as he pleased with the girl. Then, out of nowhere, there was a bullet through his skull, and it wasn't one of mine," Uri bites out.

"No doubt he would have told you what I already know. Don Locatelli wasn't at my restaurant for a friendly visit."

"I have already figured that out," Uri says.

"Yes, well. I was trying to get permission to sanction a hit on my brother. He is the one behind all of this. He has been plotting to take me out and become the head of the family.

"No one wants this. At least no one who hasn't already lost their mind. Leonardo only wants power. Give him a little; he will always clamor for more.

"However, he has taken my grief as a moment to strike. He has made friends with the heads of some of the other families. If I move against him, it will start a war Don Locatelli doesn't believe any of us are ready for," he explains.

"You were denied?" Uri says incredulously.

"For now. Leonardo knows I have no son to pass the family to. I had arranged a marriage for my Emma, but with her death, that plan died with her.

"Carmelita wasn't of Italian blood or even my blood at all, but I had planned to leave her everything regardless. All I needed was to find her a suitable husband of full Italian blood. Don Locatelli had planned to back me.

"I had planned to call Carmelita home to set up the arrangement. I believe this is what set Leonardo off. My Symphony is my last hope to continue my bloodline's name and keep the Trovati family alive.

"I will now leave my family to her. She will need an Italian husband to run the family with when I am gone. However, this places a target on her back.

"I need to keep her safe from my brother and hidden until the time comes for her and her husband to take my place. Leonardo will challenge them for the title, but he mustn't be allowed to take this from her," he says firmly.

Uri releases an amused snort. "I have known you since I was sixteen. You saved me from a life far worse than the one I live now. I have respect for you and see you as family, but I know you're not asking me for what I think you are."

"Yes, I am. You are ruthless. My brother will think twice about crossing you or the Donati family. Think of the power you will have once you become the don of the Trovati family.

"I will feel like I've left my family to a son. You are right; I have watched you grow into a man. At sixteen, I saw something in you and I know you will do right by my granddaughter and my family," Don Trovati says.

"Have you lost your bloody mind? She's fourteen. I am twenty-four.

"Will she even understand what you are asking of her? Do you think we haven't noticed? Did you think we wouldn't find out?"

"I was well aware you would do your research before going to collect her. I knew you would find out. I had hoped that would help sway you.

"You have a heart for those who need someone to protect them. You try to ignore that you do, but it's there. She is vulnerable.

"Leonardo will find her as an easy target. You are one of the best. She will be safe with you."

"So I'm to take a child bride because of our friendship? I don't even think she likes me."

I look at Uri and can see he's conflicted. Don Trovati means a lot to him. However, this is a colossal ask.

My brother has enough on his plate. He is still trying to keep me and my siblings safe from enemies who have no name or face. Only a past of violence toward our family.

"Think of all you have to gain from this. You will be Don Trovati. Your own family to run.

"All of my investments and connections will be yours. All you have to do is marry my granddaughter and keep her hidden away. You can still live your life as you please.

"Please, Uri. This is my only option. If my brother takes over this family, he will run it into the ground and he will probably start a war among the families in the process.

"You will be doing us all a favor. Don Locatelli will be in full support if you do this. Your name alone will cause my brother to think twice," he pleads.

"What if I do it?" I say before I can stop the words.

Uri whips his head in my direction and glares at me. I know I'm to be silent, but something protective rises within. I don't like the idea of leaving Symphony vulnerable to this bastard who wants power that isn't his.

She's a sweet kid. I know I can hide her away and keep her safe. I've learned so much from Uri in the last year. I have so much more to learn, but I can keep Symphony safe in the meantime.

I hold my hands up. "Hear me out. I am a Donati too.

"Word will get out that she's married to a Donati and everyone will think it's you. No one knows about me. If they see me with her by some chance, they will think I am you.

"If the goal is to hide her away, eventually, everyone will forget about her. You can continue to live your life; she will be safe, and the burden of being her husband will fall on me," I say quickly before Uri can shut me down.

"The burden of being a don will fall on your shoulders as well," Don Trovati says, drawing my attention back to him.

He looks at me as if looking through me. Searching for something beyond the surface. I keep my face expressionless.

I am the son of a don. It is in my blood. While that's not my motive here, I won't shy away from the responsibility when the time comes. My main goal is to make sure the girl goes unharmed.

"Better your brother challenge me than her. He won't find it easy to make me cower."

"Spoken like a true Donati," Don Trovati says proudly. "Uri, do you object?"

My brother pulls a hand down his face. I can feel his anger with me, but I'm decided. I will not allow Symphony to be hurt over things she doesn't know anything about.

"I need some time to speak with my brother," Uri says tightly.

"Yes, yes, take all the time you need. Symphony, come, *cara.* Let's go to the kitchen and find something for you to eat."

She looks up from the book she's reading as if just remembering we're in the room with her. Making a little face, she then places the book down beside her and gets to her feet. I wrinkle my brows as she walks by with a lock of honey-brown hair in her grasp.

I look at the back of her head and see where the lock of hair has been snatched from. I'm left to wonder if she should have been in the room during this conversation. How much of what was said did she understand?

Curiosity gets the best of me, and I stand to see what book she was reading. I go and pick it up, careful not to lose her page. When I turn it to read the cover, my brows shoot into my hairline.

It's *The Art Of War.* A grin comes to my lips. There is so much more to that kid. I think she'll be able to handle herself when she's old enough.

We just need to make sure she makes it to be old enough. I wish we could take the don's brother out and be done with it. However, I know if we do, we will face the wrath of Don Locatelli and the others who are in support of Leonardo Trovati.

"Why would you open your bloody mouth to make such a stupid promise? Do you understand what's being asked here?" Uri seethes once the don and Symphony are out of earshot.

"Yes, I understand. He's asking us to protect family. Isn't that what we do? We protect family."

Uri tugs at his hair and curses under his breath. I know what I'm doing. At nineteen, I train so much I don't have time for girls.

Being married isn't going to be the end of the world for me. It's not like they're asking me to produce an heir with her. Although I'm sure that will come into question years from now.

We'll come to that when the time comes. Besides, five years is not as big a gap as ten. Uri doesn't have to give up the women he entertains, and I'm focused on other things in my life.

"You don't just make promises in this world, Michael. Once you give your word, you have to stand by it. It would've been better if you said nothing," Uri groans.

"I've made my decision. I'm going to stand by it. I will take her as my wife, keep her safe, and help her. That is now my job," I say with my head held high.

Uri laughs at me. Then winces. "You don't see it now, but a day will come when you will regret this. Most likely, it will be because of another woman."

"You are the one who told me relationships will get me killed in this business. This marriage will be my insurance to keep me from making that mistake."

Uri laughs harder and shakes his head. "Your emotions will be your downfall, Michael. Not every situation should involve your heart."

I go to answer him, but Symphony rushes back into the room, holding a plate with a sandwich resting on it. She stops in front of me, but she won't look up at me. I smile and place a hand gently on her shoulder.

"Is this for me?"

"Yes, I will take a bite first if you like."

I give her a wink. "*Mi fido di te. Grazie.*"

She looks up and makes full eye contact this time. Her right eye has started to open again. Something passes between us, and I know for a fact I will protect her with my life if necessary.

As the youngest and the sibling of twins, I know what it's like to feel alone. It's one of the reasons I wanted to find Uri. I wanted to have a bond like Nico and Annabella have.

At least I had my siblings. Symphony has no one on top of having challenges she will face throughout her life. Not just a crazy man who's trying to wipe her and her family out, but challenges because of her condition.

I haven't even begun to think about the fact that she will be a Black woman in an Italian underworld. Being from a black sheep family, I believe I have found a kindred spirit within this kid.

"You are welcome, Michael. Thank you for taking care of me and getting me away from the bad man."

"Anytime, *mia cara.*"

I take the plate and bite into the sandwich. Her nose wrinkles as she breaks our eye contact. Her lips turn into a mix of a smile and a pucker.

Almost as if she is trying to make a silly face. However, it's more than that. It's tied to an emotion I haven't figured out yet.

When I turn my attention to Uri, he's keeping a close eye on the both of us. I sigh because I can tell he still doesn't think this is a good idea. I, on the other hand, believe this is the right thing to do.

"Don Trovati, let's talk details. My brother will do this for you," Uri says as the don enters the room.

The look of relief that comes across the old man's face is palpable. It's like I watch years come off his face. Symphony has returned to her book on the floor in front of the fireplace.

CHAPTER EIGHT

The Ceremony

Symphony

I look into the mirror at the pretty dress I have on. It's white and has pretty lace all over it. I look like one of the dolls Nonna used to have.

I loved playing with those dolls when I was small. That was before me and Mommy left Italy. I never saw Nonna again after that. Mommy was sad for a while.

I remember her crying. Nonno was really sad the next time we saw him too. I think I know how they felt.

It feels like Mommy should be here. This feels important. Nonno has tried to explain to me what's happening.

I'm getting married today. Michael Zuko-Donati will be my husband. The handsome man who saved me is going to marry me and take me away from here to keep me safe.

We're getting married in Italy at Nonno's home here. I reach up to touch my hair. The smiling lady fixed it for me and covered my patches. I'm nervous, but I don't want to mess it up, so I cross my fingers and shake my hands out in front of me.

"*Ciao*," someone whispers into the room.

I turn to look at the door and find a pretty lady standing there. She's tall with blonde hair. Her blue eyes remind me of Michael and Uri's.

Nonno said Michael's sister would be here to help me. This must be her. She gives me a smile and her eyes light up with it. I lift to my toes and go to step forward.

"*Ciao*, I am Symphony. Do you speak English, or do you wish for me to speak Italian?" I say in Italian.

"Oh, you're so adorable. I'm Annabella, Michael's sister. We can speak whichever you're comfortable with. May I come in?"

"Please, I would like that."

"How are you doing? Do you need help with anything?"

"I … I don't know. I think I am ready."

"But how are you feeling, love? You're only fourteen and about to get married."

"My marriage will keep me safe. Michael will take care of me. If something happens to Nonno, Michael will make sure I am taken care of," I reply.

"Yes, he will. I will also be around to help you. My brothers and I are now your family."

"I think I will like that. Michael is my friend. He is kind to me."

"Michael is a sweet kid. You look gorgeous. Do you want help with your veil?"

I hold my hands up and begin to tap my fingers. It's time. It's time to go get married.

"Oh, Symphony. It's okay. Breathe, love. Breathe," Annabella coos.

I realize I'm in full stim. I'm chewing, my fingers are going, and I'm seconds away from grabbing at my hair.

Annabella moves to me and wraps her arms around me. She gives me a tight hug and all the noise begins to settle down. I wrap my arms around her and squeeze back.

"There you go. It's going to me fine. Once the wedding is over, we'll have some cake and ice cream, and we'll get to know more about each other before we take you home."

"Home?"

"Yes, you will be coming home with us. Michael and I live together. Our brother Nico lives with us when his not playing football. Wait, you were raised in the States. He plays professional soccer."

"Oh, yes. Michael has told me about the soccer player. He is your twin. You are the doctor and computer genius. Michael said you won't mind if I read your schoolbooks.

"I am most excited for that. I like to read and learn new things. I didn't realize I would have to leave Nonno tonight," I reply.

"Oh, honey. Yes, you will be leaving with your husband. Will you be okay with that?"

"Yes, I will have to be. It is how Michael will keep me safe. I will do my part. I can do this."

"You are a brave girl. We will be friends. I can see why Michael wants to do this. I just want to wrap you in my arms and keep you safe myself."

I take a deep breath. "I am ready for the veil, please. Yes, I would like your help. Michael is waiting."

Annabella gives me a big smile. I like her smile. Yes, she will be someone I can trust.

I am ready. I can marry Michael.

Michael

I stand here at the altar with my brows threaded. I was not expecting Symphony to look like this. She is going to make such a beautiful woman in a few years.

Her eyes are gorgeous, so big and bright. Her lashes are insanely pretty. Her face is flawless.

For the first time, I'm beginning to question myself. Saying I do and living a life outside of my marriage feels wrong, but can this marriage ever be more than just in name.

As Symphony goes from looking me in my eyes to looking anywhere but at me, I'm not sure this is the right thing to do. However, this is the only way to keep her safe and preserve her right to the Trovati family name.

After tonight, I will be named Don Trovati's successor. Well, the son of the former Don Donati will be named his successor. I will not be announced by name.

It is our hope that everyone will assume I am Uri and fuck off. In a few years, this will all be forgotten. Don Trovati is in good health, and I pose no threat of taking his seat for now.

With any luck, Don Trovati will live a long life, and his brother will die or hide away until it's time for me to take the seat. In the meantime, I will keep Symphony safe.

"I do," Symphony says as she looks me in the eyes and holds my gaze for the first time today.

I come out of my thoughts. This is what needs to be done. I have taken the target off her back and placed it on mine. Well, they might come for Uri, but that would be a mistake.

"You may now kiss the bride."

I look down at Symphony and she's blushing furiously. I chuckle and pull her into a hug, kissing her forehead. She wraps her arms around me and hugs me, melting into me like I'm her safe place.

"It will be okay," I murmur, knowing I'm speaking the words for myself more than anything.

CHAPTER NINE

The Gift

Symphony

A year later ...

I've been getting into fights in school. Uri and Michael have talked about homeschooling me. It would be easier, but I would be isolated.

Michael doesn't want that for me. However, my temper and the incidents are drawing attention. It's not my fault. The girls at school are mean to me.

I try to ignore them, but some days, I'm too overwhelmed to block them and everything else out. I'm never the first to hit. They are the ones who put their hands on me.

I have learned to defend myself, so I do. Can anyone blame me for that? I just hate making Michael angry and he gets really angry when I get into fights.

"Symphony, come and sit. It will be okay," Annabella says from her seat on the couch.

I've been pacing since I got home. I haven't been able to calm down, no matter what I try. My nerves are all over the place and I'm overwhelmed with anxiety.

I start to walk on my toes as my nerves get the best of me. I did beat Sandra down pretty bad. She picks on me the most.

After my first six months of being married, I wanted to be different. I stopped tearing out my hair and asked Annabella to help me cut my hair off so it would grow back evenly. Sandra has made fun of my honey-brown fro whenever she gets a chance. She and her friends are always teasing me.

They are mean and hateful. I don't regret beating Sandra up. She slapped me, then pushed me to the ground and stepped on my hand.

"Where is she?" Michael's voice booms through the house.

I stop pacing and turn for the doorway as I wring my hands. It's all I can do to keep from tapping my fingers and chewing on my tongue. The music has been loud today.

I'm trying my best not to listen to it. That's why I allowed Sandra to get to me. I couldn't ignore her and the music.

Michael storms into the room and his eyes land on me. Adriano, my security guard who comes to school with me, is right on his heels. I want to groan. Adriano tells Michael everything.

"That is it. I've had enough. This shouldn't be happening. It stops now. If the headmaster won't stop them, I will," Michael seethes as he cups the side of my face.

I glance at my husband's handsome face. He looks angry but also concerned. Michael has changed so much in the last year.

His eyes have become more like Uri's. There is a darkness within them. I look away quickly.

"I'm sorry," I murmur.

"For what?"

"You are angry with me."

"*Mia cara*, I am not angry with you. I'm angry that those kids are always targeting you. I am angry with myself for not stopping this personally sooner.

"I noticed at breakfast that you were having a bad day. I should have kept you home. I knew you were overstimulated as you walked out of the door," he says.

"I will do better. I can do better."

He pulls me into a tight hug and it's like what I've needed all day. I wrap my arms around his waist and tap my fingers against him. The music begins to make more sense and it's soothing.

"I have something for you. Come with me," he says softly.

He takes my hand in his and leads me from the room. I'm surprised as he takes me to the sunroom, where I love to read and paint.

My eyes grow wide when a grand piano comes into view. Michael takes me over to the bench seat and sits me down. I look up at him and he kisses my forehead.

"This is for you, little one."

"Thank you, Michael. Thank you," I gasp.

I turn to the piano and begin to play. I've never played one before, but I play the notes playing in my head. For once, it feels like my fingers are doing what they have always wanted to do. I have never been more calm.

"You're incredible," Michael says as he sits beside me and bumps me with his shoulder.

I look at him and smile. He is always so kind to me. This is the best gift ever.

"Can I play with you?"

I nod and still my fingers. Michael rolls up the sleeves of his dress shirt, then he places his hands on the keys. I smile as he begins to play "Für Elise." I love this song.

Classical music is my favorite. I close my eyes and follow the notes he is playing. I listen closely to keep up with him.

Soon, I'm lost in the music and a sense of peace washes over me. My bad day is forgotten, and I wish it could always be like this. When we stop playing, I open my eyes and look at Michael's face.

He's smiling back at me. His blond hair has fallen into his eyes, showing he's not much older than me. A boy who is becoming a man with great responsibility.

I now understand the burden I have become to him. However, he never makes me feel like that's the case. I turn away as butterflies fill my belly.

"That was amazing, Symphony. I would never know you've never played before. This is yours. Play whenever you want. Let this room be your happy place, Sim."

"Sim?"

"Yes, Symphony Isabella Mansilla, right?"

"Yes, that is right, Michael Zuko-Donati."

"Donati, Sim. Just Donati. We are Donatis."

In this moment, I believe I have fallen in love with my husband. Michael Donati has given me the greatest gifts. A piano and a name. I will cherish both.

Michael

"A piano? You gave our little one a piano?" Nico says as he sticks his head into my office.

Looking up from my computer, I then frown. I didn't know he was home. The sound of Symphony playing fills the house.

I glance at the clock and smile. It's a good thing we don't have close neighbors, although she plays beautifully and I'm sure they wouldn't mind. The only thing that might be a problem is the fact that she's been playing "Für Elise" repeatedly for the last few hours.

"I thought you, of all people, would be happy to see it."

"I am. However, judging by the hour and the fact that Annabella says she's been playing since you gave it to her this afternoon, I don't think I'll ever get any playing time. I didn't know she could play."

My smile grows. I had no idea either. I had planned on getting her lessons. However, when I saw her slightly bruised cheek after Adriano told me what happened in school, I knew giving her the piano was the right thing to do.

Symphony tries so hard to be perfect. I always tell her to be herself and do what makes her comfortable, but teenagers can be cruel. I know it's overwhelming for her.

I remember how confusing and frustrating that time of my life was. It wasn't that long ago. I remember needing an outlet when I came home from school. I wanted to give her that. I was happy to learn she could play.

"Neither did I. I bought it on a hunch. Turns out she's a prodigy.

"I plan to find her a school for music. She obviously loves it. It might be the best thing to send her away."

"Why is that?" he asks curiously.

I take a moment to think about whether or not to share this information with my brother. Nico lives in a different world. While I've told him why I married Symphony, I haven't gone into great detail about what that means for our future.

"Things are changing. Don Locatelli and his nephew have invited Uri into something that could change everything for Sim and me." I shrug. It's most of the truth.

The Locatellis want to talk to Uri about joining an alliance they are forming. I'm still learning about it and digging for more information for Uri to consider the invitation. I'm interested. It sounds like the opportunity I need to gain the upper hand with Leonardo Trovati.

"Sim? Cute. I like it. You know I don't follow the family business, but why would you need to send her away. She's been doing so well here, no?"

I pull a hand down my face. Symphony has done great in the last year. I'm watching her flourish.

If not for the bullies at school, I'd say she's been doing wonderful. She's happy most of the time and so smart. Annabella talks to her about her university studies all the time.

My mind is blown when Symphony engages with Annabella as if she sits in the lecture halls with her. My wife holds some of the most intellectual conversations I've ever heard, and in the next moment, you realize you're talking to a child.

"Yes, she's doing well, but I don't know how much longer Italy will be safe for her. Uri's decision will affect everything. I need to place Symphony far away from any of us."

Nico pushes off the doorjamb and makes his way fully into the office to take one of the seats before my desk. I notice he looks tired. His season has been up and down this year.

He's playing great but the same can't be said for the rest of his team. It looks like that might be taking a toll. I'm sure Annabella nagging him for a visit hasn't helped.

"You are twenty. You could be out partying, but you are here taking care of a young girl, along with taking care of your duties with our brother. You take on responsibilities beyond you. I admire this, little brother.

"Your heart is a good one. If you think you need to send her away, I believe you are making the right choice for her. Although it might break her heart," he says after seeming to sit in thought.

"I have considered this, but I will always make my decisions based on what will keep her safe."

"Do what you must, Michael. I will miss her. I look forward to coming home and seeing her."

I fall back into my seat. I will miss her as well. Our talks always brighten my day.

After I've had to go to that dark place to take a life, I've become accustomed to basking in her light. However, the goal has always been to keep her safe. I don't believe staying here with me is the best choice.

I sigh as my thoughts weigh heavily. "We shall see what comes of this. If the music is bothering you, I will ask her to go to bed for now."

"No, leave her. I will go to my wing. The sound may help me to sleep." He snorts. "She has never played? *Lei è un genio.*"

"Yes, that she is. A genius indeed."

CHAPTER TEN

Sweetest Things

Michael

"Get out of my fucking way," the asshole who has bumped into me snarls.

I grin and step aside. The drunk bastard doesn't realize I'm here to take his life. He's been talking all night as he sits in this pub spewing bullshit about how he's some big shot in America.

It's all lies. He's running from his boss in America who he stole some money from. He also slept with his boss's daughter before beating the shit out of her and making a run for it.

The boss had planned to overlook the theft. Maybe find him and take a finger or two, but the beating he gave that woman earned him this visit from me. No man has a right to do that to a woman.

"You fellas have a good night," the drunk bastard calls out as he gets ready to leave.

I bet he didn't think anyone would find him here on this island. That was his mistake. He didn't know his boss had access to me. There's no one I can't find.

I follow him out of the pub as he stumbles forward, mumbling to himself. Keeping a bit of a distance, I wait for him to enter the alley ahead. Pulling my gun, I place the silencer on it.

The bastard stops and begins to piss against the alley wall. I walk behind him just as he throws his head back and sighs in relief.

The condensation of his breath in the cold night air raises as he groans. I don't give him a chance to put his shit away and zip up. I pull the trigger and put a hole through his skull.

His body drops to the ground as I stand over him. Placing two more into his chest, I then quickly remove the silencer and tuck both the gun and it away. As swiftly as I've appeared, I disappear. The job is done.

I don't need to linger. I slip into the shadows and make my way to get off the island before I'm seen. I climb into the awaiting motorboat and make my way back home. I'm about fifty kilometers out when I toss the gun and silencer into the water.

I pull out my phone and call my brother. As I wait for him to pick up, I take a deep breath and allow the scent of the seawater to fill my lungs.

"Hello," Uri answers.

"It is done."

"Good. We will talk soon."

With that, he disconnects the call. I wasn't expecting more than that. Uri can be a man of very few words.

***

I step out of my car as I arrive at the house. The lights in the foyer are on, drawing my curiosity. Annabella is away on holiday with her friends. Nico is away with his team.

I don't believe Uri has come to this side of the property. He usually lets me know if he's going to drop by. Symphony and the security team should be the only ones here.

I make my way into the house and find Symphony sitting at the foot of the stairs. She's wearing her cute little Mary Janes and a black dress.

I knit my brows, wondering what she's up to. Not taking my eyes off her, I go to sit beside her. I bump her with my shoulder, causing her to glance at me.

"What's up? Why aren't you in bed?"

"I was waiting for you to finish your business and come home," she replies.

"Oh yeah? And why is that?"

"It is our anniversary. I thought we would have dinner together."

I close my eyes and groan. I had thought about what today is. To be honest, I didn't know how to handle the occasion.

I wasn't sure if I should give her a gift or say something about it. Once the assignment came in, I decided not to do anything in the end. Now I feel like an ass.

"Have you eaten?"

"No, I didn't want to get full and not be able to eat with you. Chef George and I made dinner for us. Our meal is in the warmer."

I give her a smile. When Symphony isn't reading, painting, or now playing the piano, she loves to watch our chef and help when he allows. She is like an expert when it comes to chopping up the vegetables.

"Then let's have dinner," I say and stand.

She lifts to her feet and looks up at me through her lashes. I feel bad as I look at the effort she put into her appearance. As I take in her hair and the outfit she's wearing, she steps forward and pulls my handkerchief from my pocket.

I look back at her curiously. Tapping the cloth to her tongue, she then wipes it against my cheek. When she pulls it away and it comes into my view, there is blood on the cloth.

"I will set the table and heat our food. Maybe you should go and shower. You seem to have brought work home."

I chuckle. "Sorry about that. I will be quick. We'll make a night of it. We can watch a movie together after dinner."

"I would like that. You are just in time. We still have a few hours to do all of this before our anniversary is over."

"Then I better hurry."

I go to take the handkerchief from her, but she clutches it in her grasp. I give her a questioning look and hold my hand out for it. She shakes her head at me.

"I will toss it into the fire."

"Thank you."

Symphony

I was so nervous. I didn't think Michael would return home for our anniversary. I didn't think he would want to spend it with me.

I know it's silly for me to think he would want to celebrate the occasion. He is only married to me to keep me safe. However, I wanted to have dinner with him in remembrance of the day.

I collect our now hot plates and carry them into the dining room. I take a calming breath as the vest beneath my dress goes a long way to settle me into my skin. Annabella gave it to me before she left for her holiday.

She explained she got it from a friend who said it would work like the weighted blankets. So far, it has been working wonders. I would like to show Michael I can be a real wife.

I would like for him to fall in love with me the way I've fallen for him. I know it's silly and this crush may never be requited, but I have hopes and dreams. My disorder has not caused me to be oblivious to my attraction to the opposite sex.

My husband is very handsome and attractive. He's sexy and often makes me blush. I might be fifteen now, but it is my hope that in a few years, Michael will start to see me as more than his charge.

"Something smells delicious," Michael says as he enters the room dressed in a fresh black dress shirt and slacks.

His hair is still damp, causing it to fall down in his face. His hair is much longer than one would think when it's combed back away from his face. I have always wanted to push my fingers through it.

He pulls my chair out for me to sit. I duck my head and sit down as he scoots my chair in for me. My heart is racing.

This all seems like a bad idea now. What will I say to him? Will I sound weird to him like the girls at school say I do to them?

Will I sound childish to him? I keep my fingers hidden as I can't keep them still. I long to go and play the piano.

"George said you have been on a leaner diet. I chose chicken and steamed vegetables. We went with Italian flavors. I hope you enjoy it."

"Are you not going to eat?" he asks as he picks up his knife and fork.

"Yes, I am. I am quite hungry. It does smell delicious."

I begin to eat as he does. He groans and nods his head as he chews. I keep my gaze on him from out of the corner of my eye.

I want to start a conversation, but I'm too nervous to think of anything to say. Instead, I keep stuffing food into my mouth. I dart my eyes around as I desperately try to find something to say.

"You really were hungry," he chuckles, breaking the silence.

I put my utensils down and rub my sweaty palms on my thighs. Full of nerves, I scoot forward to the edge of my seat and finish chewing my food before I answer.

"Was your work successful?" I blurt out.

Michael places his fork and knife down and clears his throat. I turn in his direction, but I don't look into his eyes. I'm not ready for him to see me.

"I was going to ask you about that. What do you know of my work?"

"I am of the belief that you take care of bad men."

"What makes you say this?" He tilts his head to the side as he studies me.

"You train a lot, and I have seen the weapons room. You are a professional at what you do, I believe."

"You do understand that's not something you should ever share with anyone. We wouldn't want anyone to come and take me away from you."

"I would never say a word. Your secret is safe with me. I will always protect our family."

"Good girl."

I preen from his praises. He winks at me. Finally, I snap my eyes to his.

I search his gaze to see if he's angry with my words, but he looks more amused than anything. I figured out months ago that both Michael and Uri are some sort of hit men. This is why Nonno believes I will remain safe with them.

"Did your sheet music come in? How has your playing been going?"

"I love to play. The sheet music has arrived. It is wonderful.

"I have taught myself to read it and play. I also believe I've accomplished writing down the music in my head. I have composed my first piece," I reply excitedly.

"I'm glad you are enjoying it so much. You will have to play it for me."

"I would very much like that."

"We are the only ones home. You can play it after we watch our movie."

"Does my playing disturb the others?"

"No. Nico says it soothes him. Annabella has never complained. I love to listen."

"I will still try to be more mindful of the hours I choose to practice."

I make a mental note to begin to set hours for playing the piano. I can get so lost in the music and lose track of time. I would hate to annoy everyone.

"Do you think you would enjoy going to school for music?"

"Yes, yes, I would. I would like that. Is it something I would be able to do?"

"I am looking into options. We will see."

"Thank you. I am quite excited now. There is still so much I want to know about music theory. I have ordered books with my allowance to learn more, but to go to school and learn would be amazing."

He gives me a bright smile that lights up his gorgeous eyes and makes my heart skip a beat. I drop my gaze to his lips and wonder what it would be like to kiss him. Sweat begins to pour from my hands as I wish for my first kiss.

I wouldn't know how to ask him for one. It is our anniversary, but I don't believe he would be amiable to a kiss. I begin to chew on my lip as I try to think of the words to use to ask.

"How is school? Do you need anything? Are you having any more trouble with those girls?"

"My grades are still all A-plus. I have not had trouble with those girls. They have left me alone since I defended myself against Sandra."

"Good."

Something in his tone makes me wonder if those girls left me alone because I had to resort to violence or if Michael somehow stepped in. We talk more about school, my other interests, and how my day has been before we both finish our meal. When we finish, I clear away our plates as Michael goes into the butler's pantry to pop us some popcorn.

We walk together to the theater with our bowl of popcorn. Michael allows me to pick our movie. I almost have a meltdown as I can't decide what would be an appropriate movie for the both of us.

Michael walks up behind me and reaches for an old black-and-white film. His cologne wraps around me and soothes me. I nod my agreement as he shows me the cover of the film.

"I think you will like this one," he murmurs.

He sets the film up and we climb into our seats. Michael tugs me into his side and holds me close as the movie begins. I have to fight not to purr.

There isn't any place I would rather be. My lids begin to grow heavy halfway through the film, but I fight to stay awake so I can play for him after the movie.

Or at least I thought I did. I mumble and moan as my back hits the soft mattress beneath me. I open my eyes and find Michael placing me in my bed and tucking me in.

He carried me up to my room. I lift up on my elbows as he moves to pull my shoes from my feet. I blink at him sleepily.

Once my shoes are off, Michael then kisses my forehead. "Go back to sleep, *mia cara*. I will see you in the morning."

I'm too sleepy to protest or say a word. I lie back and fall out before my head hits the pillow.

CHAPTER ELEVEN

Little Secrets

Michael

"Get it together, Michael," I breathe to myself as I step out of the shower.

I continue to mumble in frustration as I head into my closet to put on a pair of sweats and a T-shirt. I had to make an early morning visit today. Someone grabbed Uri's attention and warranted an introduction to me.

It was the last introduction they will ever have. I made it nice and quick. His breakfast didn't even have time to get cold before I took his life.

"I should've dragged it out for more of a distraction," I grumble.

I need to work off some steam. I've been having these dreams of this tall dancer with shapely brown legs. I can never see her face, but her body leaves me hard and wanting when I wake.

I haven't had sex since before I got married. I didn't hookup with girls often, but I've known the pleasures of sex. I hadn't thought I would be so fazed by the lack of it.

However, those dreams are causing me to wish I had an outlet. Yet when I look at a woman, I feel wrong. I know this marriage isn't real, but the amount of guilt that rises at the thought of bedding another woman makes me sick.

I have thought of speaking with Mama's priest and devoting myself to the church. So many crazy thoughts have come to mind since those dreams have started. Last night was the worst one yet.

The dancer had her long limbs wrapped around my waist as I thrust into her tight body. It felt so real. I was on the verge of coming when I woke.

"Fuck," I mutter and run my hand through my hair.

I shake my thoughts off and head down to the gym. I hope to work off some of this energy down there. Maybe I can train my body to exhaustion.

I get down to the gym and find Uri there, standing in the doorway. He's stock-still as if afraid to move. Curiosity piqued, I move quietly to stand at his side. I am taken by surprise with what I find.

Symphony is inside. She's wearing a vest that has knives lining the front and back. She's moving fluidly as she concentrates on pulling then tossing the blades into the target before her.

Something about her expression says she's angry. When I left this morning, she was still fast asleep. I can't imagine what has led to this and where the fuck did she get that vest and those blades.

I'm well aware of the fact that she likes to watch martial arts videos, so I'm not surprised by her movements. I have told her I will spar with her if she ever wants to formally train to develop the skills. However, as I watch her now, I think I might have been underestimating her.

"Did you know about this?" Uri all but whispers after a few beats.

"No."

"Who do you think she's getting ready for?"

"I have no clue. Whoever it is, they should be afraid."

"I want to help her, but I don't know if that's the best idea," Uri muses.

I pause to think for a bit. The Trovati family is hers. Although I will be the face, it will be her right. It might not be a bad idea to prepare her.

"I think she might make a better hitter than either of us. Why not help her?"

"That is what I'm afraid of. I don't believe she has a switch to be broken. Not like we had. Teaching her would be like teaching a machine. How do we control that?"

"We'll figure it out. If we don't try, she will continue to train herself. Better to know we've trained her properly."

"Bloody hell. You have a point. I will teach Baby Terminator, but you will be responsible for her. You have to help her understand the boundaries."

"I have no problem with that. She's smarter than you think."

"I know she's a genius, Michael. I am not ignorant of this fact, but I also don't want to make any assumptions. We will have to come to know her limitations."

"Agreed."

As we finish our conversation, Sim turns to us both with her chest heaving. All her blades have been pulled from her vest and thrown.

She drops to the floor on her butt and covers her face with her hands. I have never seen Symphony cry, not even when it was confirmed to her that her mother was dead. It is as she sits sobbing that I notice a patch of hair missing from the back of her head.

Only it doesn't look like the patches she used to make by tearing her own hair out. All I see is rage. Someone did this to her. Someone who will pay.

Symphony

"Why don't they like me? What am I doing wrong? Why are they so mean to me?

"Why do this to my person? I'm doing my best. I'm doing my best," I sob into my hands as I sit on the training room floor.

I couldn't sit at the piano. Music isn't going to fix this for me. My feelings are hurt. My heart aches.

I did nothing to deserve this. I sob harder because everything has been ruined. I don't know how to fix this.

Not even the vest could calm me today. I had to go to school for science club. We had our monthly meeting.

Sandra and her friends were there for their own activities as well. Someone pulled the alarm, so everyone had to report to the auditorium while the situation was dealt with. Daphne, Sandra's friend asked me to come and sit with her.

I was already overwhelmed by the flashing lights and the noise. I thought she was trying to be a friend. She never teases me as much as the other girls.

I want desperately to begin to make friends. Michael and Annabella are my only friends. I want to make more friends and have others to talk to.

Sandra and the rest of her friends all sat behind me and started to talk trash. I had ignored them at first but then there was a loud collective gasp as I felt a tug at the back of my head.

Those mean girls cut my hair. I had just gotten it to a length I was happy with. Annabella and I have been talking about hairstyles and what I plan to do with it now.

Michael had complemented me on how pretty I looked just the other day. I'm trying. I've been doing my best and they ruined everything.

I was so angry. When I returned home, I took the extra vest Annabella gave me, and I sewed loops onto it to hold the blades I bought last month with my allowance. I had already wanted to learn how to use weapons and had been watching videos on knife throwing.

I needed to calm down, so I came down here to practice. I hadn't known Michael and Uri were watching me. I just needed the pain to go away.

"Why would they do this to me?" I sob as I'm scooped up into strong arms.

Michael sits on the floor and places me on his lap. I wrap my arms around his neck and cry harder than I ever have. He tightens his hold around me and crushes me against his chest.

"I didn't do anything to deserve this. I never bother anyone. Why would they do this to me? Why cut my hair?" I cry.

"Shh, you are still beautiful. They can never take that from you. No matter what, you will always be beautiful, and they will always be filled with hate because they can't be you.

"Stop crying, little one. It will grow back. We will make this better."

"I don't want to go back there. I have grown tired of them and their treatment of me."

"Then you will not return there. You never have to go back to that school."

"Really?" I sob into his neck.

He passes a hand over my head. I begin to hiccup as my tears subside. Suddenly, I become aware of the fact that I'm sitting in his lap and his strong arms are around me.

"Yes, *cara*. I mean it. You will not go back to that school."

"Thank you."

"Where did the knives come from, *bella*?"

"I ordered them online. They were the most suitable for my hands. I can throw them easily."

"Would you like to train with Uri and me? It is your choice."

"Yes, I would like this. I would like to fight and be strong."

He kisses my forehead. "Good. You will train, but first, we will get revenge," he murmurs while stroking my back.

CHAPTER TWELVE

Little Meanies

Michael

"This is the last one," I whisper to Sim as we step in front of the house of Sandra, her bully from school.

"She is the worst of them all. I am ready."

I nod and we begin to move forward. It gutted me to hear Symphony crying like that. She's a sweet girl and only wants to be treated like a human.

They had no right to cut her hair. I'm still livid. There is no way I was going to allow this to go unanswered.

Uri asked me to be her moral compass and yet here we are. Instead of training Symphony to protect herself, I'm teaching the girl to sneak into the homes of others to exact her revenge.

We enter the bedroom of Sandra, and I go to stand in the corner of the room of the last girl we will visit tonight. From the shadows, I watch Sim move with stealthy precision. She is a quick study.

Symphony had this down by the second girl. Five bullies in all. All five will pay for what they have done.

Sim pulls her blade and swiftly cuts the girl's ponytail off, leaving the severed locks lying on the pillow. Then she reaches for the tub of pig's blood from her backpack and pours it onto the girl's sheets. A grin comes to my lips as she comes to me for the cat carrier I'm holding for her.

She takes the carrier with the skunk inside and creeps back over to the bed. The skunk races out of the cage onto the bed and climbs up the girl's body. I wish we could stay to watch how this all plays out, but we need to go.

Sim runs to me and places her hand in mine. I lead her back out of the house safely and we climb into our waiting car. Adriano pulls off quickly as the lights from the house we just left begin to come on.

Symphony wraps her arms around my waist and hugs me tightly. My anger finally begins to dissipate. I can breathe without seeing red.

"Thank you, Michael. I do feel better now. They will all wake and find their hair lying on their pillows.

"When they return to school, they will know my embarrassment and hurt," she murmurs, causing my heart to squeeze.

"Put them out of your mind. They can never hurt you again."

CHAPTER THIRTEEN

Can't Stop Me

Uri

"She is happy and safe. That's all that matters to me," Don Trovati says as he looks over the pictures I've handed him of Symphony.

He is right. She has been happier in the last few months since we pulled her from that school and started to homeschool her. We all spend time with her to make up for the socializing Michael was so worried about.

I believe she enjoys that more than trying to make friends with kids her own age. I tend to enjoy the time I spend with the young girl. She's extremely smart and observant.

Many times, she doesn't need us to engage her. Our presence in the room alone keeps her complacent. Symphony prefers to read or play the piano. We are most times fixtures in the room as she entertains herself—reading about music, construction and demolition, architecture, medicine, and computer science.

"That is something I've come to speak with you about," I say.

"Oh?"

"Michael believes it might be in her best interest to send her back to the States. He would like to enroll her into a school for the arts."

"Will that be wise?" He threads his brows and begins to look concerned.

"No one will expect to find her there. She has demonstrated a love for playing the piano. All those photos were taken while she was playing or after she finished her practice for the day.

"I don't disagree with Michael. I believe she will thrive. I'm sure you've heard the rumors.

"Things are becoming increasingly dangerous here. If not for Don Locatelli, I would have killed your brother by now. He has my name in his mouth way too much."

"Yes, I have heard a lot. I know he has been asking about her marriage and connection to the Donati family. I have spoken with your uncle about this a number of times.

"He was ready to have my head, but I have smoothed things over with him. I believe he was amused with Michael's decision. As was I," Don Trovati says.

"My brother thinks differently from most. Symphony's wellbeing is important to him. He does all he can to ensure her happiness."

"This I am grateful for, but her safety is just as important to me."

I scoff. Her safety has never been in question. We protect Symphony as if she's a national treasure.

"If he comes for Symphony, I will kill him, and no one will be able to stop me. I do not care if it starts a war. She is my family, and I take her welfare personally. I suggest you let your brother know she is under my protection.

"Stop asking about her and stop asking about me. He is only getting this courtesy because of you. I don't repeat myself."

"Do not underestimate how much my brother wants to run this family. He will face you and whatever wrath you bring to accomplish this. He does not see that the families he has aligned himself with are only allies because he has something to offer them.

"Once they get what they want, he will be expendable. If this is what Michael thinks is best, let him send her to this school. Leonardo will overplay his hand, and we will answer when he does," Don Trovati says with conviction.

I say nothing. I meant what I said. If Leonardo Trovati steps out of line, I will put him in his place.

Leonardo

"Why can't any of you get to this child?" I seethe.

"The don has given her to Uri Donati. She has married into the Donati family. It is not as easy as you think to get to anyone in that family," Elio says like a pussy.

I turn to look him right in his hazel eyes. He's been with me for too long to think I give a fuck how hard this might be. I glare at him until he looks away from me and drops his head.

Our childhood friendship is the only thing keeping me from putting a bullet in his head. He's been more like a brother to me than my own. I certainly have more love for him than I do for my blood brother.

"Tell me something I don't know. I know who my brother gave her to. Someone kill that bastard and bring me the girl," I snap.

"That's a suicide mission," one of Elio's guys says.

I pull my gun and put a bullet through his head. All the others turn to look down at his lifeless body. I shrug and put the smoking gun down on my desk.

"Now he doesn't have to worry about a suicide. Anyone else want some help meeting their maker?"

"No, we will get it done," Elio replies for them all.

"Clean this shit up and all of you get out of my fucking face. Don't come back until you have Donati's head in a box and that little bitch in a bag beside him."

"And your brother? What is the plan for him?"

"Don't you worry about that. I will take care of him," I say with a grin on my lips.

CHAPTER FOURTEEN

Back to America

Symphony

A year later ...

I took the test and played for the audition like Michael and Uri asked me to. Now I will be attending school here in America. I miss Michael already.

Uri and Annabella were the ones to bring me here. Michael had to tend to some business. I think I'm glad he wasn't the one to bring me.

I wouldn't have been able to say goodbye. Now that I know why I took the test, I would have failed it if I knew school would take me away from him. Looking around my new room, I don't like anything about it.

I want to go back home. I swipe at my tears and continue to put my things away. I can't help but wonder if Michael wanted to send me away because he's twenty-one now.

73

I have turned sixteen, but nothing has changed between us. I've never kissed my husband, and I haven't told him about my crush. I feel silly now that I'm here and he's in Italy.

This place is so noisy. It's not like our home in the countryside back in Italy. I don't know if I will like Chicago. I will try my best to do well here, but I will long for home with each day.

"Ms. Symphony," Adriano calls as he knocks on the door and peeks his head into the room.

I drop the jeans I just took from my suitcase and turn to look at him. He is the only one here that I know. Uri and Annabella have left to return home without me.

"Yes?" I whisper.

"Would you like to have dinner soon?"

"No. I don't want to eat alone. I will skip dinner," I murmur.

"You don't have to eat alone, Ms. Symphony. I will eat with you if you like."

"You don't have to call me that. You are older than I am. My husband isn't here to scold you. You can call me just Symphony or Sim."

I give a wobbly smile as I say the name Michael gave me. I can't help wondering what I did to make him send me so far away. There had to be a music school closer to my family.

They are the only friends I have and now I have no one. I shove my hands into my pockets to keep me from falling into old habits. I blow out a breath and sniffle.

"Come on downstairs, Sim. I will have dinner with you. You shouldn't cry. This is a great opportunity for you. Michael only wants the best for you," Adriano says gently.

I nod my head and slowly start from the room. I guess it is a great opportunity. I'm happy I will get to study music.

Adriano's phone rings as he walks beside me. My ears perk up at the mention of Michael. I lick my suddenly dry lips as I try to listen in to the conversation.

"She's right here. Would you like to speak with her?"

I don't realize I'm holding my breath until Adriano hands me the phone. I take it clumsily and press it to my ear. I chide myself as I stand waiting for Michael to speak instead of letting him know I am on the line.

"Sim, are you there?"

"Yes, this is me, Symphony. Hello, Michael. How are you?"

"Hello, Sim. I am well. How are you liking Chicago? Are you getting settled in?"

"It is okay. It's not like our home. I will make do."

"I miss your playing already. The house feels so empty without you," he says.

"I will be there in spirit. At least until I can come home and be there with you."

Michael falls silent on the other end. A ball begins to form in my belly. I don't like this feeling. Something tells me I'm not going back home.

"Michael?" I whisper.

"I will always do what's best for you, Sim. I need you to understand and remember that. This is what's best."

"Okay. I will do my best. I will make you proud of me. I won't forget my training and I will try to make new friends, I promise," I say as my voice shakes and more tears fall.

"I know you will. You are my brave girl. I will talk to you soon, *bella*. Be good."

"I will be waiting for your call. Be safe, Michael. I will miss you."

"I will miss you too, *cara*."

With that, he ends the call. I stand holding Adriano's phone as I stare down at it. My heart is heavy, and I am a bit confused.

Handing Adriano back his phone, I follow him downstairs. However, as we get to the foot of the stairs, the lights all go out. I thread my brows and begin to look around.

"Stay close and keep behind me," Adriano whispers.

No sooner than he says the words, gunshots begin to ring out. Adriano pulls his guns and tries to lead me to safety. However, we don't make it across the foyer before Adriano is hit. He grunts as he stumbles back and grabs for me to cover me with his body.

"I need to get you upstairs," he grinds out.

"No, you need to hand me your pistols. It's the only way we are going to survive. My vests are upstairs. I am unarmed."

"Michael and Uri will kill me."

"No, these people will kill you and me. Now give me the guns so I can save our lives," I hiss back.

He hands me one of his guns and I roll my eyes. I then dip and grab the one I know he keeps at his ankle and the extra clip with it. With the two guns in my hands, I spin and take aim.

The streetlights illuminate my vision enough for me to see my targets and begin to take them out. I take down two and stand to my full height. Adriano limps at my side, trying to help. We work together at first, but he is hit again and falls to the ground.

Anger rocks through me. I am here alone, and someone is trying to kill me. They will not succeed.

I run across the black and white checkered marble floors and slip behind one of the large pillars for cover. I have to leave Adriano behind for now.

I focus and home in on the men shooting at me. All my training over the last year kicks in and I keep aiming and shooting. As I zone in, I count five more men moving in on me.

I narrow my gaze on the guy leading them. He lifts his hand and signals for the others to wait. I aim right for his head and take him out before he can drop his hand back to his side.

Before the other four fan out and disappear from my reach, I step slightly from behind the pillar, then tuck and roll out of my hiding place. As I come up on my toes, I aim and shoot the first two.

Quickly, I run to the next pillar and take up a hiding place behind it. Shots are fired, but they spray the floor and hit the pillar and not me. I spin out from the other side of the pillar and run toward the two shooting. I drop and slide on my hip as I take out their legs.

They both drop to the ground. I come up and go to stand over them. Without blinking, I pump two into each of their chests.

At least one of my guns is empty, but there are no more threats. I rush to Adriano and drop to his side. He's bleeding heavily. I pull him into my arms and begin to rock.

"We're okay. We're okay," I murmur as I rock.

Uri

"We need to turn around now," Annabella gasps from beside me.

"What is it? What's happening?"

"The alarm system I programmed has been triggered. The property has been breached."

"Fuck," I hiss and turn the car around.

Not caring about anything else, I floor it back to the brownstone we just left Symphony in. Symphony was accepted to schools in New York, Chicago, and Boston. We chose Chicago because when I do come to the States, I spend a lot of time here. My uncle is also here.

That might have been a mistake. Leonardo is aware of these facts. However, I didn't think he would be bold enough to pull some shit like this.

This is a show of disrespect to me and the Donati family. I am going to call for his bloody fucking head. I drive like a madman through these Chicago streets, praying I get to Sim before something happens to her.

Michael cares deeply for the girl and this will devastate him. As I turn into the block of the house, I note the cars outside that don't belong to any of the men we left here.

I race from the car before I barely shift into park. Annabella hops out with me, her own gun drawn. I wave for her to hang back, but she ignores me as we step over bodies to get inside.

I have lost a few men. Annabella stops to check our guys' pulses to make sure we have indeed lost them. I continue into the house. More bodies line the floor, along with pools of blood.

It looks like a bloodbath. However, it's once I get beyond the main foyer to the open area that feeds into the living area, kitchen, dining area, and study that I find a sight I'm not expecting to find.

"Stay with me. Stay with me. We're okay. We're okay," Sim says as she rocks with Adriano pressed against her chest.

Still holding a gun in her palm, she runs her forearm under her nose. I glance around and my chest swells with pride. This is her handiwork. She did well.

"Annabella, you are needed in here. Adriano is down," I call out as I pull my phone and get to making calls.

I haven't been here for more than forty-eight hours, and I have a mess for my uncle to clean up. I sigh. Symphony won't be staying in Chicago after all.

Boston had been my first choice. The estate there is brand new, and the place is like a fortress. There, she won't need the protection of my family because no one will get onto the property without losing their lives. Michael will just have to trust my judgment.

We tried things his way. Now we will do them mine. I will spend the next two months with her to get her settled in. Business will have to wait.

CHAPTER FIFTEEN

Snapped

Michael

I roar into the room as my chest heaves. My wife. They tried to execute a hit on my wife.

I'm supposed to ignore this disrespect? I'm seething with fury. I can't touch Leonardo, but this won't go unanswered.

I pace the destroyed office at Uri's apartment in London. I couldn't force myself to stay in the house alone. I will have to write my brother a check for the mess I have made here.

When Uri called to inform me of the situation, I lost it. I feel like such a fool for sending her away. She had been safe with me.

"What have I done?" I choke out.

I go to flop down in the desk chair after I turn it back over and right it. However, the lights go out and a commotion starts somewhere outside the office doors. I have men outside the apartment and two inside.

So Leonardo does have the balls to come after men and not just women and children. I pull my guns from my holsters, ready to take him on. I hope he has come himself and not sent someone in his place.

I want to be the one to take him down and I don't want to have to wait for permission. He needs to be dealt with. Hopefully, he has saved me the time of making the request.

The door bursts open and my two guys appear, firing at the men on the other side. I bare my teeth and rush around them. I'm not about to hide like a trapped mouse.

"Boss, no. We have orders to keep you safe. Get back," Giorgio says.

I ignore him and rush out of the room. I move like the trained killer I am. I shoot the first guy who comes into sight through the neck, then put two into his chest. My next bullet goes through the skull of the guy behind him.

I turn to my left and take three more out. The rage coursing through me fuels me to keep moving forward. I feel Giorgio and Armando behind me, but I keep my focus on the targets ahead of me.

I don't stop until both my guns are smoking and there's nothing left but the sound of my breathing and Giorgio making the call to Uri to inform him of what has happened.

My chest is heaving. My head feels like it's about to explode. This isn't enough.

I need to kill something else to feed this bloodlust that has awoken within me. It's not that I can't be the savage my brother is. I chose to be the calmer of the two. Not now.

"He wants to speak to you," Giorgio says as he holds his phone out to me.

"Hello," I say into the phone, seething.

"You know what to do."

"I do. Give my apologies to Don Trovati. His brother asked for this."

My actions from here might just start a war. I can't be held accountable for how far I take things, and I will take things far. They came for those I love. It is only fair I return the favor.

"Done," Uri says and hangs up the call without another word.

They have awoken a beast I won't be able to put to rest until I have sent a message. After all, Trovati has sent these men thinking they were targeting the man who makes them hush.

I have to set an example in my brother's name. I may not be able to touch Leonardo Trovati, but no one said anything about the ones he loves and who are close to him.

"Get a cleaning crew in here and call the tailor," I snarl as I toss Giorgio back his phone.

CHAPTER SIXTEEN

The Last Fit

Leonardo

"I'm excited for you to come back to America with me," Regina says from across the table from me.

I look into her blue eyes and smile. She smiles back at me as she runs her hand over all that thick, lush blonde hair I love running my fingers through. I plan to hold it in a tight grip while I fuck her later tonight.

"I told you if you stick with me, I'd give you the world. Look at you now. You get to travel from the States to Italy and all the other places I go," I say with a smile on my lips.

"It's all a dream come true."

"How's the apartment?"

"I love it. Although I thought I was going to stay with you," she says with a pout.

"You will. I just wanted you to have a place here of your own. My gift to you."

Her eyes light up at the mention of a gift. I have my reasons for not letting her move into my estate. None of which she needs to be worried about.

Regina has been my girl for three years now. I'm thinking about making her legit at the end of the year. She will make a good wife for a man like me.

Things are starting to look better with each day. The families I've aligned myself with have been talking about helping me move Alessio out of my way. My older brother has become set in his ways and it's time for new blood.

He knows it, they know it, and I know it. The only problem is the Locatelli family. My brother happens to be good friends with Don Alfanzo Locatelli.

We are both at a stalemate for now. If either of us makes a move to kill the other, we will tip the scales unfavorably. However, I took the risk of going after Alessio's little pet that he thinks he's going to involve in our family business.

I want Uri Donati and the girl dead. The Donatis will take over my family over my dead body. I will have news by the day after tomorrow of how my plan went.

Elio's crew was told not to contact him for two days after the hits. That way this can't come back to me. I don't need the families to know what I've done.

"I'm starving, babe. I hope the food comes out soon," Regina says, pulling me from my thoughts.

I glance around. It does seem to be taking a long time for some pasta and gravy. I note that other tables that were seated after us have been served.

Just when I'm about to make a fuss about it, our waiter appears. He places two steaming plates before us. I sit back and take a sip of my wine.

I'm sure the chef took his time to make our food fresh. My name is getting out there. I'm earning my respect.

Once the waiter shaves some parmesan on top of both our plates, I place my wine glass down and pick up my fork and spoon to dig in. I'll admit, I'm starving a bit too.

"You need to think about where we want to spend the holidays this year. I'm thinking about doing something special," I say as I think of all my plans while absentmindedly spooling spaghetti and meatballs onto my fork.

Regina gasps, causing me to look at her. I grin, thinking she has figured out my plans. However, when I look at her stricken face, my smile falls, and I pause to look down at my plate, where her gaze is fixed. I drop the fork and spoon and push back in my seat.

I can't be looking at what I think I'm looking at. I swallow hard a few times as I fully take the plate of pasta in. Anger fills me and I begin to grind my teeth.

"What the fuck?" I bellow.

"I think I'm going to be sick," Regina says and covers her mouth with her hand.

I don't move an inch. Instead, I narrow my gaze as I stare at the two hazel eyes staring back at me. One on my fork and the other sitting on a heap of pasta while fingers peek out from the pasta and gravy.

"Let's go. We're leaving," I growl as I stand.

***

I dropped Regina at her apartment when I couldn't get her to calm down. I was hoping to get her to stay with me for the night so I could fuck this rage and frustration out. Who the fuck would dare to send me that shit?

Whoever it was had some balls. I think of Donati, but I don't think that's his style. Rumors circulate through our world, but they are never what they seem.

I have no fear of Uri Donati. All that bullshit is a myth. No one man can be that ruthless and have such a reach.

The plate from the restaurant flashes in my head. I can't shake the image out of my mind. Those eyes seemed so familiar.

I'm sure they belonged to some animal. Someone is trying to rattle me. The fingers could have been fake.

I didn't take the time to dig them out to inspect them closely. Regina was freaking out and I had been in a rage. I needed to get her the fuck out of there before she caused a scene.

I punch the shower wall as a million thoughts float through my mind. Elio hadn't returned my call before I entered the shower. He has been taking care of some business for me today.

He's probably balls deep in one of his whores. He better call me back before the night is over. I want to get to the bottom of this.

Once again, my mind goes to Donati. If my men failed, this could have been him. I shake the thought off. They all know better than to fail.

However, if this gets out, it could be taken as a weakness. I want to find the source and deal with it swiftly. I will not take this lying down.

I cut the shower off and step out to wrap a towel around my waist. Grabbing my phone from the counter, I check it for messages and missed calls. Still nothing from Elio.

Tossing the phone back down, I turn and head for my walk-in closet. I freeze as I step in and find a black suit hanging over a pair of black shoes. A suit and shoes I didn't place there or have placed there.

My heart starts to pound. Rumors have said that when you are a hit Uri Donati feels is deserving, he will lay out the suit and shoes you are meant to be buried in. It is all the warning you get that the man who makes them hush has come for you.

Rumor has it that not all get this warning. You have to be a hit he takes personally. I snort. That bastard knows he can't touch me.

I glance around quickly, just in case. Then I go to pull the note off the lapel of the suit jacket. The blood drains from my face as I read it.

There is more than one way to hush a problem. You can always be touched in some way. Never underestimate my reach again. You will never receive another warning.

H

I crumble the note in my palm and stomp out of the closet into my bedroom. Who the fuck does that motherfucker think he is? As I enter the room, a smile comes to my lips.

I could use a release. Fucking Regina into the mattress is just what I need. Seeing her blonde locks sprawled across the pillow makes me hard instantly.

"I'm glad you changed your mind, baby," I croon as I drop my towel to the floor and move to climb into the bed with her.

I get under the sheets, not bothering to turn on the lights. Reaching to brush her hair away from her neck, I go to press my lips against her soft skin.

"I'm going to fuck you so good. I need to give it to you hard," I growl and go to nuzzle her neck.

I pull my face away as something wet touches my skin. I swipe a hand across my face and rub my fingers together as something thick and sticky coats them.

"Gina?" I call as I go to brush my other hand over her hair.

I startle as her hair seems to shift on her head unnaturally. Quickly, I turn to switch on the bedside lamp. When I look toward Regina, I see it isn't her at all.

"What the fuck?" I breathe as my mouth goes dry.

I grab the blonde wig and pull it off the man's head. However, as I get it in my hand, I realize it's no wig. I drop the scalp down on the bed and reach to turn the man beside me onto his back so I can get a look at him.

The body is stiff as a board. A sob tears through me as I realize it's Elio's lifeless body. His eyes have been plucked from his head, leaving hollow sockets.

I look from his body to the blonde hair now soaking the sheets. I knit my brows as what I'm looking at sinks in. There's no fucking way.

"No, no, no," I say as I pet the hair with a shaky hand.

He killed my best friend and scalped the woman I had planned to make my wife. I begin to sob silently, not able to make a sound. I have been robbed of all air.

CHAPTER SEVENTEEN

The Answer Is No

Uri

After getting Sim settled in Boston, I decided I needed to make a trip to Italy for a quick visit. I intend to return and make sure she's okay, but I need to make this trip now. I will not wait any longer to finish this deed.

Leonardo Trovati must go. He hasn't made a sound since Michael paid him a special visit, but I'm not willing to believe that's the end of it. We will hear from him again.

I need him to be hushed so that doesn't happen. I will not be made to look over my shoulder. That hit in London was meant for me because the wanker doesn't realize that I'm not the Donati Symphony is married to.

"Uri," Don Alfanzo croons. "It's good to see you. Come, come. LaSalle is here with me. We want to talk about the alliance while you're here."

I grunt and nod. I don't know that I want to be involved in this alliance business. I told him before I would hear him out, but listening is the most I plan to do.

I follow him into the dining room, where food is spread out across the table. It all looks piping hot and smells delicious. LaSalle is already seated, as are Marco and D'Angelo Locatelli.

We all say our greetings and shake hands before sitting at the table. Don Locatelli gestures for me to take the seat at his left as LaSalle sits at his right. Marco is already at my right and D'Angelo is across from him.

"I was happy to receive your call. What can I do for you, Uri?" the don says.

"I want Leonardo Trovati's head. I need you to give me clearance to take his life."

The don sits back in his seat. He looks me right in the eyes. I don't look away.

"I cannot do this for you. Leonardo Trovati is but a gnat in the middle of something greater than his ambitions. If I allow you to kill him, it will force a war I'm not ready to enter.

"It is likely that my family will win, but at what cost. This is a battle we will enter, but not a moment before I'm ready," Don Alfanzo says.

"So he gets to live and torment my family?" I seethe.

"I have ears. I know you have already dealt with him. I believe it will be some time before he is willing to come at you again."

"I don't leave loose ends. I needed to respond to him, so I did. The only reason the job wasn't finished was out of respect for you. I didn't think I would be met with resistance.

"Trovati went after a woman. A woman who is still a child. Since when is a bloody hit on a woman or child ignored," I growl.

"This is not being ignored. I am being strategic. In time, you will have a yes. For now, the answer is no."

"In that case. Thank you for having me. I have lost my appetite. I will be taking my leave," I reply.

"What about the alliance? LaSalle would like to talk to you," Don Alfanzo says.

"For now, the answer is no," I say tightly.

LaSalle

"That didn't go as we wanted," I say to my uncle once Uri Donati is gone.

Uri is a power player, whether he knows it or not. I want him for the Alliance. Logan and I both agree he will help to make our forces stronger. He has that thing we're looking for to make this work.

"He is angry for now. We will bide our time. When the opportunity reveals itself, we will offer an olive branch and open the conversation back up. There is still much time," my uncle says.

I nod. He is right; there is still plenty of time before I'm ready to make a move. For now, I will watch and wait.

CHAPTER EIGHTEEN

Time for Change

Symphony

I look in the mirror at my new hairdo. I think I like it. After looking at hundreds of videos and pictures on my tablet, I decided to go with locs.

It will be easy for me to maintain. I like the idea of that. Annabella has tried to help me with maintenance, but she doesn't know much more than I do about keeping up with my texture and hair type.

My mother was Latina, but my father was Black. I got a mix of their hair types I believe. I only have one really old picture of my parents that Nonno gave me.

"You look so pretty," Annabella says from the doorway.

I turn to smile at her as I smooth my hands over the front of my blouse. I went with a gray top and light blue jeans. My shoes are sparkly silver flats I bought while shopping with Annabella.

"Thank you. Is he here?" I ask excitedly.

"Uri sent me a text. They will be here in the next twenty minutes."

I clasp my hands together and take a calming breath. I haven't seen Michael in fifty-three days. We talk on the phone, but I haven't seen his face in almost two months.

I'm excited for this visit. I have so much I want to share with him. I hope he likes my new look.

I did my best to look pretty for him. Before I go to leave the room with Annabella, I glance over at my jewelry box. I chew on my tongue as I think about putting on my wedding rings.

I don't like the way they feel on my finger, so I don't wear them often. It's not like Michael expects me to. People would probably question me if I did.

I shake the thought off and turn to leave my room to go await Michael's arrival. Annabella takes my hand and gives it a tight squeeze as we walk.

This estate is much larger than the house in Chicago. I like it much better. I have made it home since I've been here.

Uri and Annabella have helped me to make sure everything is just right. I love having Annabella here, but I know she will be leaving soon. She has to return to her studies and whatever it is she does for Uri and Michael.

I am not her assignment. I'm okay with that. I also feel safer here.

I think it's because of the full-time military-trained staff who live with me. I don't see everyone much, but I know they're here. Uri says they are not here to make me feel like I'm in prison, but they are here to help me anytime I need.

"Don't be so nervous. He has come all this way just for you."

"I don't want to disappoint him. I'm also afraid I will start my old tics because I'm nervous. I want Michael to see I have grown," I explain.

"He will see it. We all do. I'm so proud of you, Sim. Don't worry. You will be fine."

"I hope you are right," I murmur.

"Here, take this," she says and hands me her gray hair tie.

"What is this for? My hair hasn't grown long enough to pull it up yet. Does it look bad?" I ask as I start to panic.

"No, it's not for your hair. Relax, I love your hair. It complements your face. The band is to be placed on your wrist. If you feel like you're overwhelmed, try snapping it. It might help."

"How do you always know how to help me?"

Annabella laughs and wraps an arm around my shoulders. She gives me a tight squeeze that helps settle me a bit. I lean my head against her and inhale her calming scent.

"I volunteered in the children's ward of the hospital when I was eighteen. There was a little girl there with cancer. She was also on the spectrum.

"I learned a lot of things as we tried to help her. The pain and treatments made things extremely challenging for her," she says.

"What was her prognosis? Did she beat the cancer?"

"That she did. She and her mother still write me letters."

"This is good. I am happy to hear that. Are you sure you're not going to practice medicine when you complete your studies? You will make such a good doctor. Your bedside manner will be so comforting to your patients."

"I never entered medicine to become a doctor. Not in the conventional way. I always knew my brothers would need me. I wanted to be there if something like what happened to my father ever happened to one of them," she says.

"Like you helped Adriano? He wouldn't be here if not for you. Thank you again for saving him. If you and Uri—"

"Sim. You have to stop blaming yourself for that. You saved both of your lives. No one can blame you for going into shock after what you did.

"I think you're pretty badass. I know Michael is proud of you. And Adriano is grateful. I think you earned a friend for life with him."

I go to answer her, but the front door opens as we get to the front of the house. Michael comes through the door with Uri. He drops his bags and steps forward to open his arms. I look to Annabella, thinking the gesture is for her.

She smiles and gestures with her head for me to go to him. I turn back to Michael and find him smiling at me. I gasp and run into his arms.

He wraps me in his embrace and holds me tight. I wrap my arms around his waist and squeeze him back. When he places a kiss on my forehead, I can't help but melt into him.

"I am happy to see you," I blurt out.

"It is good to see you too, little one. I want to hear all about your new school and what you have learned," he says in his deep voice.

"Is it okay for you to come to my room? I would like to show you what I have done with it."

I pull away to look up at his handsome face. He cups the side of my face and searches with his gaze. I drop my eyes to the floor.

"Yes, *bella*. Show me this room. Then you can tell me everything."

We turn and head for the stairs so I can lead him back to my room. I am talking a mile a minute as we go. I tell him about my classes and how much I love to play at school. It's nothing like the school I went to with the mean girls.

I haven't made friends yet, but no one has been mean to me. I'm talking so much; I don't realize I haven't given Michael a chance to get a word in. I pause as he stands looking around my room.

"Oh. I am sorry. I will be quiet so you can talk," I murmur.

"You are fine, Sim. I'm happy to listen to how happy you are. I can almost find it in my heart to be okay with not hearing you play every day."

I gasp. "Wait, that reminds me. I have a gift for you," I say and rush to get the box with the gift I have for him.

I retrieve the box from my bedside table and turn to hand it to him. He takes the box with an amused smile on his lips. I watch with bated breath as he opens it.

He pulls the lid off the box and pulls the pocket watch from inside. I smile as he brushes his thumb across the design on the outside. It's his initials, MD. He clicks the button to open the watch, and "Für Elise" begins to play, bringing a smile to his lips. My heart swells.

I will forever think of him whenever I hear this song. It makes me think of the time when he gave me my first piano and sat to play with me. He lifts his blue gaze to look at me and smiles.

"Thank you, Sim. I have something for you too."

I reach for the band on my wrist and begin to pop it. Michael places the watch in his pocket and turns to my vanity, where my jewelry box sits. I watch him closely.

He opens the jewelry box and reaches in for my rings. He then pulls a box from his other pocket and turns to hold it out to me. Confused, I step forward slowly.

"Wh … what is it?" I ask as I take the box with shaky hands.

"Open it."

I open the box and find a pretty necklace resting inside. I pull it out and hold it up. It's a white gold wheat chain.

Michael takes it from my fingertips and opens it. He then slides my rings onto the chain. He holds the chain up and motions me to him.

I turn and he places it around my neck. I reach to cover the rings as they rest against my skin. Looking over my shoulder, I stare up at him.

"How does it feel? Does it bother you?" he asks with concern.

"No. Thank you. I will not take it off. Thank you, Michael."

He holds my gaze as he reaches for one of my locs. "This is gorgeous on you. What made you change it?"

I turn away and take a step away from him. I love his touch, but I feel like I'm about to lose control. I begin to pop the band on my wrist and try not to start chewing on my tongue.

I'm afraid to do something to mess the moment up. The butterflies in my belly are taking over. I never told him why I don't wear my rings, but I feel as if he knows.

Michael seems to know me better than I know myself sometimes. It's in the way he watches and studies me. I get the feeling he wants to know what makes me tick.

It takes me a moment to get it together. I still don't know how to tell him my feelings. A part of me feels like it's better not to.

"I wanted to do something different. Something I would be able to maintain without a lot of fuss," I say to answer his question.

He nods. "Come, let's go get something to eat."

CHAPTER NINETEEN

Brokenhearted

Michael

Now that I've seen the fortress Uri has built around Sim I believe I might have made the right decision after all. Especially since we weren't given the go-ahead to execute Trovati.

After what I did to his right hand and his girlfriend, I know he's not going to disappear forever. He is quiet for now because he's plotting. I can feel it.

I won't chance Sim being out in the open where he can find her. Uri and I will be returning to Italy, so America will be of no interest to him. I have been in London for the last two months, causing everyone who sees me to think I'm Uri while he has been here taking care of Sim and getting her settled.

We found out that Leonardo got lucky in targeting two of the right places in search of us. His right hand used two different crews who weren't in communication with each other. I killed the only link the two crews had to each other.

There is no way for Leonardo to find out both crews thought they were targeting Uri but only one was close. I didn't regret my decision to kill his right hand from the start. After finding out this information, I was more so confident that I made the right move.

"It is best for you to be here," I murmur into Sim's hair as she sobs.

This is killing me. We've been standing in the foyer of the house for the last half hour as she clings to me crying as Uri, Annabella, and I try to leave. I have spent two weeks with her.

We went shopping so I could spoil her. I've taken her to the movies. We've been out to dinner almost every other night. Sim has had my undivided attention.

I feel so wrong leaving her behind, but Italy is too dangerous for me to take her back with me. I'm an assassin for my family. I am never in one place.

Symphony is better off here, where she can be happy and attend school for something she loves. I will remain strong and not go back on my decision. She belongs here.

"Sim, *cara*, please. You know why you are here. This is best for you. We will talk on the phone as we have been. Call me anytime you need me. Ask for anything you want," I plead.

"I want to be with you," she cries.

"I will miss you too, *bella*, but I need you to be brave for me. I need you to stay here and finish school."

"I don't want to be alone. I don't want you to leave me."

I close my eyes and tell myself to stay strong. I can't give in. No matter how much I want to, I can't give in.

"We will come to visit. You will not be alone. Adriano will be here with you."

Uri looks at me with pursed lips. He didn't want me to come to America in the first place. I can see the *I told you so* written in his eyes.

He moves forward and places a hand on Symphony's shoulder. She turns to look at him as she tightens her hold around my waist and fists her hands tighter in my T-shirt. My heart is aching.

"I need you to be brave, Symphony. I need you to be the soldier I've trained. Michael must leave to return to business.

"A part of that business is to work with me to keep your nonno and family name safe. One day, this will be your job. You will stand in your nonno's place and Michael will be there to help you. Do you understand?"

She nods and sniffles. "Yes."

Slowly, she begins to release her hold on me. My heart turns to ice as she steps away from me. Although I know this is what must be done, it feels so wrong.

"Go," Annabella whispers from beside me.

I brush a hand over Sim's hair before I turn to leave. I need to touch her one more time to let her know I care and will miss her. She has become more important to me than I ever thought she would.

As I walk to the door, she begins to wail. I turn to see she has fallen to the floor and balled herself up, holding her knees as she sobs. Adriano appears and sits on the floor beside her, leaning to whisper into her ear.

Anger and jealousy fill me. That should be me comforting her. I should be the one to stop her tears. I close my eyes when he gets her to sit up and pulls her into his arms.

Uri comes to push me through the door. How am I supposed to keep doing this? I swear, Trovati is going to die, and I will come to get my little one so she can be at home with her family.

"I'll be back, *bella*. I promise," I whisper as I leave and go to climb into the back of the car.

Symphony

I had two weeks of bliss while Michael was here. I didn't mean to break down when he had to leave. I just woke to this feeling as if I wouldn't see him again once he left me.

I have been sad all day. Adriano has tried to get me to laugh and be happy. I didn't know he was so funny and smart.

"You know if we eat any more of this ice cream, it's going to ooze out of our pores," Adriano says in his Italian accent as I grab another pint of vanilla ice cream.

"That is a lie. It is impossible for ice cream to come out of your pores because the digestive system breaks down food into tiny particles that are absorbed into the bloodstream, not transported to the skin's pores; therefore, we could eat as much as we want and that would never happen," I reply.

"I love that about you," he snorts.

"Love what about me?" I ask and blink at him in confusion.

"The way you hold so much information and know almost everything about everything. Then you spill it out without having to think about it," he says.

"I think about it. I think a lot."

"I think a lot too. I think you should remember to be a sixteen-year-old girl. I think you should live your life here.

"Let Michael do what he has to in Italy or London or wherever he will be. You are brilliant, Symphony. Make the best of what you have come here to do," he says.

I want to yell and shout at him. He doesn't know what's best for me. I know he is nineteen and older than me, but he doesn't know it all.

"I know I am sixteen. I have no choice but to live my life. I will go to school and do my best. That is what I must do for Michael to come back to get me."

"So you plan to wait for him to come back for you? What about making friends or having a boyfriend. You're very pretty. I don't think finding someone who's interested will be so hard."

"I will make friends, but I don't want a boyfriend. I have a husband. I will not dishonor my marriage."

"I just thought—"

"Please keep your thoughts to yourself. Good night."

I turn to leave the kitchen. I want to go to sleep. This day has been long and confusing.

CHAPTER TWENTY

Choosing Pointe

Symphony

I walk the halls at school, waiting for my practice hour. I need to get lost in the music. Everything has been so melancholy since my family left me.

Michael has kept to his word and calls me every day, but I still miss him and want to be with him. When I play, I feel like I'm closer to him.

I turn toward the dance rooms and breathe deeply as their music floats into the hall. The dancers are all so beautiful. I have tights and a leotard beneath my jogging suit because I love to sneak into their practice rooms after my practices.

I pass the ballet rooms and excitement fills me. The ballerinas are dancing. I'm always fascinated by how they lift on their toes.

Stopping, I watch their movements, planning to try them later. I have purchased a pair of their shoes. I have a black pair.

They spoke to me when I saw them. I slip my backpack with the shoes inside off my back and hug the bag to my chest. I believe I could move as gracefully as they do.

I'm so lost in my awe of them, I don't notice when the instructor starts for the door. She opens it and peeks her head out. I look at her with wide eyes.

"I'm sorry. I will leave," I murmur.

"If you are late you don't stand there and watch. Come inside and join in.

"I do not punish my dancers for tardiness by turning them away. Your punishment will be to perform the piece as a solo for my critique. If you don't want to be in the spotlight, you will be on time."

"Oh, no, ma'am. I'm not one of your students."

"Nonsense, I saw you practicing. Now come, stop wasting time. Put on your shoes and dance."

I see arguing with her is useless, so I open my bag and take my shoes out. Stepping into the room with her, I peel off my jogging suit and then place on my pointe shoes.

When I stand and move to the center of the room, the instructor gives me a smile and starts the music. I move into position just like I've watched the others do countless times.

Then I close my eyes and let the music guide me. I dance through the routine I've watched them perform over the last week. Moving with the gracefulness I have watched the dancers use, I dance until the song comes to an end.

I end with a leap through the air I've been practicing, then place my arms over my head and bow my head gracefully. My chest is heaving as applause fills the air. I lift to straighten as my cheeks heat.

"*Bravo, magnifique.* I haven't seen this piece performed so flawlessly in years. What is your name? Where have you been? Why do I only see you in these rooms after hours?"

"My name is Symphony. As I have told you, I am not one of your students. I am a pianist. I wanted to learn, so I have been watching and I come to practice what I have watched after my practices," I respond.

"A pianist? Ha. And I am Mozart," she scoffs in her French accent.

"I assure you, ma'am. I play Mozart. I am a music student, not a dancer."

"No, no. This can't be. You are a dancer."

I giggle and shake my head. She looks back at me with a mix of awe, confusion, and excitement. I think that's what I see.

"Class is dismissed. Symphony, you and I need to go see the dean of dance."

Michael

My phone rings as I sit scowling at the screen before me. It is midnight, but I can't sleep. I am waiting for my time to call Sim before I call it a night.

I have been irritable since leaving Symphony in Boston. I don't know what these feelings are that I've begun to have concerning her. I know I'm protective of her, but this has gone beyond that.

"Hello," I answer, feeling frustrated with myself and my thoughts.

I should be going through surveillance for my next job, but I've seen nothing as I sit here looking at the screen in front of me. My thoughts are far from here. I pull a hand down my face.

"Michael, it is me, Symphony. I had to call you with my good news," Sim sings on the other side of the line.

I chuckle, feeling my mood lighten. It's good to hear her so happy. A smile comes to my face as I sit back in my seat.

"Hello, Sim. What is this good news?"

"I'm going to be a dancer," she gushes. "A ballerina. Madam Hellene saw me dance and took me to the dean to get me into her classes. Isn't this wonderful? I think I will love to dance as much as I love to play."

My chest tightens as my dreams of the faceless dancer fill my mind. Those long brown legs wrapped around my waist. I grow hard from the memory.

Quickly, I push the thought away. Symphony doesn't have long legs, and I'm not interested in her in that way. I don't know what has come over me.

I clear my throat. "That is wonderful. What will you need? I will ensure you have everything necessary for you to excel.

"Should I put you into lessons for you to catch up? Will this interfere with your music classes? How can I help?"

She releases the sweetest giggle. "I don't need anything yet. I will let you know when I do.

"I don't need lessons. Madam Hellene says I'm a born talent. This will be good for me.

"I will be able to make friends. Dancing isn't as solitary as playing the piano. I'm so excited, Michael," she rambles.

I can't help the smile on my lips. I did do the right thing. This is the happiest I've ever heard her.

"I'm so proud of you, Sim."

CHAPTER TWENTY-ONE

Stepping In

Symphony

Two years later...

I thought I would have more friends by now. Not that I'm not trying. I must say that my developmental skills have improved. I also self-stimulate a whole lot less.

Annabella took me to a specialist my first year here in Boston. The visit was good for me. I learned to help myself.

Dr. Gideon has been kind and supportive. I don't think I would have made it through the first two years without her. I wasn't being bullied, but it was hard to get the other dancers to like me.

It was after the night I saved Ximena from that perv who tried to rob and assault her at gunpoint that I realized why they didn't want to be my friends. Ximena explained to me that the others were jealous that I had walked in and excelled, earning the attention of Madam Hellene and her colleagues. It all made sense.

However, I was grateful that Ximena decided to befriend me. I look forward to our time together. She is patient and kind.

"Hey, why couldn't we do something indoors? You want Frosty to take a bite out of my ass, don't you?" Ximena says as she joins me for lunch.

I love to eat out here in this park. The cold air is refreshing and keeps the brain alert. I often come to run here with Adriano.

I laugh at Ximena as I close the book I had been reading. Annabella has sent me copies of her textbooks and syllabus for her current semester. I'm enjoying our study sessions over the phone.

It makes me happy that I can help her study. I don't feel as alone. I still talk to Michael all the time, but he can get busy at times, and I hate to bother him.

I love that he allows me to ramble about the latest construction articles or demolition videos I've watched on my tablet. He even reads and watches some of my suggestions so we can discuss them on our calls. I love it when he asks me questions as if I'm helping him somehow.

"I will allow you to arrange our next meeting. You can choose for us to be indoors if you like. Frosty is a fictional character. I don't believe you have to worry about your ass," I say.

She rolls her eyes. "Good thing you brought your hot-ass bodyguard along. Looking at him will keep me warm for a little while," she teases.

I glance at Adriano. I never thought of him in that way until Ximena started pointing out how handsome he was. She's not wrong.

He is very attractive. He has a very handsome face, and he keeps his body in shape. I would know. I train with him a lot.

I blush as Adriano smiles from overhearing our conversation. I should be used to Ximena flirting with him, but it causes my cheeks to heat every time. It's not her words but the fact that Adriano always looks at me as if I'm the one who spoke them.

"Looking at him isn't going to keep you warm. That's preposterous."

"What's preposterous is the fact that you haven't jumped his sexy bones. There is something more you're not telling me because him being three years older than you isn't cutting it. If you ask me, that makes him perfect," she lowers her voice to whisper.

"I didn't ask you and that's an off-limits topic. Did you bring our lunch? That was your responsibility," I say firmly, closing the discussion.

She narrows her eyes at me. I've come to know her well, so I know she's not upset with me, just nosy and curious about things I refuse to share.

"I'm giving you these thick-ass peanut butter and jelly sandwiches just for that."

"Oh God, no. Please, I asked you not to make those for me. You use that chunky peanut butter, and you place it on both sides. I can't stand that in my mouth."

"Nuts are always good in your mouth."

Adriano bursts out with a laugh before he can stifle it. I look over at him and glare. He stops laughing audibly but I can see his shoulders shaking and the twinkle in his eyes.

"I wouldn't know anything about what you're insinuating. I believe you're talking about fellatio. I have never had a man's penis in my mouth, so I can't give an affirmative to your response."

Adriano chokes then clears his throat. I look at him and I'm confused by the deep blush in his cheeks. His light-gray eyes are fixed on my lips.

If I'm not mistaken, lust begins to cloud his eyes. I look away, not wanting to see what's really happening in his thoughts. I already don't like that I've become aware of his attractiveness because Ximena has repeatedly pointed it out.

"I'm going to walk the perimeter. Enjoy your lunch," he says and walks away.

"That man wants you. I've been trying to throw him hints, but he's totally crushing on you," Ximena sings as he walks off.

I reach for the rings around my neck as I think of Michael. Our anniversary is coming up soon. I've been married for four years.

I haven't seen my husband in two years. I've tried to understand why he doesn't come to see me. Uri and Annabella come to Boston at least twice a year. Nico even came for my birthday this year.

I was sure Michael would appear when I turned eighteen. He sent a gift and his apologies, but all I wanted was him.

"That will never happen. It is impossible," I breathe.

"Why?"

"You are my only friend. Why must you always ask me questions that will get you killed?"

Ximena gasps. I lower my gaze to my lap. I didn't mean to hurt her feelings.

"You don't joke, so I'm going to back off. I got you a turkey sandwich. I heard you when you said you hate the peanut butter ones."

"I'm sorry. Some things you are better off not knowing. This is one of those."

She places my sandwich in front of me and scoots closer to me to place her head on my shoulder as she wraps her arm around my waist.

"I love you, Sim. I only want to make sure you're not missing something that's staring you in the face."

"If what you say is true, I will need to send him back to—I would need to request a replacement."

"Relax, I don't think he wants to leave you. He's not going to tell you how he feels. I'm going to mind my business."

"Ximena?"

"Yeah, Sim?"

"I love you too. Thank you for being my friend. I like this sandwich. The pickles are delicious."

She giggles. "That shit is still gross."

"You have never tried it. How can you say this?"

"I asked you the same thing about sex. What did you tell me?"

I blink as I think her words over. The other girls in school were talking about boys and sex. Ximena asked me why I had been so quiet.

"When it's for me, I will try it," I say as I remember my words.

"Exactly. That nasty shit ain't for me, sugar. I'll happily make them for you but that's a no for me."

My phone rings as I go to respond. I look at the screen to find it's Michael. A smile comes to my face.

"I have to take this. Please wait for me," I say and stand.

I walk out of earshot and answer the call. Butterflies fill my belly from knowing it's him. I take a deep breath to steady my voice so he doesn't hear how happy I am for his call.

"Hello," I say.

Michael

I close my eyes as I hear her voice come through the line. Gone is the voice of the young girl I rescued four years ago. Symphony has changed so much.

Her speech still comes off as robotic at times, but she tends to find a rhythm and flow when we speak for long hours. I live for our conversations. Hearing about her friend and her classes always brings a smile to my face.

"Are you busy, *cara*?" I croon into the phone.

"I am having lunch with Ximena, but I've missed our calls. You've been busy this week. I haven't gotten a chance to speak much with you. I hope everything is well."

A grin comes to my lips. I can hear the concern in her voice. My little wife worries for me.

She doesn't have to. I have things under control. I am a problem for my problems.

"Everything is fine. I have been working. Are you all set for graduation?"

"Oh yes, I am ready. I have my dress and cap and gown. However, I am most nervous about the final recital. I will have a solo for both piano and dance," she says.

This is her last year of high school. She's been accepted to a performance arts program right there in Boston. Sim has a real future as a performer.

"You will be great. I'm sure you will."

"But you have never seen me dance. I might be terrible—"

"Never. I know you will be phenomenal. You were accepted to dance and play piano at one of the top college programs. That wasn't by accident and certainly not an easy feat. I am very proud of you," I cut her off to say.

Since her graduation is coming, I plan to surprise her with a visit. Coming back here is the last thing I want for her right now. I don't want this life for her.

While Sim has been gone, there have been several attempts on her grandfather's life. The problem is none of the attempts have had confirmed sources we can provide to Don Locatelli. Leonardo has proven to be crafty at this game he is playing.

He has involved families outside of the Italian families. Russians, Irishmen, Scotts, and others. We're not afraid to respond.

However, it would be stupid and serve no purpose. Our problem is with Leonardo. Uri and I aren't willing to burn bridges I may need once Don Trovati hands over the family.

The don has rightfully asked us not to respond. Sim's great-uncle is trying to force a war, but all he has managed to do is piss us off.

Uri and I have become like a pressure cooker. We are boiling with rage because this has a simple solution we're not allowed to enforce. This is the reason why I was happy to hear Sim applied to college in the States. We know for a fact Leonardo still believes Symphony is hidden somewhere in Europe.

After killing his right hand, I was able to infiltrate his crew with one of my men. Salvatore is smart and resourceful. Leonardo ate that shit up and promoted him immediately. Don Alessio has remained safe because of the heads-up from Salvatore each time.

The only information he hasn't been able to provide is who Leonardo is hiring and how. It's the one thing Leonardo has kept to himself. That asshole Leonardo still hasn't figured out he has a mole.

He's already proving he doesn't deserve to run a family. We've been running circles around him, even without knowing how he's getting the others to make these hits for him. We have kept him from accomplishing his goal.

"Michael?"

I'm pulled from my thoughts by her soft voice as I grind my teeth. The latest attempt was about a week ago. Because of this, Don Trovati won't be joining us for Sim's graduation.

"Sorry, what was that?"

"Can I come home for the summer?" she whispers, causing my heart to squeeze.

"*Cara*, I don't think that's a good idea. Things here are still complicated.

"Okay. I understand."

"You haven't told me what you would like for graduation. Should I call you back after your lunch for you to tell me?"

"I don't think you can give me what I want."

"Try me."

"Michael, I have to go. I hope we can talk later."

With that, the line goes dead. I toss the phone down and rub at my tired eyes. There are a number of reasons I haven't been to see Sim. However, one of the biggest reasons is the way she broke down the last time I had to leave.

It still haunts me. I don't know if I can handle that again and leave her behind. Boston is best for her. At least, that's what I keep telling myself.

CHAPTER TWENTY-TWO

Pure Beauty

Michael

I sit in the back of the performance hall with my siblings as I hold two bouquets of roses in my palms. A dozen for each solo performance. I am blown away.

Symphony plays more beautifully than I have ever heard. However, that isn't what has me in awe. My little friend isn't so little anymore. It is time for her solo.

When she steps on stage dressed elegantly in the dark-blue ballerina outfit that sparkles and glitters against the stage lights, she takes my breath away. Even from this distance, I can see her gorgeous face. Her honey-brown locs are pulled back from her face in a bun on top of her head.

I can tell the short locs have grown longer during our time apart. She has gotten taller as well. My dreams of the faceless dancer come to mind. I have been having those dreams for years.

I shift in my seat as the thought of her silky-looking legs locked around my waist fills my head. I clench my jaw and chide myself for the thoughts. I am her guardian, not her lover.

I would never force her to be a wife to me in the true sense. I don't even know if that's something she would want. I have been a friend, someone she can trust.

These lustful thoughts make me feel like I'm crossing a line that was never meant to be crossed. However, as I watch her on stage, I'm transfixed by every movement, every gesture, every leap she takes. Symphony takes command of the stage like a force.

It's clear she's been taken away by the music. I am in complete awe. The power and grace she displays are impressive and inspiring—and the smile on her face—I've never seen anything more beautiful. I haven't missed that she's dancing to "Für Elise," which is only making my heart swell more as I watch her with pride.

Then, the music changes. The classical version of the song becomes a hip-hop version, and another dancer comes out to join her. The two create magic together. Two brown visions of power, strength, and elegance.

The joy on Sim's face tells me this is her friend Ximena. She, too, is a beautiful young woman, but Sim has my full attention. To see her lost in the music as she captivates the attention of the entire audience is something I can't describe.

Symphony plays with enchantment, but she dances with an authority and power that's spellbinding. The happiness pouring from her is palpable. It has filled the air and almost has a tangible flavor.

Passion. That's what I see before my eyes. She has found her passion.

"This is where she belongs," I breathe as the dance comes to an end and the audience erupts into applause.

"Bravo, bravo," Nico croons as he claps loudly.

The thunderous applause that fills the air solidifies what I already know. Symphony is a born star. I will protect this part of her life and allow her to reach for the stars in this world. The bosses and underbosses of the Trovati family don't need to be concerned with who Symphony is.

All that comes with the underworld is death and destruction. In the last four years I have learned that more than anyone. While I'm being groomed by Don Alessio to take over his family, I'm still a hitter for my own.

I've seen it all. All the dark and twisted things this life brings into your life. This ... this is a thing of beauty. Symphony is something special.

She should forever be wrapped in music and the beauty within it. Don Alessio wants me to run his family for her anyway. I will turn my focus to that and allow my wife to remain happy here in the States.

I turn to Nico and hand him the two bouquets. He lifts a questioning brow. Uri pats me on the shoulder. I believe he, too, has come to the understanding I have as I turn to look into his eyes.

"I will see you when I return," he says, giving my shoulder a gentle squeeze then nods.

"You are leaving?" Annabella asks as she gives me a hard look.

"It is for the best."

I kiss her on the cheek and leave before I change my mind. Symphony's happiness is most important to me. This makes her happy.

Symphony

"That was amazing. You turned into someone else out there," Ximena says as we exit the stage.

I smile. It felt different. It felt like Michael was in the crowd watching me.

In my heart, I danced for him. I danced with the hope that he had come to see me dance for the first time. I felt him and the music in my blood.

"Thank you for joining my routine. You enhanced the performance. It wouldn't have been as amazing without you."

"Lies. I know my limits. I'm going to miss you so much. I can't believe this is it. You're going to knock them dead at the next level.

"You call me any time you need to talk. Don't allow those divas to intimidate you. You flash a little of that secret badass if you have to, or call me to come straighten them out," she says with a smile.

I look down at the floor as it hits me this is it. Ximena wasn't accepted to the program we both applied to. She's the one who talked me into applying.

I wasn't going to go once I learned she was denied. Once again, she talked me into accepting and following the dream for us both. I will miss my friend.

I cup the side of her face. "You mean the world to me. If you ever need anything, I am only a call away and I do mean anything.

"I would take a life for you. You gave me friendship when I needed someone so badly. There is no way I could ever repay you."

Her eyes tear up. "Being your friend is no hardship. I love everything about you, Sim and you saved my life. Friendship is the least of what I could offer after what you did for me."

"Symphony, oh my God, that was amazing."

I release Ximena to find Annabella rushing toward me. Uri and Nico are right behind her. My shoulders sag in disappointment as I look around them for Michael and he doesn't come into view.

Disappointment tears through me and I reach for the band on my wrist. I've begun to wear one all the time now. Annabella covers my hand and gives it a squeeze.

"He's proud of you. Things back home are just keeping him away from you," she whispers into my ear.

"Come here, you,'" Nico croons. He lifts me into a bear hug. "Look at you, all grown up. Who knew you could be all graceful? You're just full of magic and secrets, aren't you?"

I frown at his teasing. I don't get to see Nico much, but when I do, he's always teasing me. The fact that he does so with a smile has always put me at ease.

I have learned his words are never meant to be harsh. It's just brotherly taunting. Nico has had a smile for me since the day we met.

He places me back on my feet and smiles down at me as he towers over me. Nico is as handsome as Michael and Uri. He hands me two bouquets of flowers.

I smile and take them both to hold them to my nose. I must be going crazy because I swear I catch a hint of Michael's cologne against the paper wrapping the roses.

I wrinkle my nose and begin to look around for him again. My heart sinks when I still don't find him. I thought just maybe he would come.

"Wow, one day you will have to tell me how you know so many hot Italians," Ximena breathes.

I laugh as I look between Uri and Nico. If only she could meet my husband. Her jaw would surely drop.

"Ximena, this is my family. My brothers and sister-in … They are my brothers and sister. Uri, Nico, Annabella, this is my friend Ximena."

"Her best friend." She corrects with a smile.

"Yes, my best friend."

CHAPTER TWENTY-THREE

In Love

Michael

Three years later ...

I stare at the video chat, wondering when Sim became such a gorgeous woman. She's looking back at me with those big, bright eyes, and I can't remember when it happened.

When did I fall in love with my wife? I know, without a doubt, I love her. She doesn't know that I've been in the States a number of times to see her.

I've been to her performances. I've been to the house in Boston just to be near her for a night. Annabella hates it when I ask her to slip Sim sleeping aids for my visits.

I have only asked on our anniversaries. For one night, I climb into the bed with my wife to hold her in my arms. When the morning comes, I leave her a gift and disappear as if I was never there.

It might sound crazy and creepy but it's the only thing that keeps me sane while I deal with the reality of our life here in Italy. It is almost that time of year again and I long to hold her in my arms.

"Michael, can I ask you something?" she says, grabbing my attention.

"Yes, *cara*, ask me anything."

"When can I come home? I miss ... I miss home. I want to talk to you in person. I have enjoyed our calls, but I want to see you face to face in real life. Did I do something wrong?"

"No. You've done nothing wrong. I want to see you too. I'm just not sure this is the time. Things are still complicated here."

It's the truth. Leonardo is still a problem, and the other families are still lending him support. The attempts on her grandfather's life are starting to wear him down.

I have taken on more and more of his responsibilities. In the last three years, I've been establishing myself with his men and their crews. It's a precarious balance we have to strike to keep everyone thinking I'm the oldest son of Angelo Donati Jr.

It's not time to tip the scales and reveal our hand. For now, everyone believes Uri and I are one. This has worked in our favor in a number of ways. Believing Hush is one man who has struck fear around the world.

Don Locatelli still won't give us the green light to end this bullshit. I grow tired of it, but I'm a man of my word. I have done what I promised I would seven years ago.

Sim's sniffles pull me from my thoughts. I focus back on the screen and my heart squeezes. Her hair is now covering her face, but I can still see tears have filled her beautiful eyes. Those sexy lips of hers are trembling as she tries to hold them back.

"Please don't cry, *cara*. I thought you were happy there. You will be graduating soon, and you've been offered two jobs. My little principal dancer, or do you plan to join the orchestra, my little pianist?"

"I want to do whatever will bring me home," she says.

"There is nothing here but danger. I know you know what it is I do. You are not meant for this world.

"I want you to be safe and happy. Remain in the light of the world. This ... all of this is such crap. I lose another piece of myself every day. Please, my angel, remain where you are safe and happy," I plead.

"You keep me here because I am not like you?"

"Yes, I would rather you never come back and enter this world. Someday, you will have to, and I hate that."

"I understand. I still wish I could see you."

I pull a hand down my face to keep from telling her that I'll be there for our anniversary. Knowing that I have fallen in love with her has made it clear I won't be able to leave if she has another meltdown. This concerns me.

"I will call you tomorrow. I lo ... I will talk to you then."

"Okay, Michael. I will talk to you then."

The call disconnects and I close my eyes. What am I thinking? I almost told her I love her.

I take a breath as I begin to think about how I got here. How did I end up falling for her? It's the unfiltered way she sees life.

It's in the way she's straightforward and doesn't tell me what I want to hear but exactly what I need to hear—the unfiltered truth. It's in the way she brings a smile to my face on my worst days. I have never tried to change her, but she's always changing and adapting to her surroundings to, as she says, *do her best*.

I don't think there is anything Sim can't master. However, my thoughts remind me of a few months ago when she was upset about the other dancers trying to sabotage her. I had to explain to her why we don't kill just anyone who makes us angry.

I had to think out a list of reasons and guidelines for deciding who deserves to be erased.

Love and relationships are a bit more complicated. I wouldn't know how to address that. If I unintentionally hurt her, I would be devastated.

I have to spend so much time away from her. The restraint I show in reference to relationships and intimacy is taxing enough.

If I allow myself to grow these feelings that's only going to make things harder for me.

I never considered my deep-rooted loyalty when I agreed to marry Symphony. Once I make a commitment, it is set in stone. As a result, I have never been able to allow myself to bed another.

"God, I miss sex."

***

I walk into the dance studio and find the dancer standing by the window. She has her back to me, but there's something melancholy about her posture. I walk up behind her and wrap my arms around her.

A smile comes to my lips as she settles back against my chest. Dipping my head, I kiss the soft skin on her neck. A soft moan leaves her lips.

I grow hard as she nestles her ass against me. Wanting to finally see her face, I place my fingers beneath her chin and lift her head. A growl leaves my chest as I see the face of my little wife come into view.

Suddenly, hair is cascading down around her shoulders. I reach to touch a loc like I have wanted to touch for years. She lifts on her toes and presses her plump lips to mine.

I groan and lock my fingers in her hair. Taking over the kiss, I open her mouth to me and devour her. The kiss turns heated and passionate quickly.

She turns in my arms. I hoist her onto my waist. Her back hits the windowpane as I continue to consume her sweet mouth. Her whimpers and moans turn me on as I move my lips to her neck.

I can't stop myself. I want her so much. The feel of her in my arms makes so much sense in this moment. Here and now, nothing can take her from me.

Reaching between her legs, I fist the fabric covering her most intimate place. I twist and pull until I begin to hear the sound of tearing. With one strong yank, I shred the fabric, revealing her core to me.

Meanwhile, she has been working on the buttons of my shirt, revealing my skin to her soft touch. I look down to watch her brown hands glide over my chest. I groan as her touch heats my skin.

I find her core soaked. As I push my fingers into her sex, I rub her nub with my thumb. She cries out and drops her head back against the window.

"Michael," she gasps.

Pulling my fingers from her dripping sex, I then shrug out of my shirt. Her eyes glaze over with lust as she takes me in. I reach for her kiss-swollen lips and drag my thumb down them.

"God, you're gorgeous. So fucking beautiful, bella. I want you so much."

"Please, Micheal, I want you too," she breathes.

Her voice has taken on a sultry tone, dripping with desire. Leaning in, I take her lips once again. While kissing her deeply, I release my belt and unfasten my pants.

As we continue to kiss, I rub my length against her wet pussy lips. She wiggles her hips to get closer, causing me to slip in. Instead of pulling back, I thrust forward.

I wake with a gasp. Sweat soaks my hair, causing it to stick to my face. Reaching up, I push the wet locks from my face.

I glance around the room as I catch my breath. My cock twitches beneath the sheet, grabbing my attention. I wrap my hand around it and squeeze.

"Fuck," I grunt.

CHAPTER TWENTY-FOUR

Become Like Him

Symphony

I dress in a black T-shirt and sweatpants and put on my black jogging sneakers. Today, I put my plan into motion. Michael doesn't want me to come home because I'm not like him.

I want to go home. I want to be with him. So, I plan to become just like my husband. I will be an assassin for hire.

Uri has told me all about what they do for the families, my nonno's and the Donatis. They make the bad guys go away. Michael said we don't kill innocent people or those who don't deserve it.

I can't kill for my family like he does, but there has to be a way for me to show him we can be the same. I know just who to ask to help me. Once dressed, I make my way down to the kitchen, where I know I will find him.

Adriano is standing at the kitchen island with his coffee. He is already dressed for our morning run. I walk over to him and stand at his side. He looks down at me with a surprised expression.

"I want to talk to you. I need your help."

"Okay, you need my help with what? I'm no good at those lifts and things. I hope that's not what you need."

His cheeks flush as he says the words. I asked him to help me once as I tried to work out a new routine when I was asked to do a piece with a partner. That didn't go well at all.

"I will not ask you to put your hands next to my vagina today. You don't have to worry about that," I say.

Adriano chokes on his sip of coffee. I pat him on the back and reach for a towel to hand him. He looks at me with wide eyes.

"Some days." He shakes his head. "What do you need, Sim?"

"I need you to help me find clients."

"Clients?"

"Yes, individuals who want my services."

He looks at me skeptically. He turns to me and leans his hip against the island. I take a step back as I note that I have entered too far into his personal space.

"What service are we talking about?"

"*Morte.*"

He narrows his eyes at me. I stand with my chin held high. I try to force eye contact, but it doesn't last long.

"Explain to me what exactly is going on in your head," he says after a few beats.

"Michael doesn't want me home because I'm not like him. I have to prove I can be like him. I have trained.

"I have the skills. I've just never applied them. I will start my own assassin company.

"I will perform hits for hire. You will help me to find clients. You will also keep this secret until I am ready to expose myself," I explain.

He scoffs. "That's not going to happen. Michael and Uri both would kill me."

He folds his arms across his chest as he glares at me. I release an exasperated breath. I thought this would be easier.

"If they don't find out, then they won't kill you. Did I not say you are to keep this a secret? If you die, it will be because you are a poor liar or you spoke when you shouldn't have."

"You are crazy," he says, allowing his accent to slip.

"No. That is not a part of my disorder. I am quite sane, actually. I'm on the spectrum, not crazy. Now stop calling me names and assist me. I will pay you handsomely for your help."

"*Fanculo*, she wants to pay me for my own death," he says under his breath. "She's right. I'm the crazy one here."

"Yay, you're going to help?"

"I'm going to keep you out of trouble."

I throw my arms around his neck and hug him tightly. He returns the hug hesitantly at first. When he does embrace me, he buries his face in my hair.

"He doesn't deserve you," he murmurs.

"What?"

I pull out of his hold and take a step back. The moment has just turned awkward. I didn't mean to cross the line.

"Why do this? You dance and play like an angel. You're perfect the way you are."

"I am the heiress of the Trovati throne. I am meant to be the wife of the next don of the family. He will run the family on my behalf. How can I not match him?

"To the civilian world I can be the odd girl with no friends, no social skills, nothing more than a freakish talent, but in the underworld, I will be known to be as lethal as my family. As deadly as my husband.

"I am doing this because my mother was taken from me for this birthright. My husband has been taken from me over it. I almost lost you because of it."

"But you don't have to do this. How do you even know these things? I thought the point was to keep you innocent," he says with a voice full of concern and protectiveness.

"I know these things because they have been spoken of in front of me as if I lack the ability to understand. I have ears. I understand.

"Uri is also probably the only one who doesn't coddle me. He has answered my questions when I ask. If you're not going to help me, I will go to him," I say in frustration.

"I didn't say I wouldn't help. I just thought … Never mind. I will do as you ask."

"Thank you. Would you like to talk about your compensation? I'm willing to pay you twenty-five percent of each transaction."

He chuckles and shakes his head. "This will be on me. Come, let's go for a run."

Micheal

"I'm growing tired of these games." I seethe as I hold this bastard by his ankles over the edge of the rooftop of one of Uri's nightclubs.

Knowing Uri would be here tonight, I entered the club through the back so I wouldn't be seen. It's a good thing I did. I found this motherfucker slipping something into the food the kitchen had prepared to send up to Uri's office.

Everyone was too busy to notice his sneaky ass, but I caught him and followed him out as he went to deliver the tray. Now we are here. I would send him back to his boss with missing hands and a cut-out tongue, but he has seen us both.

Uri heard the commotion outside his office and stepped out. The look of realization on this asshole's face sealed his death. All I want to know is who sent him.

"My boss is Jacques Dubois. A call came in from someone he owed a favor. Italian accent.

"He asked us to kill the man they call Hush for two million dollars. Jacques refused the job. I called the number back to accept it. That was a lot of money to turn down," he chokes out.

"Too bad you won't get to spend a dime," I snarl and release him.

"Fuck, Michael. Have you lost your bloody mind?" Uri bites out.

"I dropped him in the alley. I couldn't leave him alive. I will have him cleaned up before anyone notices."

"You are becoming unhinged. Your work is beginning to look more like mine."

"That isn't much of a problem, is it? Shouldn't we be uniform?"

He growls and gives me a look of exasperation. I shrug and dust my hands off. I did what needed to be done.

"Don't get cheeky with me, you arrogant brat." He pauses to take a breath and pinch the bridge of his nose. "I think it's time for you to take some time off.

"You've been under a lot of pressure. Let things cool down a bit and then you can get back to it. Killing dodgy bastards like that filthy fucker can wait."

"I'm fine," I grunt.

Swiftly, he moves to get in my face. He glares into my eyes, making my inch of height over him disappear. In this moment there is no doubt I'm the little brother.

However, I don't look away or cower. He's not expecting me to either. Uri demands respect, but he is also willing to give it. I know I have earned his respect, which is why I listen.

"You will take a fucking break. Deal with your shit. Clear your head. We are not to get sloppy now. Do you understand me?"

He is right. I have been becoming unhinged as of late. I'm sexually frustrated, I keep having dreams about Symphony, and there seems to be no end in sight of this bullshit with Leonardo.

The Locatellis have enough power to give us the green light. They are strong enough to handle a war if it comes to it. I grind my teeth at the thought because even I know that all could lead to uncalculated disaster.

"I hear you."

I turn and walk away. I have a lot to work through. London and Italy may not be the places where I need to be to sort this out.

CHAPTER TWENTY-FIVE

Taken Off Guard

Symphony

Emory Lawson walks through his bedroom door at eight fifteen on the dot. He is a man of routine, making my job easier. I was able to slip into his private estate easily.

His staff moves in sync with his demand for punctuality. All I had to do was move to the beat of their schedule. I danced my way right in.

Mr. Lawson meets all the guidelines Michael set. He is a disgusting man. Children have died because of him. He is responsible for the deaths of many innocents.

He and his company have knowingly distributed medications that would harm the children they were meant to save, all for profit. I guess he never thought about the families left behind to grieve.

My client is a wealthy stockbroker whose son was a victim of Mr. Lawson's. I wasn't sure I would take this one until I hacked

Mr. Lawson's company system. The documentation was right there. He knows. They all know.

The data is clear that the medications are more harmful than helpful, especially for humans under the age of thirteen.

"Allison, what's going on with the lights," Mr. Lawson calls as he continues to flip the switch.

Allison won't be answering him. I put her down for an evening nap. When she wakes, it won't be to shed any light on things.

"It seems you're in collections," I say as I step from the shadows.

His eyes grow wide as I aim my gun with the silencer. I put one between his eyes and two in his chest. Quickly, I leave out the way I came.

I follow the path that will ensure I won't be detected by any of the surveillance. Once I get to the designated location Adriano was to park and wait in, I slip quietly into the car.

"I think I enjoyed that one," I say to Adriano once I'm back inside the car.

This will be my third assignment since I started a month ago. I am making a name for myself. My clients have been quite satisfied.

Most of all, I'm learning to become better. My kills are untraceable. I get the job done and my clients get results.

I pull out the dance magazine that arrived this morning with me featured on the cover. A smile comes to my lips. As promised, I am doing my best.

Michael

Uri was right, I need some time to clear my head. I don't know how it happened, but I ended up in Boston. For four weeks, I warred with whether or not to come here.

Annabella has accompanied me, wanting to visit Sim herself. What I wasn't expecting was to find that Sim isn't home, and no one can tell me where she and Adriano are. I never should have sent him here with her. I had once thought it wise to leave her with someone closer to her age.

I thought she would be more comfortable with a younger bodyguard. Most of my guys are older. Uri assigned all the guys who started with me.

Adriano is the younger brother of Salvatore. At the time when Sim was fourteen it made sense. Adriano was seventeen and had finished his schooling early. He wanted to join Uri's crew, and his brother vouched for him.

He had been in training for a year by the time I assigned him to Sim. Uri had been impressed with him. That alone made me decide to trust my wife with him. Uri isn't impressed by many.

Now, I wish Sim had let him die in Chicago. The thought of him being near her turns my stomach. She should have been here when I arrived.

"Annabella, what are you doing here? I wasn't expecting you and Uri at this time," Sim says as she enters the sitting room we have been waiting in.

I have my back to her as I stand at the window with a drink in my hand. She would think I am Uri from this angle. Some of the tension leaves my body and a smile comes to my lips.

"Uri couldn't make it this time, but we wanted to come see you," my sister says.

"But—"

Sim's words are cut off as I turn and place my glass down. I give her a smile and open my arms. It only takes a second for the shock to wear off and for her to fly into my hold.

I'm taken by surprise as she leaps up and wraps her legs around my waist. I have to stifle the groan that creeps into my throat. She feels so good in my embrace, and she smells delicious.

I'm growing hard down the leg of my pants. I clear my throat as I squeeze her tightly in my arms. I want nothing more than to cup her face and bring her lips to mine. Instead, I cup the back of her head and hold her close as she trembles against me.

"You are here," she breathes into my neck.

Then suddenly as if she's just remembering herself, she drops to her feet and takes a step back. She looks up at me as if in awe.

"Wow, you have gotten so tall since the last time I saw you. I ... I thought you were Uri, but you are even taller than him."

"Come here," I croon, pulling her closer to me. "I've missed you. I wasn't done with my hug."

"Oh, I thought I overstepped."

Tugging her back into my embrace, I begin to chuckle as she inhales deeply as she buries her face in my chest. As I rub my palm up and down her back, she melts into me. I dip my head to kiss the top of hers.

"You have gotten tall as well. You've changed a lot," I say through my laughter.

"I am five-nine, weighing in at one hundred and thirty-six pounds. Although my instructor would like me to come down five or six pounds. I will do my best, but I keep telling him it is all muscle.

"I look thinner than all the other dancers my height. The scale just says differently. They shouldn't force us to weigh in anyway. They are shaming us," she says.

My heart swells to hear her voice in person. When she lifts her gaze to mine, I can't help but smile as she gives me her eyes and doesn't look away from me. I reach to brush my fingers against her blushing cheek.

The warm purpling hue stands out against her flawless brown skin. Her locs are pulled up in the front, with the rest flowing down past her shoulders. They are as neat and pristine as they were when she first got them.

"You are perfect just the way you are," I murmur as my gaze drops to her lips.

Fanculo, I want to taste them to see if they are anything like in my dreams. She is perfect. Her legs look long and toned beneath the tight leggings she's wearing. The zip-up jacket she has on molds lovingly over her full breasts.

My hard-on is raging in my slacks. I have to remind myself that's not what I came here for. I'm here to spend time with her and make sure she's okay.

"Um, I should shower and change. I will return momentarily. I'm so happy you are here, Michael.

"We can have breakfast and talk. I will have Chef make us something. Please don't leave. I will be quick."

My chest squeezes from her words and the way she glances at me out of the corner of her eye as if I'll disappear. I pull her to me for one more hug.

"I will be here waiting. Take your time."

My words earn me a tight squeeze around the waist and a shy smile. I kiss her forehead and release her to go take her shower. I knit my brows as she walks away, flicking at the band on her wrist.

I remember her wearing bands the last time I was here, but I thought it was a part of her outfit. I'll have to ask about it later. Annabella has informed me that many of Sim's tics have ceased, or she's developed new, less severe ones than tearing out her hair.

I feel like I need to learn everything about her all over again, but I have this excitement for it. I'm hoping this time can bring me some clarity and answers. Those dreams are driving me crazy, but I don't know what to do about them.

CHAPTER TWENTY-SIX

Our Anniversary

Symphony

I am so excited I can't contain myself. He is here. Michael is here.

He looks so different but the same. He's gotten so tall. He has to be at least six-six. I know Uri is six-five, but Micheal has to be an inch or two taller than him.

Being in his strong arms felt so right. I didn't mean to jump on him, but I was so shocked and happy to see him, and I wasn't thinking. He smells better than I remember. It's the same cologne, but somehow it smells different. More mouthwatering.

I'm digging through my closet like a madwoman. I need to find the perfect outfit. I want to look nice for him.

I did need to take a shower to wash the GSR off from the hit I had just executed, but I also wanted to make myself look presentable. I look in the mirror as I hold up a dress against my body.

It's cute, but I don't think it's right. I toss it aside and rush back to the closet to look for something else. I wish I had known he was coming. I feel so ill-prepared.

"Come on, Symphony. Think. What will look nice?"

I cover my face with my palms, feeling like I might burst into tears. I never put this much thought into what I wear, but it's been so long since I've seen Michael, and I want to look my best.

"Knock, knock. Do you need help in here?" Annabella asks as she peeks her head into my room.

"Yes, please. I don't know what to wear. How should I do my hair?

"Should I wear makeup? Does he even care? I'm so nervous."

"Relax, love. Of course he cares. He came all this way to spend time with you.

"Let's see what we're working with first. You should definitely show off that cute little body and those long legs. Oh, how about this?"

She holds up a soft-pink dress I had passed over a few times. I thought the color was childish. However, now that she's holding it up, it does look cute.

"Oh, wait. No, not this one. I think you should go with this one. It will look great with your skin tone and hair," she says as she grabs another dress; this one is a burnt-orange color.

I groan as I remember the day Ximena talked me into purchasing the garment. She wanted me to go to a party with her. I never made the party.

Adriano saw me in the dress and grumbled about it under his breath. When it was time to leave, suddenly all the cars had flats or some other issues. I was relieved and called Ximena to beg off from going to the party.

I never put that dress on again. It's a few years old, but it might fit. It might look nice.

"I will try that one on. It is certain to make me look like a woman. Yes, that is the one."

I take the dress and slip it on over my black lace bra and panties. When I turn for the mirror, my mouth falls open. The stretchy fabric fits my body like a glove.

Annabella is right, the color does work well on me. I look ... I look like a woman. I've never thought about that before. I'm no longer a fourteen-year-old bride.

I've become a woman and my husband is here. Will Michael notice too? I reach for the band holding my locs up in the front and pull it from my hair, allowing it all to flow freely.

The front of my hair falls into my face. I push it back out of my eyes. A couple of locs fall back into my face. I'm grateful that I just washed and freshly retwisted it yesterday.

"Wow, you look gorgeous. Here, put these on."

She hands me a pair of nude heels from my closet. I take them and slip them on. I'm in even more awe of my reflection. My eyes look brighter, and a smile is on my lips.

Annabella pulls my hair over my shoulder. "This looks great on you. You're so pretty.

"Don't be nervous. You will take his breath away. Things are different now.

"You are a grown woman. He will see that. You should tell him how you feel," she says with a playful smile.

"I ... I don't think I wish to do that."

"Why not? You have always been in love with him."

I begin to pop the band on my wrist. I can't look her in the eyes. I've never told her about my feelings for Michael.

I didn't know anyone else could see this crush I've been carrying. I start to pop the band faster as I wonder if Michael knows. Is that why he stays away from me?

My heart drops. My mind begins to swirl, causing me to chew on my tongue. What if being an assassin isn't enough?

What if he sees through me and knows what I've been up to? Will I lose him forever this time because he figures it all out and he doesn't want me the same? What if my best isn't enough?

"Oh, Sim, love, look at me," Annabella coos. "It's all right. You don't have to tell him. It's fine."

I look around me and realize I've spiraled into a meltdown. I'm sitting on the floor with my head between my knees as I rock and whimper. I've even started to twist one of my locs and can feel it tightening against my scalp.

If I keep twisting it like this, it will snap. I dart my gaze around, trying to find something to focus on. Annabella climbs behind me and cradles me between her legs as she wraps her arms around me.

I sag into her tight embrace and try to focus. My eyes finally find a crack in the tape in the corner of the wall. I keep my gaze there and begin to count in my head.

Annabella leans into my ear and begins to whisper. "You've got this. Breathe; you don't have to do anything you're not ready for.

"Don't listen to me. I don't even have a relationship. What do I know about a husband?

"You be you. That's why he's here. He wants to spend time with you," she says soothingly as she hugs me supertight.

"I'm being ridiculous. He will never return my feelings. I shouldn't try to get his attention. I am being foolish."

"I don't think you realize how much my brother loves you. Everything he does is for you. Your happiness is the most important thing to him. Did you know he was the one to ask me to find Dr. Gideon for you?

"You are always on his mind. I think he feels the same way you do. I'm not saying this to overwhelm you. I just want you to know you can relax and be yourself," she says and kisses the back of my head.

I hear her words, but I don't think they fully sink in. I'm too focused on calming my anxiety. Slowly, I begin to relax.

I hate that Michael is finally here and I'm having a bad day. It's been so long since I've had a bad day. Dancing and playing have made bad days all but non-existent.

When that doesn't work, I train. Exhausting my body calms all the noise. It stills the anxiety.

Right now, I either need to dance, play, or throw knives. Anything to ease my thoughts. I'm so afraid Michael will see me.

All this time, he was right. His being in Italy is for the best. There, he can't find out that I've started a hit-for-hire business. There, he can't see how much I've fallen in love with him.

"I need to play," I breathe.

"Will you allow me to do your makeup first? Can you handle that?"

"I like the sticky feeling of the lip gloss and popping my lips. I will allow you to place gloss on my lips. Maybe some mascara. I am not able to handle more than that. Not right now."

"That is more than enough. I am here for you, Sim. Talk to me whenever you need."

"Thank you, Annabella. I would like for you to keep my secret. Michael doesn't need to know how I feel. Please don't tell him."

"Oh, Sim. I would never embarrass you like that. Although I do believe the feeling is mutual. I will allow you both to figure it out on your own," she coos and gives me one more squeeze.

"Thank you."

Michael

I turn my gaze from glaring at Adriano. He's been sitting on a stool in the corner as Symphony plays the piano. Of course, I gifted her another when she moved here to Boston.

I had this one custom-made for her. There is even an engraving under the right side, but I'm not sure if she's aware of it. I guess I have been in love with her for way longer than I've allowed myself to admit.

The engraving says, *To my love. Play to your soul's content.*

Someday, I will tell her where to find the words. Someday when I'm sure she can handle the weight of them.

However, today isn't that day. There's been something in the air with Adriano since he found me here. I didn't miss his shock or the scowl that followed.

I also didn't miss the look in his eyes when I hugged Sim as she returned from her shower. It was a mixture of lust and jealousy. I understand the look of lust.

Symphony looks sexy in the body-hugging dress and nude heels. Her physique is exquisite. I almost swallowed my tongue when I saw her.

Her lashes are always long and pretty with her big brown eyes, but she's wearing some type of makeup that's making her eyes pop. Then there's the lip gloss that makes her full lips look sensual, inviting, and taunting. I have never wanted to kiss a woman more.

However, something has changed since she returned. To top it all off, Adriano's presence is pissing me off. I know he's doing his job, but I'm here. He doesn't need to be.

I stand from where I've been sitting, listening to Sim play while I sip at some cognac. I place my drink on the piano and sit beside her on the bench. She scoots over slightly, bringing a smile to my lips.

She's been shyer than usual. It's endearing. I wonder if she has a clue of how beautiful she looks. I don't think she does, which only makes her sexier.

"Can I play with you?"

She pauses her fingers on the keys and looks out the corner of her eye at me. I reach to brush a few of her locs out of her face and tuck them behind her ear.

I love them on her. The middle-sized locs compliment her face. They are very neat and the scent coming from them is intoxicating. She almost smells like candy.

"I ... I would like that. Yes, you may, Michael."

I place a hand on her back and the other on the keys. I start to play "Für Elise" as I rub her back soothingly. She joins as a little purring sound leaves her throat. My cock twitches from the sound.

I grind my teeth as Adriano jumps from his seat and storms from the room. Sim stops playing and starts to pop that band on her wrist. Not wanting to draw attention to the action and embarrass her, I don't mention it.

Instead, I reach beneath her hair to cup the back of her neck and give it a gentle squeeze before I begin to massage her soft skin. She releases another little purr. Not able to help myself, I lean in and brush my lips against her temple.

"Is there something going on between you and Adriano I should know about?" I ask as I pull away.

"Are you asking me if I'm involved with him?"

"Yes, that is the question," I say harsher than I mean to.

"No. We are friends, that is all. I have never had a boyfriend."

A low growl emits from my throat before I can help myself. I feel like an ass as she begins to dart her eyes around. I take a calming breath.

It takes a moment for me to calm down as I fight not to tell her she should never have a boyfriend because I'm her husband and I won't share my wife with anyone. I want to claim her lips and show her why she is mine and only mine.

Instead, I go back to playing softly. When she doesn't join me, I stop and turn to look at her. She's watching me out of the corner of her eye once again.

"Do you remember what tomorrow is?" I ask to break the silence.

"It's our seven-year anniversary. We have been married for seven years tomorrow."

"That it is, *cara*. What would you like to do? Anything you want, it is yours."

"Anything?"

I know I shouldn't, but I nod. There isn't anything I would deny Sim. If it makes her happy, it is hers.

"I would like to have my first kiss," she all but whispers. "That is if it's appropriate to ask for such a thing."

My lips are sealed to hers before she can finish her words. Her lips are softer than I could have ever imagined. The lip gloss adds a silky feel. Reaching to cup the back of her neck once more, I then tip her head back.

She moans and I growl into her mouth as I cup her face. She gasps and her mouth opens to me as I palm her breast in one hand. I take the opportunity to stick my tongue in her mouth and deepen the kiss.

The whimper that comes from her lips breaks all my restraint. I lift her from her seat and turn her back to the piano as I lift with her, still devouring her sweet mouth. Sim locks her fingers in the top of my hair as I grasp ahold of her waist.

The keys cry out as I lift her onto them. Cupping her ass in one hand, I lift her enough to close the lid over the keys and gently place her on it. I wasn't expecting this kiss to be so passionate, but the chemistry between us is sizzling.

I break the seal on our lips to kiss my way down her chin to her neck. I have my hands tightly grasping her hips as I kiss my way down her body. When I get to her breasts, I move to one nipple and suck it into my mouth over the fabric of her dress before moving to the other.

"Michael," she pants.

I feel as if I'm going to burst through my pants. How does she do this to me? The breathy sound of her voice calls to something deep in my groin.

Reaching for her long, silky legs, I run my hands up them as I continue to kiss my way down her body. I push the short dress up over her ass, revealing her black panties underneath. I should stop this. I know I should, but I can't find it in me to do so.

This is my wife, and I want her. I want her so fucking bad. I want her to feel my love.

Sitting back on the bench before her, I reach for the waistband of her panties and hook my fingers in to peel the fabric away from her body. I look up and find her eyes right away. Reaching between her legs, I then find her wet center and begin to coat my fingers with her juices.

She's so wet for me. I play with her little pussy, making her cry out my name. However, that's not enough for me. I need to taste her.

I scoot forward and toss her legs over my shoulders. Leaning in, I inhale her delicious scent. It's a mix of cocoa butter and champagne. Whatever fragrance her body lotion is should be banned from her possession. She smells of pure sin.

The need to devour her is overwhelming. I can't hold back any longer. I glide my tongue through her juicy lips and groan as her flavor bursts on my tongue.

Grasping a tight hold of her waist, I keep her hips rocking against my face. She arches her back and rides my face as I consume her sweet pussy. I have never been so ravenous.

"Michael."

The way she sings my name drives me over the edge. I move my hands to her curvy tight ass and squeeze. I hum into her as her legs begin to shake on the sides of my head.

"Oh," she gasps.

I glance up to see her eyes rolled into the back of her head as her lips form an *O* shape. Her body is convulsing as she rains into my mouth. I begin to kiss my way back up her body to take her lips.

She grasps my ears as I take her lips in a searing kiss. I'm so lost in the kiss it takes a moment for me to register the popping sound behind my head. I pull back and look at her.

"What's wrong, *bella*? Are you all right?"

"I ... I. Excuse me, I need to go upstairs," she says, pushing to get free from my embrace.

I stumble back and allow her to go. Feeling like an asshole, I flop onto the bench as she races away. What the fuck did I just do?

Oh my God, I'm an idiot. I drop my head in my hands and tug at my hair. That was incredibly stupid.

I just royally fucked up. All she wanted was her first kiss. Why couldn't I give her that and walk away?

"Fuck, fuck, *fuuck*."

Symphony

Stupid, stupid, stupid. Why did you run? Why did you ruin everything?

As I rush into my room and kick my heels off, I already know the answers. I'm not ready. As the lust began to clear away, and I tasted myself mixed with the alcohol on Michael's tongue and lips, my thoughts became clear.

What if he regrets everything in the morning. It was better we stopped before he had even more to regret. I will never forget my first kiss and everything that came after.

That was amazing. I didn't know my body could feel like that. It's still buzzing from his touch.

"What have you done, Sim?" I huff as I climb into the empty tub while still fully dressed.

I wrap my arms around my legs, and I try to process what just happened. I don't know how I'm going to face him in the morning. I'm so embarrassed.

"Just great. I really fucked this one up," I grumble and gasp, slapping my hands over my mouth.

I sigh. It's time I go to bed. Today wasn't one of my best.

CHAPTER TWENTY-SEVEN

Bitter and Fed Up

Micheal

Three years later …

"You were looking for me?" I say as I walk into Uri's office.

I saunter to his desk with a scowl on my face. These days, all I do is scowl. I rarely have anything to smile about. My days and nights have been darker than ever.

I don't talk to Symphony anywhere near as much as I used to. That means I remain in the darkness. It is rare that I come across any light.

That night three years ago still haunts me. I took things too far and the two months that followed were awkward until the day I left. I ruined everything.

I wish I could turn back time. However, I can't, so I've become a brooding shell of a man. I run things for Don Trovati, I carry out hits for the Donati family, and I brood.

I'm still in love with my wife, but I clearly don't know what I'm doing when it comes to her. She's brilliant, gorgeous, and so damn sexy, but I'm an idiot when it comes to her. I don't know what I did wrong that night—whether I moved too fast or if she hated how I made her feel.

I can't say I'm the most experienced. The whole thing kind of made me question myself. Maybe I'm just terrible at eating pussy.

I haven't been able to bring myself to test that theory with anyone else. All I see is Sim when I even think about trying. The whole thing has me at a loss.

"I'm heading to America. I have someone I need to visit. I need you to get me a location," Uri says, bringing me from my brooding thoughts.

"You have a name?"

"Howard Russ. He is a child molester and woman beater. This time, he put his hands on the wrong woman. Uncle Nicholas has made this request personally. The victim was Crivello's niece."

I release a low whistle. Crivello is a capo for the Donati family. It's no wonder Uncle Nicholas made the request.

Russ is a dead man walking. I drop into the seat in front of Uri's desk and pull my laptop from my bag. It takes me all of two seconds to have an address for him.

"Looks like you're going to Connecticut." I pause to think. I may not have much contact with Sim, but I know all about her life. She has been performing right outside of Connecticut.

"I can handle this one for you," I offer.

"That won't be necessary. I'm due for a visit with Uncle Nicholas and I should check in on Symphony while I'm there," he replies absently.

Once the words are out, he stops what he's doing with the papers on his desk and looks up at me. He studies me for a moment as if looking through me.

"If you want to go see her, do not use family business as an excuse. She would be happy to see you," he says as if reading my mind.

"I'm not looking for an excuse," I mumble.

"You lie. Is this how you repay my love by lying to my face?"

I give a genuine smile. A rare smile for a rare occasion. Uri doesn't express his affection often. I know he loves me but it's not often I hear him admit it.

"I have things here to look after. She's better off without me."

"You have things to do here, yet you offer to do this job. Piss off. I'm not going to play this game with you. I don't know what happened when you went there last, but it has changed you.

"You can lie to yourself, but don't try this with me. Don Trovati has noticed the change as well. I don't want you losing yourself in all of this.

"You are my little brother. If this has become too much, say so. I will take over the responsibility.

"We can file for a divorce or have the marriage annulled or whatever. You don't have to continue to carry this weight. You were a child when you agreed to this.

"I shouldn't have allowed it. You just speak too quickly and … I should have put you first," he sighs.

Hearing the guilt in his voice stings. This isn't his fault. I wanted to do this. Even now, anger rises as I think of what he's suggesting. If I'm not married to Symphony, then who?

The thought of another man taking my place makes me want to spit fire. I rub at my chest where I wear her name tattooed across my skin. I had it done the year after the incident.

It felt wrong to have Annabella drug her for me to spend the night with her in my arms. Not knowing what triggered her the year before, I couldn't bring myself to do it. The chance that the sleeping aids could wear off and I would be there to frighten her turned something once innocent into something absolutely, without a doubt, creepy.

"I am fine. I have not changed my stance. Things are just complicated," I say.

He snorts. "I do remember telling you they would be. I find I understand Sim more and how to handle her when I ask questions and allow her to do the same.

"Her unfiltered honesty reveals everything you need to know. I don't think it's as complicated as you make it. *Capisce?*"

"*Capito.*"

Symphony

"Ninety-nine," I murmur to myself as I stand over my last two kills.

This husband and wife deserved this. They stole a child and have done nothing but abuse him for as long as they've had him. It was a visit to the hospital from one of their beatings that revealed the two weren't his parents, putting in motion an investigation.

The boy's parents turned out to be a wealthy art dealer and heiress to an oil family. The father was the one to seek out my services. After seeing the pictures of what was done to the boy and the mountain of hospital records, I would have done this one for free.

Never the same hospital more than once. The severity of the injuries increased with time. Black eyes and broken eye sockets, broken bones, and injured organs.

I want to go after everyone who neglected to get the child help, but they don't fall into the guidelines. I will have to let it go and be satisfied with kills number ninety-eight and ninety-nine.

I turn and leave quietly the way I entered. My assignment is complete. Adriano nods to me as he opens the car door for me to slide in when I get to the location where he's been waiting for me.

"I wish to speak with you," I say once he is behind the wheel and pulls off.

"Oh really? What's up this time, boss?"

"I keep telling you I am not your boss. Especially since you haven't touched a dime of the money I pay you. Which is the topic of the conversation I wish to have."

He sighs and glances in the rear-view mirror. I fold my arms over my chest. I don't understand why he refuses my payments.

"How do you know I haven't touched it?" he asks and lifts a brow.

"I hacked your account. I had a suspicion, so I've been underpaying you the last few jobs. When you said nothing, I hacked the account," I reply.

"*Bella*, you do know that's an invasion of my privacy?" he chuckles.

I've become a great hacker since starting my business. I was subpar before then. I had watched enough videos for the basics.

Now, I would call myself an expert. I bet I could match Michael or Annabella's skills. Again, Uri shared information with me when I asked about my family.

I have learned a lot about who they are and what they do. What he doesn't tell me, I use my skills to find out. I smile as I think of Uri.

I never get the sense that he tells me things because he thinks I don't or won't understand. It's more like he wants me to know and understand who we are. It's not like when others speak around me, assuming my intelligence is too low to comprehend what's said or how to apply the knowledge.

I'm okay with that. I have used it to my advantage. Needing to know more about organized crime organizations, I've inserted myself into a low-level Irish family here in Boston.

They hired me for my computer skills, but I have played my role and have come to earn their respect or at least their tolerance, leading to my presence in meetings they probably wouldn't allow me in if they knew better.

I understand the ins and outs of a family like mine much better. Uri has filled in the blanks for the things I found challenging at first. Most of which were more of a cultural difference.

The Italians do things a bit differently. I believe I've learned of ways to help Michael and my grandfather run my family more efficiently. I will share these things when the time is right.

"What privacy is there between us? You know everything about me, and I know everything about you. You have spent your life with me, so tell me, why is my money no good for you?"

"You misunderstand. It is not that your money isn't good enough. It is that I don't believe I have earned it. You do all the work. I only helped you get started."

"You drive me to every job. You have kept my secrets. You tell me when you feel I should pass on a job. You were the one to get me in with the O'Shea family. You have earned it," I say firmly.

"Connecticut is such an easy place to travel through. I will get you to rehearsal early this evening, or do you wish to make a stop?"

"Traffic will make us late if I deviate from the scheduled course. I will go straight to rehearsal. I can shower there and be on time."

"As you wish, boss."

I grumble under my breath. I have not missed his avoidance. We will discuss this at a later time.

CHAPTER TWENTY-EIGHT

A Peace Offering

Uri

"To what do I owe this visit, mate?" I ask as Sam Mairettie appears in my club.

I sit back in my private booth and spread my arms across the back of the plush booth seat. I came down to the main floor to monitor a situation that got my attention from upstairs. Once the wanker saw me enter the main floor, he and his mates left my establishment.

I decided to sit for a bit and let my presence be known. I wasn't expecting to see this guy walk into my club. He's actually the last face I expected to see.

I've been keeping my distance from the Locatelli family since I was denied the right to hush Leonardo Trovati. I have nothing else to say to them. I'm not into underworld politics.

149

I don't have it in me to play nice with everyone. Especially when I'm the only one required to make concessions. However, he has come all this way, so I will listen at least.

He lifts his hand and beckons one of his men forward. Being a capo looks good on him. I see before me more than the pompous, wet behind the ears, entitled boy who tried to establish his rank when I first met him.

This man standing in my club tonight might earn my full respect someday. His reputation has paved the way so far. However, it will be his character that seals the deal with me.

"I come with a gift from me to you. You might want to open it under a little privacy," he says as his guy holds up a gold case.

I tilt my head to the side curiously. I've heard about LaSalle and his golden gift boxes. I too, have an affinity for the flair of sending such gifts. If I'm right, his words of warning hold validity.

"Come, we will go up to my office. We will have privacy there. Choose only one of your men to follow. You will both be disarmed before we reach the office suite. Choose wisely," I say and stand, buttoning my suit jacket.

To my surprise, he takes the gold case and gestures with his head for his man to leave. He then follows me, leaving both men who arrived with him behind. Ballsy, I'll give him that.

That or he doesn't have the proper amount of fear toward me. I get the feeling it might be a bit of both, given those I've heard he keeps company with. Sam Mairettie and I keep some of the same company if you look in from a distance. Or should I say LaSalle Locatelli?

I get the feeling that's who I'm dealing with tonight. We make our way into my office, and I offer him a seat. He moves to the sitting area and sits on the couch, placing the case down on the table.

I move to the bar and go to pour myself a drink. I'm in a scotch sort of mood. I pour two fingers and turn to hold the bottle up in offering.

He shrugs. "Why not?"

I grab another glass and the bottle then head over to join him. I pour him a drink and sit back with mine. I eye the case out the corner of my eye suspiciously but make no rush to reach for it.

"What is this about, LaSalle?" I ask as I glare at him.

"May I?" He points at the bottle for another drink.

"Drink up. I assume you've come as a friend. Drink like one, mate."

"I have come as a friend. A friend who you can feel welcome to call on. I brought you something I believe you were on your way to collect."

Now my curiosity is piqued. I reach for the case and turn it to me. The craftsmanship of the gold case-like box is stunning.

I open it and the scent of rotting flesh burns my nose. A glance into the box reveals two severed hands. The ring on the left hand grabs my attention.

Another on the right confirms my suspicions. I close the case and purse my lips. I guess I won't be going to Connecticut.

"What do you want in return?"

"I ask for nothing. You had a problem. As a friend, I solved it.

"You called me, LaSalle. Just so you understand, I've come as a Locatelli. We want you to know you have friends within our family. Times are changing and the right friends are good to have."

"Does this change involve an affirmative on my request?"

"If you have time, I would like to tell you all about the benefits of your friendship with me. Things will be different. I'm looking for a few who would like to share the world with me.

"I'm not after Italy. I want it all. For men like us, *no* should never be the response you receive. I understand why it was what you were met with. Doesn't mean I agree," he says.

"So you would have given me the green light?"

"You would have a seat at the table. You wouldn't have had to ask."

Michael

I stand between the hidden panel to Uri's office and the door to the exit, my hands dripping in blood. Rage and anger are seething within me.

"Thank you for hearing me out. I look forward to our future if you decide the Alliance is for you," the man in Uri's office says as Uri claps him on the back.

"You have given me much to consider. Only time will tell from here," Uri responds.

"Yes, that it will."

"I will see you again, LaSalle."

I lift a brow. LaSalle Locatelli is a name that rings bells, but much like Uri, he is an enigma. I can't help wondering what all of that was about.

"Come out. My phone has been buzzing incessantly. Tell me what has happened," Uri calls once LaSalle is gone.

I slide the panel back and step forward. Uri's eyes go wide. I must look a sight.

"Fucking Christ. What in the bloody hell? Tell me none of that is your blood."

"No, none of it is mine, but a lot of it belongs to the don. Leonardo Trovati sent men to ambush us at the meeting at Don Alessio's restaurant," I say in explanation.

It was after hours, but our men were there. The old bastard took a bullet before I could get him covered. He's one strong son of a bitch.

"Fucking hell. I grow tired of this." He swallows hard. "Trovati?"

"I got him out of there and he's going to survive. However, we both lost men. That bastard Leonardo lost more."

"Did you recognize any of them? Can we use this against him this time?"

"No, once again, not Italians. He has managed to cover his tracks again. My concern at the moment is Salvatore. He didn't warn me this time."

"Fuck," he growls and pulls a hand down his face. "That can only mean he has been caught, or he will be soon."

Those are exactly my thoughts. I came here to inform Uri of the situation and see how he wants to handle it. Salvatore has been loyal. If we can extract him, I want to do so.

"If we're going to get him out, it has to be done as soon as possible," my brother says as if reading my mind.

"He can come with me back to Italy. London isn't safe for Don Trovati."

I am also putting Uri at risk while I stay here. The two of us have been in the same place for too long. I need to be where I'm not seen.

"I've taken on too much power. I'm beginning to draw notice. This is what Don Trovati wanted to meet about," I say to Uri.

"This is true. I am aware that Leonardo knows this as well. My name has been circulating more as of late.

"Talk is that I have muscled my way into the Trovati family since I have no chance at taking over my own," he scoffs.

"Will this alliance change anything for me or Symphony?"

I gesture with my head for the door LaSalle Locatelli left through. Uri places his hands on his hips. I can see the wheels turning in his head.

"Brilliant. That's bloody brilliant," he murmurs to himself. Then he looks to me. "It just might. *If*, which is one big fucking if, I decide to join them, it will be because of you and Sim."

"I think you should do it. We're going to need their power. I can do this.

"I can bring her home, but it would be a lot easier with the power he just offered. It would stop Leonardo in his tracks as well. No more outside help."

Uri moves closer to me and cups the sides of my face. He then kisses my forehead before looking me in the eyes.

"Done."

CHAPTER TWENTY-NINE

Crossing Paths

Symphony

Four Years later ...

"Ugh, I don't know why I allowed you to talk me into this. I feel like a beached whale and I'm hungry. What's with all this finger food. Are these people rabbits?"

"We will go once I confirm the information I need. Thank you for attending this event with me."

"You are lucky I love art," Maribel grumbles.

I have enjoyed having her with me. I wish it were under better circumstances, but I have taken pleasure in her company either way. Besides, it was better I bring her along instead of Adriano. He knows nothing about art and this charity event has some heavy players who could expose my cover.

I glance around the room for my target. I haven't accepted this job. I'm only doing recon to see if it meets the guidelines.

Sam Mairettie comes into view, standing beside his wife. I glance away quickly as I find her eyes on me. I don't think I will be accepting this job.

I only have a few hours to decide. Mairettie and his wife will be returning to New York in the morning. The client wants the job done here in Boston.

"Oh, look at this one. I love it. She looks like she's leaping from the photograph."

I turn my attention to the photograph Maribel is speaking of. It's a black-and-white of a hip-hop dancer. It makes me think of Ximena and how she tried to get me to mix ballet and hip-hop while we were in school together.

"Do you think you could do this for me?" I ask as I think of how Michael has never seen me dance.

"You mean for your husband, don't you?"

"Yes, he did come to mind. I would like to gift him a photograph like this."

"Sure, we can do that. I think it would be cool. Have you decided what you will do about him?"

I chew on my lip as I think her question over. Her words have been on my mind since we rode to her appointment and she asked me about Michael. Guilt rises as I remember not giving her the full truth.

"I don't know what I will do," I reply honestly.

"I don't mean to be in your business, but I've been thinking about it. I think you should go to him if he's not willing to come to you.

"It sounds like you guys have a lot to talk about. At least clear the air."

"I will consider your words. Thank you, Maribel."

"Girl, I need to consider a potty. My bladder is about to go off."

I chuckle as she turns to wobble off. I wish I had more friends like her and Ximena. I have been wondering if things would be different if I had confided in Ximena more.

"This is a stunning piece."

I turn to find Mrs. Mairettie standing beside me. Ellen, that's what the dossier said her first name is. She's staring at me again with a smile on her face.

"I'm sorry. I just wanted to come over and tell you how stunning you look. You and your friend have stood out in this crowd," she says and reaches to place her hand on my arm.

She pulls her hand back quickly as her eyes glaze over. I force myself to focus on her. I want to know if her behavior will reveal her husband's character.

I found none of the things my client told me about him. He seems to be a businessman with a little family he's raising. Nothing to trigger me and make me want to end his life.

"You are a very special and powerful woman. The answer is no. You don't want to do what you're being asked to do.

"He's a friend of your family. He will be a friend of yours. If you do this, you will lose everything you've been hoping for," she says as her eyes refocus.

"Excuse me?" I breathe.

She moves in closer and leans into my ear. "You don't want to kill my husband. He is connected to your future. Don't make things more difficult than they need to be.

"You will already have a challenge on your hands with your husband. There will be at least two more years before you can remain at his side, but if you do this, you will lose him forever," she whispers.

She pulls away and I search her gaze. How could this woman know any of this? I glance around the room to see if her husband is watching.

Did he put her up to this?

"How can I know your words are true?" I ask.

"You will mean a lot to my son. I would never take that from him. He will know what's possible for him because of you."

"You don't have a son. You have a little girl. You are lying to me."

She places her hand against the full fabric of the dress she's wearing. It is then I can see the bump forming. Okay, she's having a boy.

"No, I am not lying. After this daughter, I will have a son. His name will be Sammy. You will mean as much to him as your husband and brother-in-law.

"I can't prove any of this today, but you will know I have told you nothing but the truth when you see the dancer within the music. When you see her, not only will you know I have spoken nothing but the truth to you, but you will also know you have to be the strong one and walk away.

"Before my time is up, you and I will meet again. Then you will know that we are your family, not your enemies."

"Walk away from what?"

"Him. The one who bears the dancer. If you stay. He will lose his life saving yours."

With that, she turns to a returning Maribel and rubs her baby bump. Her eyes light up and a warm smile comes to her lips. She turns to me and winks.

"Friends for life. They will be family too."

Maribel looks after her as she walks away. I watch Sam pull her into his embrace and kiss her forehead. I knit my brows as I watch the two.

"Who was that and what's with these white people? No one has asked if they can touch my belly before doing so. It's just plain rude," Maribel says beside me, causing me to snicker.

"She is a friend of a friend," I say and shrug, not knowing how else to explain.

CHAPTER THIRTY

Following Advice

Symphony

Three months later …

"Are you sure this is what you want to do?" Adriano asks as we climb into the car after arriving in Italy on a private jet.

I've come to see my husband. After four months of thinking about it, I decided to follow Maribel's advice. I still don't know if I will ask for a divorce, but I've considered it.

"This is where he is. It is where I need to be," I reply.

Adriano sighs and shakes his head. "She is sure to get me killed," he grumbles under his breath.

"I have not seen a single member of my family this year. If they are too busy to come to America, I have come to them."

"*Fanculo*, have you thought that maybe things here are keeping them from coming to you?"

"That is likely, but I can only be sure if I'm here to find out."

"You are here for him. You have stepped into danger because he is a coward and ignores you exist."

"Enough. You will not speak of my husband like this. Michael and I have our issues, but that is our business," I growl.

The car falls silent. I have started to pop the band on my wrist. Adriano's displeasure with Michael is something I am very aware of.

I don't need a reminder. Not now. I'm nervous enough.

I lied to Maribel. I told her I hadn't seen my husband since I was sixteen because I was too embarrassed to tell her what happened the last time I saw him. I was twenty-one and freaked out because my husband gave me cunnilingus.

Things have been so strained between Michael and I since that night. I want to fix things. I want to be with him.

I believe Maribel was right. I need to go to Michael and let him know how I feel. I have chosen to ignore Ellen Mairettie's warning. I have nothing to prove her words mean anything.

I need to see Michael. I don't believe I should just call. Calling leaves room for complications and misunderstandings.

This is hard enough for me. I can learn to become a black belt fighter by watching videos. I've become a weapons specialist in the same manner. My tablet has always been my friend.

It has brought the world to me. If I want to know something I spend hours diving into knowledge, separating myths from facts. Once the information begins to play in my mind like a symphony, I find that I'm satisfied and have the knowledge I desire for that subject.

It is how I learn. However, emotions and relationships can't be taught through my tablet. Trust me, I've tried. I haven't found an answer to what I'm doing wrong with Michael.

"I'm sorry," Adriano says as he reaches to cover my hand to keep me from popping the band.

"It's okay. I am under a lot of stress. I might be overreacting."

"You are not. I have overstepped."

"I don't speak of Michael to anyone. It is hard to explain how I feel about him, about what I know he has sacrificed for me.

"He doesn't neglect me out of cruelty. Other things keep us apart. I want … I …" I shake my head as I have trouble finding the right words.

I'm so frustrated. I hate it when I can't draw my words together. It's like the words are right there, but I can't express them the way I want.

"You don't have to explain it to me."

"But I want to."

"It's okay, Sim. I can see you are overwhelmed. Take the rest of the ride to gather your thoughts for him. That's who matters."

"You matter too. You have become my friend. I couldn't have done this or my business without you."

He reaches to pat my knee. "You saved my life. I will always be here for you."

"Thank you, Adriano."

***

We pull up to the gate of the property and Adriano pulls to a stop. I am startled when he throws the car into park and jumps out. One of the guards at the gate looks just like him.

Adriano and the man tug each other into a tight embrace and begin to speak in rapid Italian.

"I have come with Symphony. She's here to see the boss," Adriano says in Italian.

The man knits his brow. "Why would you bring her here? This is not good. Michael will be furious."

"He did not bring me here. I came on my own and he followed. Let us in. Michael can chastise me himself," I reply in Italian as well.

"This is my brother Salvatore Cattaneo. He means no disrespect," Adriano says with a smile as he pats his brother's chest.

"Hurry, take her to the house before someone sees her here," Salvatore says with concern in his eyes. "Benito, I'm going to ride to the house with them. Will you be fine here?"

"Gino is on his way. Go on, I'll be fine."

Adriano and Salvatore jump back into the vehicle, and we pull through the gate. Salvatore talks with his heavy accent as we head to the house. I watch out the window, remembering the first time I came here.

As we get closer to the house, my heart begins to pound. I don't know what greeting awaits me. Adriano could be right. This could be a very bad idea.

I hold my breath as we park, and I step out of the vehicle. I move to the front door as I used to do every day after school. Pushing through the front door, I inhale deeply.

It's like I'm welcomed home by the familiar scents of simmering sauce, fresh flowers, and the manly colognes of Michael and Nico. As if summoned by my thoughts, Nico comes up the hall with an apple in his hand as he takes a bite out of it. He pulls the apple from his mouth as he knits his brows.

"*Bella*, you are a sight for sore eyes. Come give me a hug," he croons in Italian.

I rush forward into his arms. He gives me a tight squeeze. I squeeze him tighter, not realizing how much I've missed him too.

"What are you doing here?" he asks.

"I could ask you the same thing. Why aren't you with the team?"

He gives me a blinding, mischievous smile. I drop my gaze away and dart my eyes around. Nico and his cheeky behavior will always exasperate me.

I don't take offense. I get that it's brotherly love. Nico would never do anything to harm me.

"I've missed you. Now that there's a possibility Uri will be in the States more, I have signed a new contract to play for an American team. I had planned to drop in on you at the end of this week, but here you are," he says with a teasing grin.

"Uri is moving to America?" I gasp.

Before he can answer me, Michael appears. He takes my breath away. He has a scowl on his face while grumbling to himself as he looks down at his phone.

He's dressed in a light-blue dress shirt and light-blue slacks with cream-colored shoes on his feet. Everything is so crisp and pristine. His blond hair is neatly combed into place as it always is.

"What's going on? I dropped my phone in the sink. The front gate was calling before I dropped it," he says. "Well, this is shit."

He tosses the phone to the guy walking beside him and looks up. Our gazes lock. It's like all the air in the room is sucked out.

I stand stock-still. The intensity around us cracks like a whip. I can almost feel it brush against my skin, sending a shiver down my spine.

"What are you doing here?" he bites out.

"I am twenty-eight. I have never had coitus. You are my husband. I would like to have it with you."

A collective gasp fills the air. Michael's mouth drops open. Nico bursts into laughter and I think Adriano is stifling his laughter behind me.

"Um … I think you two should go have a private chat. I will get my hugs later," Annabella says.

I hadn't noticed her as my focus had been on Michael. Her words cause me to realize I've chosen the wrong time to speak honestly. They also snap Michael into action.

He closes the distance between us and grabs me by the wrist. Even with my long legs, I struggle to keep up with his stride. He tugs me to the stairs, not saying a word.

When we get to the top, he doesn't turn for my room. Instead, he turns for his wing of the house. At the end of the hall, he pushes the door open and tugs me into the room with him.

Quickly, he closes the door behind us. I jump when he rounds on me and cages me against the door. I keep my gaze on his chest.

"You put your life in danger to come and demand sex from me?"

"I am not demanding. I would like for you to deflower me. If you don't wish to, then at least I will know and can stop waiti—"

My words are cut off by his lips. He kisses me like a starving man. I wrap my arms around his neck and lift on my toes to kiss him back.

He groans as he moves his hands over my body. With shaky hands, I move my fingers to the buttons on his shirt. I only manage to get two undone when he coaxes my arms up so he can take my sweater off.

"*Merda*, you drive me crazy. Whenever I'm around you all I want is to be near you, to touch you. I only stay away because I can't have you."

"Why can't you have me?"

He places his forehead against mine. Slowly, he drags one hand up my side, stopping just below my breast. He grasps hold of me, resting his thumb beneath the cup of my bra. Then he tightens his hold.

"That was never a part of the deal. I'm your guardian, your protector—"

"My husband. I was there, Michael. I know what was said.

"What was asked of you. Nonno never said you couldn't touch me. I'm your wife. Who else do you think he expected to take my virginity?"

"*Fuck*," he growls and lifts me onto his waist.

He's devouring my mouth once again. I whimper into his as he sticks his tongue into my mouth and searches my cavern like he has lost something within it.

He moves his lips to trail kisses against my skin, moving across my cheek, to my neck, and then down to my collarbone as he presses into me. My heated skin meets the cool surface of the door behind me, causing me to gasp and arch my back.

Micheal takes the motion as an opportunity to unclasp my bra. My breasts bounce free, and a groan comes from deep within his chest. He palms one and lifts it as if testing its weight.

"You are mine. No one else will touch what belongs to me," he says huskily before he takes my nipple into his mouth.

I throw my head back and look up at the ceiling. His sucking has made the light pulsing of my vagina turn into a throbbing beat as if my heart has dropped between my legs.

"Michael," I cry out.

He pulls away and looks into my eyes. There is so much lust there. I reach for his face and run my thumb across his wet lips.

"*È questo che vuoi, amore mio? Vuoi che io faccia l'amore con te, sì?*"

"Yes, Michael, please. That is what I want. I want you to make love to me," I reply.

"You are so beautiful. I have wanted you for so long. How can I tell you no?"

"Please don't. I don't think I can take it if you do. I have wanted you too.

"I've longed for you to come to me. I am here because I want you, Michael. I am ready. Please," I plead.

He kneads my breast as he takes my lips again. I love the way he kisses me. I feel wanted and cherished.

His touch sends my skin buzzing, but I don't want it to stop. The music in my head is playing, but it's the most beautiful song I've ever heard. He releases me from his waist, causing me to whine.

"We are not done, *cara*," he says with so much lust in his voice.

He chuckles darkly as he works on the buttons of his shirt. I unzip my pants as I kick off my shoes. Then I wiggle out of my pants. Eager to feel his touch again, I make quick work of taking off my socks.

"Fuck, you're gorgeous. So perfect," he says as he stands before me naked.

I glance at his penis and my cheeks heat. It's long and seems to be thickening before my eyes. My mind goes to all the literature I've read.

I can't help wondering what his sexual preferences are. I want to do my best to please him and not just receive pleasure. I have no doubt he will make my body feel amazing.

If his cunnilingus is any indication of what it would be like to have coitus with him, I know he's going to leave me more than satisfied. I drop to my knees in excitement as his penis twitches.

I will perform fellatio for the first time. With a smile on my face, I pull the band from my hair and gather all my locs to tie them all back, not just the front. I look at his penis as I'm now face to face with it and lick my lips.

Michael

If I wasn't so painfully hard, I would laugh at the way her eyes cross as she looks at my cock. The wicked grin that comes to her lips as she licks them causes me to groan.

She lifts those beautiful big brown eyes to me and smiles. I know I should slow down, and we should talk first, but I haven't had sex in years. I'm tired of jerking my own cock.

It feels like I've become a virgin again from lack of sex. When Sim palms my length in her hands and runs her tongue through the precum dripping from the tip, all I can do is groan.

"What are you doing, *bella*?"

"I have never given fellatio. I want to give you pleasure first," she says happily.

I growl. "We are not going to have coitus, Sim, and you're not going to give me fellatio. You are going to suck my cock and I'm going to fuck you. Can you say that for me?"

Her encyclopedia explanation of what we're about to do makes me feel like I should stop this. Is she really ready? It's been so long since I've had a real conversation with her. I have no idea where her head is at these days.

"Yes. I am going to suck your big fat cock and then you're going to fuck me with it. Do you have toys to stretch my ass? I will let you fuck me there too."

My mouth drops open. What happened to my sweet little Sim? The lust in her eyes tells me she's all woman now.

This isn't the same twenty-one-year-old who asked me for her first kiss, then ran from me. I grasp her face and bend at the waist to crush my lips to hers. I love her sweet mouth.

I could spend the day drinking from her full lips, but neither of us wants that. She begins to stroke me as I consume her mouth. It's effective in getting me to head in the direction we are going.

I straighten, ready to carry her to my bed. However, my love has other plans. I drop my head back and hiss as she takes me between her lips.

"*Fuck.*" The word comes through my teeth, almost sounding pained.

I glance down at Sim as she sucks me like she's a professional. Why wouldn't this woman be perfect at this, like everything else she does?

I cup the sides of her head as I thrust my hips forward. My heart swells as she looks me right in the eyes. This is a gift in itself.

I always want to connect with her, but I never want to force her to look into my eyes when she doesn't feel comfortable doing so. This intimacy is more than I could ever have asked for. I nearly come from the eye contact alone.

That and the insatiable way she's sucking my cock. I pull from her mouth before I blow my load. I can't help licking my lips as I see her long fingers between her legs as she plays with her pussy.

"Come, love. Let me take care of that for you," I say as I lift her to her feet.

I then lift her so she can wrap her long legs around my waist. The heat from her pussy has me growing harder. I turn for my bed and walk across the room.

With a playful smile on my lips, I toss her onto the bed and watch her bounce. She looks amazing sprawled across my bed. Reaching for one of her ankles, I drag her body back toward me.

Dropping to my knees, I then lock her legs around my neck as I dive in to devour her hot little pussy. As she begins to writhe against my face, I place a hand on her belly to hold her still.

"Michael," she cries out breathily.

I lift my gaze to look up her body and find her up on her elbows, watching me. I groan into her pussy as her juices fill my mouth. She takes me by surprise when I feel the power of her thighs as she tightens them against my ears.

Bringing her to climax twice, I then pry her legs open and climb onto the bed, moving her up the mattress as I position myself to hover over her while resting between her legs.

"Michael, you are so gorgeous," she pants.

"No, *cara*. That is you. Are you sure you're ready?"

"Yes, I am."

I take her lips as I palm her breast, then pinch and roll her nipple. She whimpers into my mouth, but I swallow the sound down and deepen the kiss.

Her scent has surrounded me and taken over my head. She always smells so good. My mouth waters for her.

Hard as steel, I begin to push into her tight sheath as I drink from her mouth. As I meet her barrier, I pull back. Sim nips at my lower lip.

I return the gesture as I drive back into her. She bows her back as she wraps her legs around my waist. I pause as my eyes roll back.

My brows knit as her pussy grips me tightly. It's the best feeling in the world. Better than I could ever have dreamed.

"Are you okay, baby?" I breathe against her cheek as I try to regain control while she adjusts around me.

"Yes, I am fine. I believe I need you to move."

I kiss my way down her neck as I begin to move slowly. Her tight pussy ripples around me, sucking me in. She moves her legs higher as I thrust my hips down into her. My pace increases with her moans and cries of pleasure.

"Fuck, you feel amazing."

"Michael ... oh my God, Michael. Yes, yes, more please," she pants.

She's so wet and tight. I slide in and out of her, feeling her tightening around me. I can't believe I have her in my arms.

As she claws her nails across my back, I growl and shift my angle to get deeper. When I can't find the angle I want, I pull out and move to my knees. Sim sits up, looking at me as if she's confused.

I smile at her as I grab the base of my shaft in one hand and reach for her thigh with the other. Tugging her to me, I angle her hips and thrust back into her.

We both watch as my length moves in and out of her tight body. I throw my head back and look up at the ceiling. I pray to God for an answer to bringing this mess to an end so I can bring my wife home for good.

I don't know how I will stay away after this. Sim screams loudly in pleasure, causing me to tighten my hold on her thigh as I look back down at her. She's so fucking sexy.

The sight before me makes me so much harder. Her head is thrown back, her breasts are bouncing, and her pussy looks amazing sucking me in. I lick my lips, wanting to taste her again.

However, she has other ideas. She pushes at my chest, pushing me onto my back. In the next breath, she mounts me and begins to slide down onto me.

"Easy, baby. Don't hurt yourself. Slow down. We don't have to rush," I grunt as I grasp her hips to slow her down.

My eyes begin to roll back as she bounces on me. She finds her rhythm and rocks her hips as I clench my teeth to keep from coming.

Sweat begins to glisten across her gorgeous brown skin. Her hair is coming loose from the ponytail she placed it in before sucking me off. A vision of pure beauty.

"Yes, baby. Ride me just like that. You wanted to fuck, show me what you like," I groan.

"Michael, you're so hard inside of me. I didn't know it would feel this good."

She reaches for one of my hands and places it on her mound. I use my thumb to rub her clit as she grabs the other hand and places it right over the other. As she bites her lip, she drags that hand up the center of her body. I curl my fingers to claw at her skin as she drags my hand.

"Fuck, baby. Your pussy sounds so fucking wet. Ride me harder. Use me for your pleasure."

"Michael," she gasps.

I lift to palm her breasts and take her sexy lips once again. She kisses me back with just as much passion. I break the kiss to take one of her nipples into my mouth and then move to the other to give it some attention too.

Her walls begin to spasm against me as she cries out for more. I give her everything she wants. When she begins to convulse on my shaft, I flip her onto her back and drill into her.

Sim cups my face to look in my eyes and I slow down. There's that intense connection again. I begin to make love to her as my heart stirs.

"You are everything to me. I'm glad you came to me. I'm doing everything I can to make—"

She tugs my head down to her and kisses me, cutting my words off. I pin her legs back into her body as I swivel and thrust my hips. She throws her head back and screams my name.

I keep stroking as I watch her take pleasure from my body. She's so beautiful as she comes. As she comes down from her orgasm, she cups my face.

"We don't have to waste words now. I'm not going to listen to anything you say right now that doesn't have anything to do with you fucking me. Shh. Just make me feel good."

I grab her wrists and pin them over her head, then I fuck her into the mattress. When I release my seed into her, it dawns on me that I've finally consummated my marriage. Symphony is mine.

CHAPTER THIRTY-ONE

Could Lose Him

Symphony

I wake wrapped in Michael's big, strong arms. He is snoring heavily as his chest is pressed to my back. My body is sore all over and I need to use the restroom.

I go to wiggle free of his hold and freeze when I look down at his forearm. He has a tattoo I've never seen. It's of a ballerina. She is dressed in black with red slippers. However, what takes my breath away are the musical notes she looks to be dancing through.

Ellen Mairettie's words come back to me. They are so loud and clear as I stare down at the tat. I fight to trap the sob that rises in my throat.

I can't prove any of this today, but you will know I have told you nothing but the truth when you see the dancer within the music. When you see her, not only will you know I have spoken nothing but the truth to you, but you will also know you have to be the strong one and walk away.

I cover my mouth to hold the sound in. Michael groans and rolls away from me. Not thinking twice, I leap from the bed and rush into the bathroom.

Closing the door behind me, I then rush to climb into the tub. I sit inside and wrap my arms around my shivering body. I'm trying my best not to hyperventilate.

"No, no, no," I whimper.

It's Michael. Michael is the one who bears the dancer. After what we just did, I am going to have to walk away from him? If I don't, he will lose his life because of me.

"*Why?*" I sob loudly.

As Ellen's words fully set in, I can't hold in the sobs. The agony of having to leave him rips through me and more sobs tear from my lips. Hot tears slide down my cheeks.

I have to find Adriano. We have to leave. I can't stay here and lose the man I love.

Michael

I jump from my sleep and take in a sharp inhale. Looking around, I try to catch my bearings. The sobs that woke me were coming from my bathroom.

I run a hand through my hair. Symphony. She was asleep in my arms when I passed out after we spent hours making love.

Well, some of it was fucking. Who am I kidding—a lot of it was fucking. However, now she's in my bathroom sobbing.

"Fuck. Not again," I mutter.

Earlier was amazing, but what if it wasn't for her? I knew I should have slowed things down. Why am I such a moron when it comes to her?

Frustrated with myself, I climb from the bed and head to the bathroom. I'm relieved when the knob turns and I'm able to push in. I find her in an empty bathtub, sobbing as if she's just lost everything.

"Sim," I say gently.

She doesn't answer. I move farther into the bathroom and climb into the tub behind her. Wrapping my arms around her, I hold her against my chest.

"Baby, are you okay? What's wrong? Did I hurt you?"

She shakes her head, but she keeps sobbing. I kiss her shoulder and tighten my hold. I can't believe I've allowed this to happen again.

As much as I want my wife, I don't think we're going to be able to make this work. I don't know what I keep doing wrong. I thought this was what she wanted.

She came here to me. I thought we both enjoyed the experience. She pleaded with me for more.

Stupid. Stupid. Stupid. You thought with your cock, Michael. She wasn't ready.

I will never forgive myself for this. All I can do in this moment is hold her in my arms and comfort her. She turns in my embrace and climbs into my lap, wrapping her body around me.

Leaning back against the cool tub, I hold her close and hum "Für Elise" in her ear. I don't want to lose her, but this might be too much. I can't have her crying every time we're intimate.

Soon, my lids grow heavy, and I'm finding it hard to keep them open. I'm too tired to stand and carry her back into the bedroom, so I surrender to sleep with her pressed against my chest. We will talk in the morning.

CHAPTER THIRTY-TWO

Gone

Michael

I wake and groan, my back is aching and my ass is cold. I open my eyes to find I'm still in the bathtub, but Sim is no longer with me. I sit up and rub my back.

"*Merda*," I grumble.

As my mind clears, I realize I need to find Sim so we can have a conversation. I want to know why she keeps melting down after we are intimate. Is it something I'm doing or something else?

I need to know if it's something I can fix because I want to fix it. It may not be safe for her to be here, but I would like to start making trips to America to spend more time with her. Uri will be in the States more with his new wife, Valentina.

They will split their time between New York and Chicago. I had already been thinking about spending time in Boston. This conversation will determine a lot.

"Shower first," I say to myself.

I stand and head into the shower, turning on the hot spray to release my tense muscles. As my frustration with myself builds, I move through my shower faster. I need answers now.

Turning the water off and climbing out, I then wrap a towel around my waist and head for my closet. I glance at my bed and see the evidence of our lovemaking and Sim's lost virginity. I chastise myself even more for my actions.

How do I keep hurting someone I love so much? Her sobs from last night are haunting me. She cried as if she lost someone. I don't know how to feel about that.

I'm lost in thought as I dress in cream slacks and a cream dress shirt. I roll the sleeves up as I move to look in the mirror. I take in the outfit as I loop a brown belt around my waist.

The tat on my forearm catches my attention. I got it after seeing Sim perform about a year and a half ago. She was dressed in black with red ballerina slippers on her feet. It made for the most stunning visual as she danced across the stage.

I had wanted to let her know I was there that night. I wanted to hold her in my arms then. Instead, I had this tattoo inked on my skin.

I had the musical notes wrapped around the dancer because that night, I truly thought I could see the notes floating around her. She was wrapped in the beauty of the sound. A pure vision of magic.

Each time she leaped through the air, my heart jumped with her. I was mesmerized and in awe. The woman is magnificent.

I shake the thought off and turn to find her and answers. My thoughts go to how long I can keep her here. Leonardo has been up to his old tricks.

I would destroy him if anything happened to Sim. However, I'm not willing to risk it. She shouldn't remain here long.

A few days. I want to keep her with me for a few days before she returns to America, where I'll know she's safe. I wonder if that will make her happy.

"There you are," Nico croons as I enter the kitchen.

I get this feeling in the pit of my stomach. Something doesn't seem right. I look to Annabella and she has a sad look on her face. My heart tightens and I feel like I can't breathe.

"She's gone?" I choke out, not asking a question.

I already know. She has left. This heartache is so sharp and painful.

I've hurt her enough to send her running from me. This isn't going to work between us. My love will never be enough to fix what's broken.

CHAPTER THIRTY-THREE

Lost Monsters

Michael

Five months later ...

Uri has asked us to come to America. He wants to introduce us to his wife before the baby is born. I think he has made a mistake. His wife was right on our property, and he chose to keep us hidden.

I know who his wife really is. She is one of us. A hitter.

At times, I have wished Sim could be by my side in all of this. Then I realize how ridiculous that is. This darkness shouldn't belong to anyone.

"I may not have a choice," I mutter to myself.

I may have to go to America. Italy has been compromised. Leonardo has gotten too close to our home.

He is forcing my hand. I will either have to reveal myself or I will be revealed. This vise grip and my confusion about what happened with Symphony have strained my vision.

It feels like I no longer have a purpose. I feel nothing. Bitterness always fills me.

I've been lost since the day Sim left without a word. Leonardo kept me from running after her. He had me ambushed the day I decided to head to Boston for answers.

Sim wouldn't answer my calls. I had no idea what I did wrong. However, after the attack, I knew her leaving was for the best.

It happened between the properties, so I couldn't be sure if it was an attack meant for me or Uri. The real supposed husband of Symphony. Now that Uri is married to a Caprisi, this cover we have kept will be blown soon.

I'm infuriated with the situation. Not that my brother has found happiness, but the fact that his new life threatens all I have been protecting for the last fourteen years. Now, I move with rage.

It's only been five months, but I have been on a warpath during this time. Leonardo has only fueled my rage and the fire building inside. If I can't get to him, I will kill everyone he sends and anyone connected to them until they give him up or give me the proof I need for the families to okay his kill.

These German bastards are only the latest victims he has sent my way. It wasn't hard to find them. Their arrogance led me straight to them. I enter the old run-down hideout I've followed them to from the bar.

To sit in one of my cities and speak so freely of your crimes is like buying the Grim Reaper a first-class ticket to your funeral. You might as well go running through the streets screaming *silenzio*. I don't think they know they have been calling my fucking name, but I'm here to answer.

Pulling my gun with the silencer already in place, I shoot out the lame surveillance cameras they have in place. Then, like a thief in the night, I move through their hideout like a freight train. I hit hard and fast. There are about twenty of them to one me, but you wouldn't know that by the time I have the last one by the back of his hair as I walk him through the carnage I've left behind.

"Please, I have son," he says in a heavy Czech accent.

"Not German," I murmur to myself.

"No, I get job through cousin smuggling in Germany. He runs with Germans. I come along to drive. I know nothing more."

"That's a shame. I hope your son learns to make better choices from his next father."

With that, I blow his brains out and drop him in front of the door I came in through. I double back to a room on the second floor that grabbed my attention. There is blood everywhere.

As I walk into the room in question, the sound of someone gasping for breath fills the air. I grab the case I noticed then turn to put a bullet through the head of the gasping bastard leaning against the wall. Stepping over another body, I leave as quickly as I came in.

Symphony

"Shit, Sim. How do you plan to get out of this one?" Adriano hisses through the comm.

His assistance was needed for this job. I don't normally take jobs like this one, but I needed to get out some of this pent-up frustration. I miss Michael.

All I could think about when I woke up on his chest in that bathtub was Ellen Mairettie's words. I've done some more research on the woman and found she's from a family of Gypsies.

A few of them are known for fortune-telling to the underground world. Before meeting Ellen, I don't think I would have subscribed to such things, but now I refuse to play with Michael's life to find out the truth from experience.

"Answer me. Are you okay in there?" Adriano demands.

I sigh and roll my eyes. If I'm supposed to be hiding, how can I answer? And people talk to me and treat me like I'm slow.

I roll my eyes again. I'm going to have to fight my way out before he storms his way in here and gets us both killed. Now I wish I had come on my own.

The dojo beneath me holds my three targets, but they have security with them. This shouldn't be the case. I was told it would only be the three.

Looking through the vents, my eyes land on the wall of weapons. If I can get to it, I can get out of here. I will need to disarm the big guys first and then take on the targets.

This might be the challenge I need. I have never truly tested my combat skills other than in training with Uri and Adriano. However, these three are masters.

I had planned to use bullets to take them out from a distance. Now, if I speak to let Adriano know that I'm okay, I will lose the element of surprise and I'll be cooked. If I take action and attack, I will need my bullets for the guards, not the targets.

I don't know how I got into this situation. This client will have a lot to answer for. I will never work for them again.

As silently as I can, I move through the vent to the other side of the room where the weapons wall sits. I hold my breath, hoping not to make a sound over their heads.

I shift my body in the small space so I can slide instead of crawl. I already know the vents are thin and the sound carries. It was the first thing to grab my attention from the time I entered them.

"Sim, I'm coming in. If you can hear me, hang tight. I'm on my way."

I hold in a groan. I don't need him to charge in here. I can handle this. Ugh, this is why I work alone.

I purse my lips and release an annoyed breath. Here goes nothing. Reaching the vent, I pull my gun and drop down through the opening. Landing in a crouch, I take out the first two big guys—one to the head, two to the chest.

Not taking a moment to think about it, I then put down the other two. One of them gets a shot off before I drop him. The bullet hits the wall behind me. Unfortunately, the shot rings out, alerting the others outside.

Two more rush into the room, I take them both out then drop my gun. I need to get to the weapons behind me. The three targets snap into action, ready to take me on as they get into fighting stances.

"I don't know who you are or who sent you, but you have come to die," the first woman says.

I grin before I turn and run at the wall to my left. I use my momentum to walk the wall and get to the swords I have my sights on. I grab the hilts of the two I want and flip down to my feet.

One of the targets laughs at me. "Do you know who we are? You will be dead in seconds. I won't even bother to remove my coat for you."

I chuckle back. "I didn't ask you to. I know who you all are. It will be an honor to take your lives."

I have slowly moved into the center of the room as they have begun to surround me. I channel the anger I've been feeling since the morning I had to leave Michael in Italy.

I drop into a pose with the swords held out before me. They have begun to circle me like I'm the prey. From the sound of it, Adriano entered the building as he promised.

I need to finish here to help him. These three women have earned this death. They have lied to families, promising to give their daughters a better life.

Instead, they have used the poor girls to traffic them. One of the families had someone contact me and offer to pay the fee to make these women disappear. Because of the masters they are in the arts, not many were willing to take the job.

I fear no one. If you deserve to die. I will make sure I do my job.

The music starts to play in my head, and I begin to dance. I am abrupt and smooth as I move through their attacks and dodge their blows. I move swiftly as I swing up and cut through the center of the smallest one. She reaches for her open chest right as I spin and bring the other blade across her throat.

"One down, two to go. I believe I have made it at least a minute already," I taunt.

The final two begin to work together. I move fluidly like the ballerina I am. Dipping back, I avoid a kick as the tallest one's leg glides over my body.

When I come up, I slash behind her leg. She drops to her knees. I spin quickly and bring my blades up to block as the other now has a set of blades from the wall.

She is fast and fluid, but I am faster and more careful. She tries to back me down as the other one tries to rise back to her feet. I block her and force her to go on defense.

"You are skilled. I would have loved to be your teacher," she says.

I grin before I spin and bring one blade across her body and the other across her center, separating her torso from her legs.

"No," the last one cries. "Who sent you? How dare you?"

"How dare you?" I snarl. "They are all little girls. Why would you hurt them?"

"We only did what the world would someday do? It was done to us. We treat them better than we were treated."

"All the more reason for you not to show them such a fate."

With that, I move forward. I spin around her as she tries to fight me. This time, I slice through the backs of both knees, dropping her to the floor.

Spinning out on my toes, I then leap into the air and spin back in her direction. Her head is bowed as if in surrender. I take it for the respect that it is.

They fought hard. They didn't make it easy on me. I just danced with grace and fought with skill. I did my best.

I land at the same time that her head falls from her body and rolls across the floor. Chest heaving, I stand and take a bow. This job is done.

I smile and turn to leave, finding Adriano standing right outside the door, shaking his head at me. I shrug my shoulders and start to walk out.

"You never needed me, did you?"

"No, *Andiamo.*"

CHAPTER THIRTY-FOUR

In My Dreams

Symphony

"Come here, cara," Michael croons as he sits in the window seat of my bedroom.

I stand from the bed and move across the room to him, stopping before him in all my naked glory. He bites his lip and reaches out for me.

The moment his warm hand connects with my skin, I moan and shiver. My heart skips a beat. I close my eyes as he glides his palm up my side.

I've missed him so much. It's been so hard to be away from him. There aren't enough jobs to work off my sexual frustration. I need his touch as much as I need my next breath.

"Come, sit on my cock, baby. I want to feel you around me, cara."

Opening my eyes, I move to straddle his hips as he guides me over his length. My head falls back as he enters me. I'm already so wet for him.

"Michael," I breathe.

"You are everything to me. I only want to bring you pleasure," he groans into my ear as he thrusts into me.

He's so hard and thick. I work my hips, enjoying the way he fills me. As if he isn't already pushing me to the edge, he palms my breast and pulls my nipple into his mouth.

"Yes, Michael, yes," I cry out.

My walls begin to tighten around him, but I'm not ready for it to end. Lifting up, I then climb from his lap and drop to my knees. I need to have him in my mouth.

He groans and drops his head back against the window as I take him in deep. Reaching for my hair, I move it out of the way as I keep sucking. His moans make me excited.

I'm bringing him pleasure. I'm undoing the man before me. A man I know is powerful.

"Sim, baby. That feels so good."

I work him with my hands and mouth happily. I never want to stop. He gathers my hair into his hands and begins to pump his hips.

His silky hardness in my mouth makes me want to ride him again. Feeling all that power inside me is so thrilling. I take him as deep as I can and hold him inside my mouth.

"Holy fuck, Symphony," he hisses out.

I don't stop until I begin to choke. My eyes begin to water, but I can't get enough. I want more. I want him to come in my mouth.

However, Michael has other plans. He pulls from my mouth and lifts to his feet. Then he lifts me to stand and shifts our positions until I'm in front of the bench and he's behind me.

Pushing me down with a hand in the center of my back, he then enters me from behind. I grasp at the pillow of the window seat and hold on tight as I cry out his name.

"You like the way I fuck you, Symphony? Do you miss my cock? Do you regret leaving me?

"Your pussy is so wet for me. Are you keeping it tight for me? When I come for you, will you still be mine?"

I pop up from my sleep and look down. My vagina is throbbing. I can feel that I'm wet.

I can't believe this has happened again. It's the third night in a row. I palm my forehead and groan.

"How long am I to put up with this?" I say into the empty room.

Michael

"You feel so good, cara. Sing for me. Let me know how good it feels," I demand as I fuck Symphony from behind.

I have her bent over the piano as she takes me. Looking down at her smooth brown skin, I lick my lips. The ripple of her ass as I thrust into her has me growing harder.

"You feel so good. I don't want you to stop. I never want you to stop," she sings out.

My heart swells. How can I not love this woman? She fits me perfectly.

The grip she has around me have my eyes crossing in my head. I want more. I need more. I can't get enough.

Reaching for her breasts, I hold them as I thrust into her harder. She begins to scream my name as she throws her head back. Leaning over her, I take her lips for a hot, passionate kiss.

She whimpers into my mouth as her sex clenches around me. Bending my knees, I begin to thrust deeper. The sound of our skin slapping echoes through the room.

I'm getting closer. Her tight pussy is going to make me come. Moving my lips to her shoulder, I nip at her sweaty skin. Kneading her breasts, I then begin to play with her tightened nipples.

"Michael, please. Yes, I want more. Please," she pleads.

"I will take care of you, bella. Just keep taking me."

Her legs begin to shake as she lifts onto her toes. I lick the sweat from her back, moving to her neck. I bite her earlobe and growl as she comes around me.

The feel of her juices dripping down my balls is like a trigger. I spill right inside of her. My knees go weak, and I drop forward against her back, panting heavily.

"What the fuck?" I breathe as I wake, my stomach convulsing as I come against my sheets.

Tossing the covers back, I look down in disbelief. I'm too fucking old to be coming from a fucking dream. Tugging a hand through my hair, I try to catch my breath.

"What have you done to me?"

CHAPTER THIRTY-FIVE

I Don't Like You

Uri

A year later …

I've just come out of a meeting with Sam Mairettie and Wyatt Black. Now that things have settled and the threat is gone, we'll be moving forward with the plans for the Alliance. There are only a few more pieces that need to fall into alignment.

I believe Michael will be happy to hear the news I have for him. Shutting Leonardo down will be within our grasp shortly. It couldn't have come at a better time. I'm concerned with my brother's choices and the dark mood he's always in.

Things have been busy since I got married. For the first time I've gone an entire year without going to visit Symphony. Knowing deep down she is the cause of Michael's brooding; I have felt guilty for not giving her more attention.

The reports I get always say she is thriving. She's been traveling with her dance company or playing in concert halls. Since no one here in America has any clue who she is, I haven't worried about her safety as much.

Not that it would be wise to target her. I grin as I think of how lethal my sister-in-law is. I only got to train her briefly, but she's a quick study. I can only imagine the chaos she's capable of now.

Not to mention the fact that we keep her guarded like a precious gem. Adriano takes caring for her seriously. When offered to be reassigned, he refused.

"Did everything go okay?" Michael asks as I walk into the sitting room our family is gathered in.

"We will talk later. You have decisions to make. You and the don should talk."

He frowns and nods, understanding this isn't the time or the place. Everyone has broken off into families to begin to make plans to leave the Briggs' compound. I, for one, am ready to return to my home.

Tina needs to see a doctor about our little one she's carrying, and I would like to have my privacy back. I'm sure the Briggs feel the same.

I walk over to my scowling wife and lift her chin to place a kiss on her lips. As I take in everyone in the room, I groan. This isn't going to make my mood any better.

"Does she have to stay with us?" Val asks, referring to this Julissa woman, completely ignoring that she is standing in the room with us.

Valentina has made it no secret that she doesn't like Julissa, or should I say Vanessa. Many of the women aren't a fan of hers now that they know the history she has around here. I can't say I'm fond of the idea of her staying in our home either.

However, since Roberto is dead and everyone has begun to return to their homes, this woman needs to go somewhere. Michael has offered for her to come along with us. I don't think that's a good idea, but at thirty-five, I can't tell him what to do with his life.

Michael has lived for another for so long I feel it's wrong to tell him he shouldn't do as he pleases. I can only hope he's wise enough not to do anything to hurt Symphony and make me kick his arse.

"She will be my guest, Valentina. I will find her other accommodations as soon as I can. For now, staying here under the Briggs' roof isn't going to cut it," Michael says.

I cut my eyes to him as I don't care for his tone. He takes a calming breath and turns to begin pacing. Michael has a heart for those who are in need of help.

I understand why he wants to help this broken woman, but she might be more of a challenge than his wife. Julissa is fragile. She is not made for a man as complicated as Michael.

"I would like to say something," Julissa speaks up.

"Please don't," Val and Annabella say in unison.

Annabella is another who's not in favor of the relationship Michael seems to be developing with this woman. This is going to need an alternative solution. I will not have this tension in my home.

"I only wanted to say that it's okay. I am safe from my past. I can handle myself from here. I will get a room at a hotel while I figure things out," Julissa says.

"That sounds about right to me," Valentina sings.

"Love, come on now—"

"Uri, don't even bother." She cuts me off and rolls her eyes.

"I will move somewhere else, and you can stay there with me," Michael says.

"Ugh," Val grumbles.

"Oh, great. Will you be going to Boston and taking her there with you?" Annabella taunts.

Michael's expression turns to a murderous one. I quickly move to his side and place a hand on his shoulder. This is not the time for this, although I agree with Annabella.

"Michael, it's okay. I'll be fine," Julissa says.

As I stand beside Michael, Tina stands from her seat and walks over to where Julissa is sitting. She leans down into her face. I clench my jaw and tighten my hold on Michael's shoulder.

"I don't like you. I don't know what kind of spell you put on my brother-in-law, but I'm going to find a way to break it and get your ass away from my family and friends.

"After all you have done, I'll be damned if I sit around and allow you to smile up in their faces like you belong here. We have no more use for you. You should be gone. You're lucky you're still breathing," Val snarls.

With that, she straightens and walks out of the room with Annabella close on her heels. I close my eyes and thank Christ Val didn't pull a gun to shoot her. I'm sure it crossed her mind.

"That could have been worse," I breathe.

"We shouldn't be judged by the sins of our past. Name one of us who would be free of judgment," Michael snarls and tugs away from me.

He storms from the room without a glance back. Looking after him, I narrow my eyes. This isn't about Julissa.

She is only a symptom of the turmoil he's going through regarding something else. She is something to focus on so he doesn't have to deal with his reality. I don't think she will be around for long.

This too shall pass.

"Uri, I—"

I hold up a hand to cut her off as I move to leave the room. I am not a fool. I will not be placed in a situation that could cost me everything.

"If you want to keep your life, never talk to me while my wife isn't in the room. Never find yourself in any room I am in alone. If you want these women to respect you, you have to start with giving them respect first. Build their trust back or disappear now," I say as I leave the room.

Michael

I know I shouldn't be angry with Valentina or anyone else here who doesn't like the idea of Julissa's presence. She has done some foul things. However, I don't know that side of her.

Since we met, I've known a timid, gentle woman. I have been around her enough to know she's uncomfortable here and only wants to belong. I've done my best to be kind. However, I believe I've been kind for selfish reasons.

"Will I have to write a check for that punching bag before we leave?"

I close my eyes and hold the heavy bag still. I came to the gym to blow off some steam. Val has a right to say when she doesn't want someone in her home.

"Are you ready to talk to me about what's going on? This has nothing to do with Julissa, does it?"

"I don't feel like talking," I bite out.

"Fine, then we fight until you are ready to talk."

I turn to find Uri taking off his shirt and folding it neatly. I sigh. He might be forty, but Uri still kicks my ass when we spar. However, today, I'm in the mood for this. I take my shirt off and toss it aside. Uri lifts his fists, and I move to join him.

"At least your fighting has improved even if your decision-making hasn't," Uri taunts after we trade a few combos.

"What is that supposed to mean?"

"You are angrier than usual. Nothing that you are doing is about Julissa. You can talk about it with me, or you can continue to sulk like a bratty child."

"What have I done any of this for? You have married and now we are exposed. It is all falling apart."

"You have done this for Don Trovati and Symphony. You have done this to be the don," Uri says back.

"I don't care about being don. It was never about that," I bite out.

"You still aren't making sense. I've been married for almost two years. Why are you so angry now? Why are you taking up with a woman you know isn't for you?"

"Because I need this pain to stop. I feel as if I hurt the one person I love and I don't know how to fix it. I don't know what I did wrong," I yell.

"Now we are getting somewhere. This is about Sim. You think you have hurt her, but know your actions are sure to hurt her. Do you hear how that sounds?"

"I do, Uri. *Fanculo*, I do, but how do I make this right?"

"Don't drag that woman into things. You are playing with her life."

"When I'm with her, it's the only time I feel sane other than when I'm hunting and hitting for the families. What do you want me to do? I'm losing myself," I bark back.

"You continue to work. I have a series of hits you can handle for me. I will handle the rest. You wanted us to have a seat at the Alliance table. Now we make it work for us."

CHAPTER THIRTY-SIX

The Other Woman

Valentina

Five months later …

I kiss the top of Vita's head before I place her into her crib. Then, I turn with my hand on my growing bump. DJ is looking back at me with a smile, the corners of her lips turned up.

In the last few months, I've come to really like her. I was taken by surprise when Felix Black asked me to do him a favor and hire her without letting her know he was involved. When she showed up at the interview, I knew I would like her before Uri began to question her.

She's been taking such good care of my little Vita. It doesn't hurt that I know she can protect them both if needed. We have worked out and trained together almost every day since she's been here.

Uri mentioned something about Brooklyn O'Brien claiming her, but I still don't know why Felix asked me for the favor. The one thing I do know is she's my family now. I have her back, and she has mine.

"Do you really think you will find something? Uri is crazy about you. I can't see him cheating on you," DJ says as she eyes me warily.

"I don't know what I will find, but his behavior has been off. What are these trips to Boston and why have they become so frequent?"

She looks behind her, then drops her voice. "He is the don now. His responsibilities have changed. Could it have something to do with the family?"

I think her words over. DJ knows more about us than most of the other staff. I believe she understands us and who we are on a more personal level.

I shake my head. "No, this has nothing to do with his promotion. If he were going back and forth between Italy and Chicago, I might believe that was it, but Boston?"

"I don't blame you for following your gut. You go on. Vita will be fine here with me. Don't go busting any windows," she says, her Irish accent slipping just a little.

I wink at her and laugh. "I promise not to take any pages out of your book. I only want to know what's going on."

"Safe travels, love. You make sure to give him a good shag in apology," she snickers.

"Yeah, sure," I grumble and leave.

I have a flight to catch. I will suck the life out of Uri's dick if I'm wrong. However, I have this feeling there's another woman behind these trips.

I'm going to empty my clip in both their asses if Uri is cheating on my big pregnant ass.

Symphony

I had one of those dreams again. Which is embarrassing since Uri is here on a visit. I blame Adriano for this.

I had a little fall and sprained my ankle. Yes, I was on a job when it happened, but I didn't want him to call Uri. Since the incident, Uri has been coming in more often.

"Ah, you can't sleep either?" Uri says as he turns from the refrigerator with a pint of ice cream in his hand.

I chuckle. That is my ice cream, but I don't mind. I don't get to indulge often, but I keep the freezer stocked with my favorites.

"No, I came down for some water."

I amble over to the sink to fill a glass, ignoring Uri's chiseled bare chest. He has on a pair of silk sleep pants and his gun holster. I guess that's a family trait.

I have my holster on under my robe. I never roam the house unarmed, not after that attack in Chicago. Besides, the weight of the guns soothes me.

I can use all the soothing I can get tonight. I'm having those stupid sex dreams more often. They seem to become more vivid each time.

"You want to talk about it?" Uri asks as he takes a seat at the island.

"No, not at all," I reply and gulp down my glass of water.

Refilling the glass, I then go to sit with him. It's been a while since we've had one of our talks. I am happy to see Uri, so I'm eager to spend a little time with him.

"How have you been? How's the ankle? You're not limping as much," he says.

"I am fine. It was only an ankle ligament sprain. A few weeks of rest and it was back to normal. I was fine when Adriano made a big fuss about it."

"You speak as if you're not a dancer."

"I am, but you can't believe that I dance and play year-round. I take breaks from the company to focus on the orchestra. This happens to be offseason for dance."

"Have I told you how proud of you I am? I'm sorry I have been so busy in the last year. I want to have a meeting with you and Michael.

"You should be with family. I want you to come to New York. This distance serves no purpose any longer," he says as he stabs at the ice cream.

"Does Micheal know about this? Has he asked for my return?"

Uri sighs. "I believe it is time I intervene. He has been angry since you left Italy. He's not himself any longer."

"I had to leave," I whisper.

"No need to explain to me. Italy wasn't a safe place for you. It was a good thing you left when you did."

"Can I think about it?"

"Of course, love. Take your time. It might be selfish of me to want you all in New York with me."

"You seem happier. How is Nico? I would like to see him if that's all right."

"He is recovering, but he has a long way to go. You are welcome whenever you are ready."

"There are a few more shows booked for this season. I will have to look at my schedule and ... I have some other things to sort out."

I pause to think about my secret business. I will have to shut it down if I move to be with my family. However, that's not what's holding me back.

I need to find a way to get in touch with Mrs. Mairettie. I need her to tell me it's time to return to Michael. If he's not safe, I won't return. I can't.

"Look at me, Symphony," Uri says.

I turn my gaze to his and hold it. He gives a nod of his head and smiles. I reach for my band and pop it a few times. The sweet sting filters out all the anxiety that's building.

"I know about your assassin operation. I have allowed it because Adriano believed it suited your needs and you're good at it. While it's not something we've allowed the women to do in the family, I've decided our family will make an exception.

"Michael may not feel the same, but I have someone in my life who's proving the old ways wrong. Your work is professional and clean. Your decision-making shows wisdom.

"When I say I'm proud of you, Sim. I mean everything about you. I already know the truth."

"Is that why he has never spent a dime? Because he ratted me out. Stinking buttface." I seethe.

Uri roars with laughter. "Adriano cares for you. Maybe more than he should."

"You're not angry?"

"Why should I be? You have become who your grandfather has wanted. Michael has also exceeded the don's wishes.

"I think I understand the plan he has had all along. I have fallen into a plan myself. I now understand the plotting and planning of old men. Sometimes it works out better than you can imagine."

"I hope you are right."

"I know I am. I just need you to decide if coming to New York and living with Michael is what you want."

"Will he forgive me? Is that what he wants? I know about the woman he is seeing," I murmur down at the countertop.

Uri leans over to kiss my forehead. I fight back the tears that burn the backs of my eyes. I was devastated to learn about this Julissa woman.

I hate her, but I can't be mad at Michael. I ran away. Annabella has told me how upset Michael was.

"She doesn't mean as much to him as you think. He has been losing himself without you. She has been a friend, but she can never remain in his life.

"Sleep on it, love. If coming home with me is what you want, I will make it happen. It is time."

I finish my water and nod. I have a lot to think about. I will get in contact with Mrs. Mairettie. I'm tired of living here alone.

I am ready to face my destiny. I will not hide forever. Michael needs to know I've become like him. I can stay with him now.

"Try to go get some sleep, love. We will talk again before I leave."

"Thank you, Uri."

I get up and head back to my room. My ankle is a little tender, but I refuse to limp and cause Uri to worry about me. Especially now that I know he knows.

I'm going to kick Adriano's butt. I thought I could trust him. Now I wonder how long Uri has known.

"Put it down, or I will blow your head off," I growl as I pull my gun and spin to face the woman in my home.

She glares back at me through blue eyes set in a brown face. She has a gun pointed in my face as well. I cock my gun, letting her know I mean business.

"So Uri has a thing for women who carry guns," she says calmly and tilts her head to the side. "At least you're pretty. I would have been pissed if he were cheating with someone ugly."

"What are you talking about? Why are you in my home?"

She cocks her gun. As she does, I notice her heavily swollen belly. Who is this woman to Uri?

"What the bloody fucking hell?" Uri barks as he enters the space.

I see him out of the corner of my eye, looking utterly shocked. The woman now looks pissed as he stands there in nothing but his holster and sleep pants. I'm confused, but I haven't taken my gun off her.

"Symphony, this is my pregnant wife. Put the gun down, love. Tina, this is Michael's wife, Symphony. I need you to put your gun down too.

"On the count of ten." He begins to walk toward us slowly as he counts. "One ... Two ... Three ... Four ... Five ... Six ... Seven ... Eight ... Nine ... Ten."

By the time he gets to ten, neither of us has put our gun down. Instead, we both stare at each other, confused. She is pretty, I will give her that.

Uri grabs both of our guns and begins to lower them. However, she pulls another and aims it at me. Just as swiftly, I pull my other one.

"Michael's wife, my ass. Since when has he been married? Uri, you have me so fucked up right now."

"I am Symphony Isabella Mansilla-Trovati-Donati. I am Michael's wife. Uri is my brother-in-law.

"I have been married to Michael for sixteen years. We were married in Italy when I was fourteen. You can put your gun down."

I release the clip and the one in the chamber from mine and hand them over to her. She looks at me then back at Uri. Then to me again.

"Oh hell no. You keep those. Uri, you hand her back that other gun. Michael and that home-wrecker are going to answer some questions for us."

"Michael and I have spoken at length about what's going on with him. I've been coming to Boston for wellness checks, but I also would like to bring Sim home to Michael."

"You know what? You and your hidden family and family secrets are about to make me lose my shit, Uri. A whole-ass wife. I'm going to need a list of all your properties by the morning."

"Why is that, love?" Uri says through an amused smile.

"I'm going to check them all to see if you have any more hidden siblings and in-laws."

"Don Alessio Trovati is my grandfather. My husband is to be his successor. I am being kept a secret from my great-uncle, who wishes to take that from me and Michael."

Her eyes widen. "Does Sam know about this?"

Uri purses his lips. He looks annoyed. I begin to pop the band on my wrist as I feel like I might have said too much.

"Yes and no. He knows about Leonardo Trovati and that I want him dead. I will accept my seat at the Alliance table because of Michael and Sim. Leonardo Trovati isn't as smart as you are, *bella.*

"He hasn't figured out that Hush isn't one man. Now that we have married, it doesn't make sense for her to continue to hide. Leonardo will figure it out soon enough that I was never married to Don Trovati's granddaughter. It has always been my baby brother," Uri replies.

"Then we make him hush. What's the problem?" This woman shrugs.

"We were forbidden from touching Leonardo because of some of the other families. Now that the Alliance is picking a fight with everyone, it is open season. We just need to wait for Sam's promotion.

"Don Trovati also plans to hand the family over officially. Things are lining up. Sam's promotion and Micheal's will have to align for us to move forward. No one will touch Sim before then."

My mind is filling with information I'm trying to filter through. I freeze as one detail stands out. I look to Uri's wife.

"You are a hitter too?"

"Yes, I am Valentina Caprisi-Donati, by the way. Sorry about all of that. Pregnancy hormones will make a girl crazy," she says and gives me a smile.

"I am not offended. Welcome to my home. I would like to get to know you. You are the first female assassin I have met," I say and chew on my lip as I bounce my gaze over Valentina's head.

Uri

"I like her. Okay, she's a little odd, but I like her better than that home-wrecker," Valentina says as I lead her to my bedroom here at the estate.

"Symphony is on the spectrum. She may stumble to communicate sometimes or come off as awkward, but she's brilliant and talented," I say proudly.

"Oh, now that makes sense. Talented at what?"

"Everything she puts her mind to. She is a professional ballerina and pianist." I chuckle. "I guess I should add hitter to that list."

"Oh, wow. I can see the ballerina. I was actually jealous when I first saw her. I can't be surprised about the piano. That seems to be a Donati thing."

"Oh, love. Not like Sim. We are tinkering when we play. Symphony embodies her name. I will get another ticket to her show tomorrow evening and you can accompany me."

"I would like that. It only makes sense for me to stay and return with you now that I'm here."

"Yes, but what doesn't make sense is how my wife, my *bella*, got it into her head that I come here to Boston to cheat on her. When in this lifetime have I given you a single thought that made you think I could fathom cheating or wanting anyone other than you?" I growl into her neck as I pull her into my arms.

"Oops."

"Oops is right, you little cheeky monster. You followed me here to do what exactly?"

"Let's not talk about that. I want to apologize. I might have allowed my hormones to carry me away," she says as she pushes me back.

I flop down onto the side of the bed. A smile comes to my lips as I watch her begin to peel her layers of clothes off. Her trench coat is the first to hit the floor. She then pulls her black sweater over her head.

When her swollen belly comes into view, my smile grows wider. How could she ever believe I would want someone else. I love this woman with my entire soul.

She kicks her heels from her feet, causing me to shake my head. I don't know how she wears those things while carrying our two little ones. Another sign that she's magical.

My cock begins to tent my sleep pants. While she wiggles out of her black leggings, I remove my holster and place it on the table beside the bed.

Before I can turn my attention back to her striptease, she drops to her knees and pulls me from my pants. I cup her face and look into her eyes as she lowers her head to cover me with her mouth.

The hum of pleasure and the tight suction of her mouth have my eyes rolling in the back of my head. I drop my head back and grab ahold of the sheets on either side of me.

"Fuck, show me how sorry you really are," I bite out. "I'm certainly going to spank you for each transgression."

She smiles around me as she keeps sucking. This isn't enough; I want to make good on my promise. Pulling from her mouth, I then move to stand. Holding my hand out for hers, I wait for her to place it in mine. Then I help her up from her knees and place her on the bed.

Once she's on the bed, I climb on and lie on my back. Placing my hands behind my head, I grin and look at her pointedly. She licks her lips as my shaft jumps, awaiting her attention.

"Come, love. Arse to me. I'm going to spank your arse while you suck my cock."

As I finger her pussy and spank her arse while she sucks me to completion, I make sure we both remember why there is no one else for either of us. She never has to worry about another.

I am hers and only hers.

CHAPTER THIRTY-SEVEN

Hello Again

Symphony

Four months later ...

"Hello again," Ellen says as I take a seat before her in a little café.

She's been sitting alone as if she's waiting for someone. I have been watching her and waiting for someone to arrive. I still have things to do, so I've decided to come to sit with her.

"Hello, Mrs. Mairettie."

"Please, call me Ellen. How can I help you?"

"I would like for you to tell me if it is safe to return to my husband."

I hold my hand out to her, not sure how it works. She smiles and tilts her head to the side. I glance into her eyes then glance away.

"Your family is waiting for you. It is time for you to become who you were meant to be. He needs you. You both are ready.

"Go home. Our families need you. It's time for you to take your place," she says warmly.

"Thank you. How can I repay you?"

"You will repay me with the gifts you teach to my son. You will show him how to ground himself to function in all things. You will also give him the words to know he can love and be loved. Others will try, but it won't sink in until he hears it from you," she says.

"I will do my best to help him. Let me know if there's anything else I can do for you."

"Accept the role you are given. You are important. Your thoughts matter."

With that, she stands and leaves. I watch her go, wondering if the person she's been waiting for arrived. However, she leaves the café and climbs into a car, then it pulls off.

Sitting back in my seat, I look around the café. Was she waiting for me? Excitement fills me as I realize I have the green light to go home.

I must go and make calls. I need to pack my things. I'm going home to my husband.

I pull out my phone and dial the person who has been encouraging me the most. I begin to pop my wristband as I await the answer on the other end.

The sound of infants crying fills the line as it's picked up. "Hello?"

"Hello, Valentina. This is Symphony. I am sorry for the disruption."

"Don't worry about it. Call me Val, Sim. How can I help you?"

"I wish for you to inform Uri that I'm ready. I want to come home."

"Thank God."

CHAPTER THIRTY-EIGHT

I Want More

Michael

"Where to, Boss?"

"Home. I have had enough celebrating for one night," I reply to my driver.

While I'm happy for Nico and his win and the fact that he's going to be a papa, I need some time alone with my thoughts. I have a lot on my mind. A lot to figure out.

After I completed the hit Uri sent me on, I took his advice and went to Sicily to spend some time with Don Trovati. He's been staying on a private, heavily guarded estate there.

I've been back from Italy for three and a half months. We spoke a lot about the time coming for me to lead things. I am soon to become Don Michael Donati of the Trovati family. An official *fuck you* to Leonardo Trovati.

However, there were things that happened in Sicily that were unexpected. Don Trovati made sure to make it known that I am

204

the husband of Symphony, not my brother. I will never have to hide who I am or pretend to be my brother again.

It has been so freeing to know that not only am I free to use the name Donati, but I'm free of Roberto Zuko and the bullshit he forced us to believe. Leonardo Trovati has been more of a threat than the phantoms we thought we had to hide from ever were.

We have always been the real ones to fear. Now, we have the power to prove that and ensure we never have to answer to anyone ever again. Not only will I have my own empire to lead, but I met with Don Locatelli while in Sicily at the request of the don himself.

To my surprise, I was informed that although my rank won't be as high as Uri's, I have my own seat at the Alliance table if I choose.

I had no idea Don Trovati planned to initiate this. However, Don Locatelli didn't seem surprised by any of it. It was as if he was waiting or something.

He knew I was the Donati married to Sim all along. I'm still trying to wrap my mind around all that's happened while I was gone. Everything has changed.

Reese's words during Nico's game earlier today brought up the feelings I've been warring with. My wife should be with me. I want her to be, but our relationship is still so complicated.

While I care for Julissa, I'm not in love with her like I am with Symphony. Julissa kept telling me she wanted more. I can't give her more.

My trip to Italy sort of proved to me that things could never work between us. She needs way more than I can give. What I need is to understand what went wrong with Symphony.

What am I doing that keeps triggering her and is it something I can fix? If I can answer that, I'll be able to move on. I hated the way it felt to be questioned about my love life.

"You're home, boss," Massimo says, pulling me from my thoughts.

I look out the window at the house. It might be time for me to begin to look for my own home. Here at Uri's, I have plenty of space to myself and I don't have to see him and Valentina if I choose not to.

However, I've grown accustomed to being surrounded by family, I'm not sure if now is the time to part ways and be alone. I shake the thought off and get out of the car to head into the house. To my surprise, I find Uri and Val standing in my wing of the house, talking at the top of the stairs.

I pluck Vita from Uri's arms and kiss her cheek, then toss her into the air. Her sweet baby giggles surround me, reminding me why I haven't found a place of my own.

This house has been filled with baby Donati laughter now that my nephews have been born, and I wouldn't want to miss any of it. I look at my brother and note the smile in his gaze. My heart swells for him.

After our childhood ... after his childhood, it is good to see him happy like this, with a family of his own. I can only hope to have the same someday.

I turn for my room with a babbling Vita in my arms. I will have my evening snuggles with the little bella before I hand her off to her nanny. It has become our routine at least twice a week.

Vita loves Nico so much I have to build some type of bond to have a shot at being a favorite uncle. Although, I might have a better shot with Inzo and Nori. I chuckle tiredly at the thought.

"Hold on, where do you think you're going?" Val calls after me as Uri blocks my retreat and takes Vita from my arms.

"Not tonight," Uri croons with an amused look on his face.

I sigh and lean in to kiss Vita's forehead. "Sorry, *bella*. Uncle Michael is too tired to fight them for you tonight. I will see you in the morning. We can have breakfast, and I will fill you up with sugar before I hand you back in the afternoon."

I chuckle as Val glares at me and folds her arms over her chest. Uri shakes his head at me as Vita coos happily in his arms. We all know I would never do such a thing.

Not because I don't want to torture her parents, but because I wouldn't be able to stand my little bella with a tummy ache. I hate to see her in pain. God help her future boyfriends.

"Good night," I call over my shoulder and throw my hand up in a wave as I walk away to my bedroom.

I begin to unbutton my shirt, eager to make it to my bed. It has been a long day. Between my thoughts and the excitement of Nico's return to the soccer field and his win, I'm ready to fall on my face.

I enter my bedroom and note something is off. I pull my gun faster than I can think about the action. It's almost second nature to me at this point.

"Don't shoot. It is me, Symphony. Don't shoot."

I grunt tiredly and place the safety back on the weapon. Returning it to the holster, I then shrug the holster off to hang it. Slowly, my tired brain begins to catch up.

Just as slowly, I turn for the bed where Symphony is sitting in a white tank top and panties. At least, that's what I can see in the dimly lit room. I shake my head as if she's a dream.

"Sim?" I breathe.

"Yes?"

"You are here?" I say in Italian.

"Yes, but if you don't want me here, I understand. I will leave and find one of the guest rooms to sleep in for the night. I can have my things sent back to Boston and I will return there."

I make my way to the foot of the bed and stalk toward her until we are nose to nose. Not able to help myself, I peck her lips gently. Then I pull away and look into her eyes.

She tilts her head and studies me. I remain still as if not wanting to frighten a small bird. She gives me a small smile.

"I want you here. Don't leave. If I do something to trigger you or if I hurt you in any way, I need you to tell me. Don't run from me, tell me."

She palms the side of my face. Confusion is painted all over her expression. I can't breathe for fear this isn't real, that she isn't here.

"You have never hurt me. If anything, I feel safest when I'm with you."

"Then why do you keep crying and running from me? What am I doing wrong?"

"Oh," she says as if recognition hits. "The first time you had been drinking before ... before our kiss. I didn't want you to regret anything in the morning.

"In the days that followed, I wanted desperately to talk to you about it, but I couldn't find my words. I was too anxious about what you would say. Then you were gone."

"Okay, I can understand that." I sigh. "But what happened in Italy? Why were you crying and why did you leave?"

"I ... I met this woman at a charity event in a gallery. She told me some things. One of them being about someone with a ballerina dancing in music.

"When I saw the tattoo on your forearm, I wasn't willing to take a chance. I couldn't lose you. You couldn't die trying to protect me. I love you. I wouldn't allow you to die."

I crush my lips to hers and kiss her passionately. I feel like a fool for all the time we've missed together. I've stayed away because I thought I had been doing something wrong and didn't want to pressure her.

My tired mind is still processing all she has said, but the main thing screaming at me is that I never hurt her. She can handle our marriage and our relationship. She wants to be here.

"Say it again," I breathe into her mouth.

"Say what?"

"That you love me."

She cups my face in both hands and pointedly catches my eyes as she ducks her head to look up at me. "I love you, Michael. I always have. I don't want to be away from you.

"But I will not share you. You are my husband. If you can't love me back. I deserve better.

"I have thought long and hard about whether or not your friend Julissa fits into the guidelines for a kill. She doesn't, but she will be my first exception—because I just want to—if you continue to see her and share what's mine."

I scoff loudly before I take her lips again. I have no idea how she knows about Julissa, but she never has to worry about her. I deepen the kiss to pour all my love into it.

"Michael, please don't try to distract me or deter my thoughts. This is important to me. I am your wife. Ellen says it's safe for me to be here now.

"I want you and I want your love, but I don't want to share you with another woman. I would like for you to be tested before I allow you to enter my body again. I will not be given an STD because of your exploits."

"Sim, baby. I have never touched a woman other than you since we've been married. Julissa and I took a break because I couldn't give her my heart. It has always belonged to you.

"I have never even kissed another woman. I love you more than you could ever know. But, Symphony?"

"Yes, Michael?"

"Hearing you say you would kill for me has me so hard. I miss being inside you. Do you wa—"

"Yes, I would like for you to fuck me. Please."

She tears my shirt open, sending buttons flying. I don't know whether to laugh or groan. This feels right.

I know I could never bring myself to be with another because my heart has always known that someday she would be right here—in my arms, where she belongs. We both work feverishly to get my clothes off. I move my lips to her neck and begin to suck on her skin.

The flavor of coconut bursts against my tongue and I realize that's the scent I've been smelling since I climbed up the bed. I reach to palm one of her breasts and the fabric feels saturated with liquid.

I pull away with my brows knit and reach for the light switch. Light begins to illuminate the bed area, revealing my wife to me. I growl and quickly get my pants off.

I need to have her now. In the light, I can confirm she's in a thin white tank top and white panties. Her nipples straining against the thin, moist-looking fabric. Her long legs look like silk as they glisten with oil.

Her little white panties seem to be saturated as well, as they cling to her pussy. She's covered in oil, making her warm brown skin look like something I want to devour with my mouth.

"*Symphony*," I groan as she reaches into her panties and begins to rub her pussy.

"I have waited a long time to have you inside of me again, Michael. I'm aching for you. Please, I need you so badly."

I'm torn between answering her plea and watching her bring herself pleasure. When she reaches to squeeze her breast, I'm done for. I will blow my load all over my stomach if I don't join in and take her soon.

"Michael, yes," she cries out as I move the soaked fabric aside and begin to feast on her pussy.

Her flavor, mixed with the coconut oil, assaults my mouth, causing me to hum in satisfaction. I wrap my arms around her thighs, holding them open for me. The more she cries out, the more I dive in.

It's so good that at some point, I find myself on my knees, trying to crawl into her to get deeper to have more of her in my mouth. Sim is on her fifth orgasm when I can't wait any longer.

I move to hover over her as I peel her T-shirt over her head. Then I make quick work of peeling her panties down her long legs. For a moment, I can't help staring down at her body.

It's as perfect as I remember. Wanting to feel her around me, I align my length with her sex. I plan to go slowly, but Symphony has other ideas.

She locks her legs around my waist and pulls me into her. I bare my teeth as I slide into her hot, sucking, wet channel. As I'm sucked in, I can feel the veins in my neck pop as I try to hold on to my restraint.

She feels better than the first time. I palm her ass and thrust my hips. I would walk a million days in a dry desert if it meant I could quench my thirst in this pussy once it was over.

My sweat-slicked body moves with her oil-slicked one like we were designed for each other. We fit perfectly together. My body knows we belong to her.

"Michael, oh my ... yes, just like that. I've missed you so much. I'm going to reach my summit."

"You're going to come. I am fucking you and you're going to come," I growl as I tighten my hold on her ass as I thrust deep into her.

"Yes, Michael. I'm going to come all over this fat fucking dick. I want you to fuck me all night. I don't want you to stop."

I kiss all over her face. Her dirty talk shoots through me as it becomes raunchy and crass. I take her lips in a searing kiss to show her how much she pleases me.

As I plunge my tongue into her mouth and my cock into her tight pussy, I know I'll never want another. Give me my Symphony with all her quirks. I love them all as much as I love her.

"Fuck, I love you," I roar while I throw my head back as I feel her explode around me.

"I love you too, Michael. Give me a moment. I will get us some water so we can continue. My legs feel a little shaky."

I kiss her forehead. "I have not finished, love. Once I do, I will get us some water and fuel."

"Oh, I thought I felt your semen."

"You did," I chuckle, thrusting my still-hard member into her.

CHAPTER THIRTY-NINE

You Failed

Leonardo

I sit down in this dank winery cave with the men who once offered me protection. In this moment, I feel like I need protection from them. Had I been given a choice, I wouldn't have come.

Too bad I was ambushed and brought here against my will. Things haven't been the same since losing Elio. Nothing but rats and snakes surround me.

I unbutton my suit jacket and get comfortable in my chair as I prepare to hear what it is they want from me this time. It is always what I can do for them, never what can be done for me.

They wouldn't even assist when that Donati bastard had a spy under my nose and pulled him from my grasp. I was forced to let that go as I was with Elio and Regina. I should have destroyed them all then.

I would have if I didn't need them. The joke is on me. They have done nothing for me and now I'm here.

"We offered you an opportunity. All you had to do was prevent Alessio from cementing his connection to the Locatellis and this plan that's been brewing. You have failed."

Oh, how convenient. We're going to blame everything on me. Not that I hadn't expected this. I grind my teeth as Don Accetta continues.

"They have more pieces on the board than ever, and you are allowing them to get your family. One of the largest pieces of them all. Do you understand the weight of this?" he snarls at me.

This is humiliating. As if I'm not already humiliated enough now that I know I've been chasing after the wrong man. None of this is my fault.

If they weren't such cowards when it comes to the Locatelli family and Uri Donati, this never would have happened. But no, they wanted me to throw the stones while they all get to hide their hands—serves them right. My gut tells me my head was always up to be placed on a platter.

Once I got Alessio out of the way, they were going to erase me and take all that's ours to divide among themselves. I know how this all works. I took the risks I thought would position me for a better opportunity.

Now everything looks like it's turning to shit. I've played most of my cards. My brother is still alive. He plans to promote that piece-of-shit Donati, who wouldn't have even been in line to become Don in his own family.

The third son. The insult. Alessio knows I deserve more respect than this.

"Women and Blacks involved in business. It's a shit show, this *alleanza*. We want it shut down."

"Your brother will not make fools of us. We know he will only give the family to Donati in name. He intends for that girl to be the head behind the scenes," Don Romano bites out.

"Why have you been so sure of this?" I ask, not bothering to care about formalities.

The writing is on the wall. They have already written me off. I plan to do what I want when I leave here.

If I leave here. Which I will. Even if I have to take them all down to do so.

"Because he has been promising this would be since she was born. Do you think he found the Donati boy and took him under his wing by chance? This has always been his plan.

"He wanted to marry off the girl's mother, but the Donatis and Locatellis declined. Oh, but Alessio didn't give up there. The girl was born, and he began his plotting again.

"However, he learned something was wrong with the child and her mother took her back to the States. He never wanted you to have the family. That was never going to be an option," Don Romano explains.

Some friend this one is. He and Alessio grew up together as boys. He knew my brother long before I was ever born. There was a time when you would have thought they were brothers. Now, here he sits, plotting along with my brother's enemies for his demise.

"You have all brought me here for what?"

"One more opportunity to prove yourself," Don Accetta says.

"You fail us this time and we will wash our hands of you," Don Romano adds.

"The girl and the brother. There isn't to be a Trovati—by name, birthright, or marriage—connected to this alliance," Don Marino wheezes.

CHAPTER FORTY

The Business

Uri

"If I give you my credit card, will you make sure your mama doesn't spend all of my money?" I coo to Vita as I hold her up in the air as I walk to the kitchen.

She giggles excitedly like she understands exactly what I'm talking about. Showing off her tiny teeth while kicking her chubby legs and clapping her little hands. In her excitement, she drools right into my mouth. I close my mouth and pull a face.

"Why on earth is it always so bloody cold?" I grumble. "I'm starting to think your mum tells you to do this."

I move her onto my hip as she continues to talk gibberish. My phone pulls me from my conversation with my daughter. I frown and pull it from my pocket.

"Hello," I say into the phone as I put it between my ear and shoulder while I brush at the drool that missed my mouth and landed on my shirt.

"Donati, this is Brooklyn. We're going to need to meet about all the transplants on the roster. We should know who belongs to us and who doesn't. Things are going to move fast once Logan gets home."

"You don't have Michael's number? This is something the two of you should address."

"Aye, you would think that. Dealing with the McGowans isn't going to work that way. LaSalle wants them in. They will send Ronan if they agree to this.

"I'm like one of his nephews. He's not going to listen to me. I don't care how many men's blood I have on my hands. He's been doing this shit since I was in diapers.

"Besides, Michael isn't a don yet. As a New York member, I think you should sit in on the conversation, at the very least, as a show of respect. He probably won't speak slowly enough for you to understand him, but if we show a united front, he might listen."

"Why isn't LaSalle handling this directly?" I ask as I hand Vita to Tina.

Then I take one of our sons from the little contraptions in front of her. As I cradle him in my arms, I lean to kiss Tina's lips, then place a hand over the chest of our other son.

"Because once things are in play, Logan and LaSalle aren't going to micromanage any of us. Older members are going to want us to handle them with a different kind of respect.

"Ronan McGowan will be one of those members. I'm just looking to get ahead of things. I will call Michael to handle everyone else, but Ronan should get the red carpet. Logan would want me to show him that respect," Brooklyn says.

I sigh. Politics, I hate them. This is why I've always done things my way.

Symphony's laugh fills the kitchen, grabbing my attention. I look to where she and Micheal are. Michael is sitting on one of the bar stools at the kitchen island and Sim is sitting in his lap. He's feeding her mini quiches and fruit while they smile at each other and laugh as Michael murmurs low to her.

My brother finally looks happy. Symphony buries her face into his neck and inhales. Michael tightens his hold around her and kisses her forehead. Watching them reminds me why I'm doing this in the first place.

"Done. Set it up. Call Michael later. He's taking care of family business at the moment."

Brooklyn chuckles on the other end. "Maybe it's time I stopped by. I still have some unfinished business under your roof."

I snort. "Do so at your own risk. You know where to find her."

"Aye, I do. I'll be seeing ya soon, Donati," he says, allowing his Irish Brogue to slip.

With that, he hangs up. I put my phone away and turn my attention back to Michael and Symphony. I note something right away.

The way they look at each other. The way they move together reminds me of me and Val. Michael should know. I want him to know.

Symphony

"Symphony," Uri calls as Michael whispers dirty things in my ear.

I turn to look at my brother-in-law. He is standing with his wife and their babies. Vita, Inzo, and Nori.

I have a little niece and two nephews. Their names are Vita, Inzo, and Nori. I find this very exciting, although I haven't been willing to hold them yet. Val has offered, but I am not ready.

"Yes, Uri?"

"Have you closed down the business?"

I gasp and widen my eyes. Why would he ask me this in front of Michael? My heart begins to race.

"No. I have not. I don't have any clients currently, but I haven't shut down the operation," I reply as steadily as I can.

"What business?" Michael asks near my ear, but still loud enough for Uri to hear.

A shiver runs through me. I ignore the way his breath tickles my skin. It was a fight for us to climb out of bed this morning to come down to breakfast.

"Would you like to explain?" Uri asks.

"Yes, please."

I turn in Michael's lap so I'm looking directly at him. I fight against the need to pop my wristband. I knew I would have to tell him about this at some time.

"I have been running an assassin-for-hire business. When you told me I couldn't be with you because I wasn't like you, I did my best to become just like you. I have done very well."

"Wait a minute. You knew about this?" Michael hisses at Uri.

"I learned about it after some time. I allowed it to continue once I was made aware of the results. You weren't the only one allowing the jobs to keep you going."

"Seriously, Uri?"

"Why is it that this is a problem? Is it because you think I am not capable? Valentina does the same thing. Why are you upset?"

"Valentina isn't my wife. You are. How long did you plan to keep this from me?"

"I don't know."

"I would like you to see her in action. She is quite impressive. I have witnessed one of her jobs."

"What? How?" Michael and I say in unison, causing the baby in Uri's arms to begin to whimper.

I believe he's holding Inzo. Uri kisses his head and places him back in the bouncy chair in front of Valentina.

"Adriano. I requested he send me footage. Don't worry. It was encrypted and immediately destroyed," Uri replies.

"What the fuck have I been paying him for? How did this happen?"

I am getting angry. Michael still wants to treat me like a child he needs to protect. I've become more than capable of protecting myself. I am smart, I have skills, I always do my best. I jump up from his lap and glare at him.

"Things cannot continue like this. I want to be your equal. Nine years, sixty assignments, one hundred and forty-two kills.

"Not once have I taken a hit. Not once have I missed my target or failed a mission. Why do you treat me like I can't do this?

"I thought you, of all people, would be proud of me. I did this for you. I did this so you wouldn't have to worry about me, so we could do what Nonno wants. Together."

Michael stands and closes the distance between us. He cups the back of my neck and places his forehead to mine. I feel the tears building up.

"I have done my best. I am one of the best," I choke out.

"I know you are. You are the best at anything you put your mind to. That doesn't mean I'm okay with the woman I love placing herself in those types of situations.

"Can you give me that? Do you understand how that makes me feel? I've been trying to keep you away from all of this for as long as I can.

"Your grandfather plans to give me the promotion soon, but it's your family now. I know I can't keep you hidden forever. I will have to allow you to become who your grandfather wants you to be, but that's not going to be easy for me.

"Not because I want to be the don, but because I always want to keep you safe. Your grandfather's wish is for you to be known as the head of the family. I have every intention of making that happen.

"We *are* making that happen. Just give me some time to wrap my head around this. I'm still reeling from the promotion and all the other shit that will come with it."

"How do you think that will happen when you have kept me away from knowing anything about the family?" I ask.

"Because I've been slowly preparing you. Or should I say guiding you," Uri says.

"What do you mean?"

"Adriano has introduced you to the right element to move you in the right direction."

"The O'Sheas? You know about that too?"

"I am the reason he connected you with them. I am also the reason they pulled you in close. Nothing has happened in your life that I haven't had knowledge of."

"So you're okay with her being a hitter but I had to retire?" Valentina snaps.

Uri snorts. "As if you have remained retired in any sense of the word."

"We will talk later," she says tightly.

"I'm sure we will, love," Uri says and kisses Val's forehead. "Michael, I have a reason for bringing the business up."

"I bet you do."

"You two should work together. Allow Symphony to show you what she's capable of. Things are changing and I believe we will all need to be open to this change.

"Despite making the world believe it's so, we can't be everywhere all the time. You will rest easier knowing she's capable of returning home to you no matter what. I say this from experience."

"Way to save your ass," Val says under her breath.

I snicker. I like her more and more. She is the one who told me I needed to stand up for myself when it comes to Michael.

Michael sighs and turns me in his embrace so he can wrap his arms around me—my back to his front. He kisses the side of my neck. I close my eyes and soak him in.

"We have a lot to talk about. You should know what's going on in Italy. We will call your nonno as well. He will be happy to know you are with me."

"I would like that."

CHAPTER FORTY-ONE

Better Together

Michael

I still don't know how I feel about this. It's not that I don't think Symphony is capable. This just isn't what I want for her. If it were up to me, she would dance or play on a stage for the world to see.

How did we get here? I am on a kill and my wife is with me. My sweet Symphony is here to help me silence a few lives.

With each second that passes, I'm beginning to feel a little more insane. If anything happens to her, I will lose my fucking mind.

"Michael, I will be fine. I am a professional," Sim says through the comm.

"We move in and out. There are five targets. Do not separate from me."

"I know what to do. It will be easier if you trust me."

"I trust you, Sim. It is them I can't trust."

"You are making me angry. Let's just do this. I want to go home and play for a few hours to work off my anger."

"Symphony, I'm sorry. I—"

"They have all arrived. Our focus should be on the task. Focus, Michael," she growls, cutting me off.

I release a heavy breath and get ready. Blocking out that this is my wife I'm about to do a hit with, I pretend I'm working with Uri instead. It is all I can do to keep focused on the task at hand.

"Let's move."

Symphony

I push my anger aside and lock in on the job at hand. I will not allow Michael to cause me not to do my best. He will see I am a professional.

With my tablet, I shut down all their comms, then I cut the lights. Once done, I tuck the tablet away and pull my guns, my silencers already in place.

Allowing the music to play in my head, I dance. Michael becomes my dance partner. I move with him.

We enter the building with our night vision glasses on. I take out the two confused-looking guards before they can find their bearings and shoot us. Michael nods and we keep moving.

We turn the corner and come up behind three more guys. Michael takes out two and I take out the third one.

A door opens on the left and a guy steps out. Michael uses his body to shield me, much to my annoyance. However, I arabesque, lifting onto one leg and stealing enough height to aim over Micheal's head to shoot the guy once in the head and twice in the chest.

Michael looks over his shoulder at me, but I don't have time to poke my tongue out at him like I want to. Two more guys pour out from the room the last one came from. I toss one gun in the air, then place my palm into Michael's back to reposition him out of my way.

Catching my gun, I then take them down and move around Michael to move forward. Once we clear this floor, we move swiftly to the next, where we should find our targets.

We enter a wide-open room. It has the feel of a gallery, which I believe it once was from the recon I did on the building. I take a deep breath as everything changes. Our targets are here, but so are at least twenty other men. The only good thing is the fact that they haven't noticed us.

I reload quickly. I'll need the fresh clips to clear this room. Michael seems to have the same thought as he does as well.

"I love you, Sim. Don't—"

Before he can finish whispering his words, I take out two of our targets. They are taller than the others, giving me clear headshots. However, that alerts the others to our presence.

Michael hits one of our other main targets as I move forward behind one of the pillars surrounding the perimeter of the room. Bullets are now flying our way. Our final two targets are on the move, trying to escape.

Michael has started to chart the same path as me on the other side of the room. My focus is on the last two targets. We can't allow them to escape.

I move faster, then I leap into the air, landing in the perfect firing range as they get to a door at the back of the room. I pull the trigger and take out both their knees. The two men drop to the ground and the men who were trying to get them out turn and begin to fire on us.

Michael takes two out swiftly. The third fires a shot at me, but I duck out of the way. Michael shoots him in the shoulder, then runs up behind him and viciously snaps his neck.

I move to stand over the last two, who are groaning in agony. Michael reaches my side as I put two in the first one's head. Michael finishes off the other.

Quickly, we head out of the exit they were trying to escape through. Michael bolts the door behind us, and we rush down the stairs. The exit at the bottom dumps us right out into the back lot, which will lead straight to our vehicle.

Job sixty-one done. One hundred and fifty-five kills. Still never touched once.

CHAPTER FORTY-TWO

Synergy and Fire

Michael

I'm still in awe as we pull up to the house. I haven't been able to find the words I want to say to her to express how amazing she is. The synergy, the electrifying way we worked together.

The job had been unpredictable from the start. We had to go in blind in order to get all five targets at once. It had to be done simultaneously.

For all my worries, Symphony proved me wrong. She handled herself like a well-trained assassin. With each day that passes, I have been seeing the errors in how I have handled Sim.

My protectiveness may have done more harm than good. Uri is right. Symphony is a natural.

After what I witnessed tonight, I would fear her as much as Hush or *Morte Nera.*

225

Without a word, she steps from the car, leaving me to stare after her. She's still angry with me. I get out and follow her into the house.

She goes in through the side door and straight to our bedroom. The last two weeks have been heaven, waking up with her in my arms and going to bed with her next to me. It makes me question if I have done anything right.

As I'm lost in thought, Sim strips down and climbs into the shower. I bag her clothes, then strip from mine to do the same. Then, I walk the bag to the shoot that leads to the furnace to toss it in.

Uri now has one of these shoots in all the hitter's bedrooms of this house and his office. It has been convenient, to say the least. Once I'm done, I head back to the shower. I owe my wife an apology.

Symphony

"Stupid buttface. I know how to do my job," I grumble to myself.

I am stewing. I have never been so angry. Michael could have gotten himself killed with his behavior.

I wasn't in harm's way. I had it under control. I growl in frustration. I haven't been underestimated like this since my freshman year in college. One of my professors only saw my disorder.

He treated me like I didn't belong until I outdanced every dancer in the program. I worked harder than everyone else. I lived in the dance studio when I wasn't practicing piano.

When the professor would try to change the routine mid-session to throw me off, I homed in my focus and picked up the changes before anyone else. It was exhausting at times.

I would return home and have a meltdown many days, but I showed him. I did my best like I always do. I became the best.

When I master something, I master it. Killing has been no different. Those men tonight were all bad men.

I knew what we were there to do, and I did it. I've been working on my own for nine years. Adriano rarely assisted me.

How dare Michael doubt me? This may not have been as controlled as I liked, but I was still able to handle it. I got it done.

"*Bella*, I can hear you cursing me out in your thoughts. I am sorry, Sim. Forgive me," Michael says in my ear as he steps into the shower behind me and cups my soapy breasts.

He begins to kiss my neck as he kneads my mounds. I cling to my anger. This is important to me.

I want his respect. I have already stepped up in the last two weeks. I've demonstrated what I've been learning while working for the O'Sheas.

He goes from kissing to sucking while pinching my nipples. I fight a moan as I wish to keep my anger. I do my best to ignore him.

"You were amazing. I am sorry. I will never doubt you in anything ever again."

Lifting one hand to my chin, he turns my face toward him and dips his head to take my lips. I don't open my mouth to him. When I don't, he squeezes my breast in one hand and wraps his other arm around my waist, pulling me tightly against him.

"Baby, please. We have lost so much time already. Let's not spend more time being angry."

"I have a right to my anger."

"Yes, you do," he says and kisses my lips. "I will do anything you want for me to make it up to you. Name it and it's yours."

I stand with my gaze on his chest. His growing erection is poking me in the leg. Through my anger, I'm still becoming wet for him as he roams his hands over my back and butt.

"Anything?"

"Anything."

"I want a dance studio. I miss the one I had at the estate in Boston."

"Would you like a new piano as well? The one you have been using is a rental. I should have realized Uri was up to something when he rented it."

"Yes, I would like that too."

"I will find us a house and I will give you your studio and piano."

"We are leaving?"

He pinches my chin between his fingertips and waits for me to meet his gaze. Sadness fills me at the thought of moving from here. I like Val and I miss Uri.

"You don't want to move into our own home?"

"No. I am finally surrounded by family. I want to stay here. Val is kind to me and Annabella is here. I like playing with the babies. I think they likes me.

"I would like to live here. Before I came, Uri said there was plenty of room here for us. I have learned that to be true. I wish to stay."

"Then we will stay. I will discuss your studio with Uri and order your piano in the morning. Is there anything else that you would like?"

"I want to go on a proper date. We have never been on one."

A huge smile comes to his face. He tightens his hold around me and kisses my forehead. My anger finally begins to melt away.

"We will have to fix that, won't we?" he croons.

He takes my lips in a searing kiss. I wrap my arms around his neck and return the kiss this time. I moan into his mouth as he deepens the kiss.

"One more thing," I say as I pull away.

"Yes, my little killer."

"You have to do another job with me. This time, you have to trust me as a partner."

He searches my gaze for a bit. At first, I believe he's going to say no. My anger begins to rise again.

"I leave for a hit in Greece in a few weeks. Something a little more intimate. Come with me. We will do it together."

I nod and lift on my toes to kiss him again. I whimper when he breaks the kiss and steps back. Reaching for the bodywash he begins to wash my body and then allows me to wash his.

Once we are clean, he shuts the water off and steps out to grab a towel. He dries me off and wraps the towel around me, then wraps one around his waist.

I remove the cap and wrap from my hair and move to the mirror to oil my scalp and fix my locs. Michael brushes his teeth, then turns to lean his butt against the sink as he watches me.

"I remember when you first changed your hair. I thought it was pretty on you then. It is gorgeous on you now."

"Thank you."

"I remember once asking you why you changed your hair, but what made you choose that style?"

"It ... I ... I needed something I could manage on my own. Annabella never really knew how to care for my hair. Then there were the patches from my stimming.

"As a teenage girl, I started to think about my appearance more. It took a long time to decide on what to do, but I chose locs because, if needed, I could twist them to serve my stim.

"I'm just a lot more cognitive when I've placed the strands under too much tension. I thought the women in the photos who wore locs were pretty and fierce. It also tamed the mass of hair I had when it wasn't damaged and ugly," I say.

Michael moves to stand behind me. He gathers my hair and places it into the bun I keep it in for bed. He then kisses my shoulder and looks into my eyes through the mirror.

"There has never been anything ugly or damaged about you. I'm sorry I didn't know how to take better care of you. I should have found someone to handle your hair and assist you with anything else you needed.

"If I could do it all over again, I would do so much differently. I would have given you so much more."

I turn to face him. "You gave me everything I needed and so much more. You were my friend when I had none. You were a shoulder to cry on when life was so overwhelming and confusing.

Michael, you have been my safe place. The reason I always want to do better.

"You are the reason I play music. The reason I breathe. The reason I always want to do my best.

"The reason I know I can do anything. I have always felt your love even before I knew it was romantic love. I will never regret the day the pretty boy with the blue eyes saved me and took me away from the bad man."

Before I can finish pouring my heart out, he crushes his lips to mine and cups the back of my neck. The kiss quickly turns heated. He pulls my towel loose and it falls to the floor.

I cry out and toss my head back as he cups my breast and wraps his lips around my nipple. He has his fingers working in between my legs, driving me crazy. I claw my fingers through his damp hair and moan as he makes my body bloom for him.

"What do you want, Sim? What do you need from me?"

I think his words over before I deliver a clinical answer. I pause my reply as I think about how he loves to hear me talk dirty. I think of what I want and the most crass way I can say it.

"I need you to fuck me from behind. I want you to pin me down and fuck me," I say.

Michael pauses in his movements. He pulls away from my breast to look up at me. I search his eyes to see if I've done something wrong.

"Did I say the wrong thing?"

"No, not at all. You just took me by surprise."

"I think I will enjoy being dominated in the bedroom. I would like to know what it's like to get fucked hard."

"You want me to dominate you?"

"Yes, fuck me, choke me, take my body for your own. You are a strong male. I think you would be good at it."

"*Cazzo. Potresti essere più perfetto? Ti scoperò finché non potrai più urlare. Così forte che i tuoi occhi si incroceranno.*"

"Yes, please. I want my eyes to cross, my toes to curl. I don't care if I lose my voice. Fuck me as hard as you want. You are the perfect one."

"Spread your legs for me," he growls.

I open my legs wide as he gets to his knees. Swiftly, he places my legs over his shoulders and begins to feast on me. Michael is so good at cunnilingus.

My eyes roll back in my head, and I grab hold of the edge of the sink. I come screaming, having to cover my mouth with my hands.

Michael looks up at me and releases a dark chuckle. Lifting to his feet, he scoops me up into his arms and wraps my legs around his waist. He kisses me deeply as he walks us into the bedroom.

I begin to kiss his neck and inhale his scent. Bending his knees, he opens the bedside table on my side of the bed and pulls out one of my bottles of oil. He then allows my body to slide down the front of his.

I lower to my knees and look at him through my lashes. He looks at the oil, then back at me. I smile and wait for him to pour some on his penis.

"That wasn't my plan, *cara*," he laughs.

"Is this not what you want?"

His penis jerks in my face. I lick my lips, wanting to return the pleasure he just gave me in the bathroom. He pours some of the oil onto his shaft and begins to stroke himself.

"Open your mouth."

I do as he says happily. I have been doing some research and think I know more about how to bring him pleasure. I have a few tricks I want to try.

He slides his length into my mouth as I relax my throat. I take him as deep as I can, but he pulls out way too fast. I pout up at him, wanting to demonstrate what I have learned.

He smiles down at me. "Open again. Hold your mouth open and stick your tongue out."

I do as he says, and he taps his penis against my tongue. The precum on his tip drops onto my tongue. I hum and lift to follow his retreat with my mouth this time.

I'm rewarded as he slides into my mouth, but he tries to pull back out again. I wrap my lips around him and suction my cheeks.

I have a tight seal on his thick member, trapping him in and pulling a groan from him.

Placing my hands on his powerful thighs, I take over and bob my head. As he begins to make more sounds of enjoyment, I reach for his balls and begin to massage them gently.

"Sim," he hisses through his teeth.

I hum happily as I alter the pressure of my touch to gauge what he likes most. Suddenly, the slick feeling of the oil dripping over my breasts grabs my attention. I look up at my husband through my lashes and find his gaze locked on my oil-slicked breasts.

With my free hand, I begin to rub the oil on my mound, pinching my nipple until it comes to a hardened peak. Micheal grunts and cups the back of my head, holding me in place.

I choke a bit, but I don't back off. He has to pull out for me to catch my breath. When he does, I run my forearm across my mouth.

The raw lust in his eyes makes me so happy. I'm ready to continue, but he lifts me to my feet and turns me until my back is to his front. He pours more oil onto my body before he places the bottle down and palms both of my breasts.

I moan as he nuzzles my neck and kneads my chest. Lifting one breast up, he leans over me and takes my nipple into his mouth. The action shoots straight to my core.

I push my fingers into his hair and hold on tight as he continues to suck and lick at the tightened peak. I lift on my toes, trying to get closer to his mouth. He splays a hand between my belly and my pussy as if trying to hold me up from tumbling to the floor.

My heart swells. He's always trying to protect me. In this moment, I realize that's never going to change. It's ingrained in the core of who he is.

My angel, my protector. My strength, my love, my Michael. My husband.

"Michael, I need you so much."

"Be patience, *mia moglie.*"

He nudges my feet apart with his foot, then grasps my upper arms in his palms. In the next motion, he thrusts in between my slick petals. I lift up on my toes, but he tugs me back down to take him.

"Michael, I'm so full," I pant.

"This is what you wanted. You said you wanted me to take you from behind. I'm giving you what you want, *mia moglie*. Is it not good?" he breathes into my ear.

"Yes, it's so good. So fucking good."

"That's my girl. Take it and tell me how good it feels."

"It feels amazing. You're so thick and so deep. I can't believe you're so hard inside me."

I don't understand how this can keep getting better. Just when I don't think it can go to another level, he bends me over at the waist and begins to thrust harder. He now has my wrists crossed above my butt in one of his hands.

"Oh God, Symphony. You feel so incredible, baby. So fucking wet. Can you handle more?"

"Yes, please. I can take more. I want more."

He pulls out and pushes me to climb onto the bed as he climbs on behind me. I moan loudly as he begins to kiss and suck at my butt. He has his hands everywhere, caressing my skin and heightening my arousal.

When he begins to eat my pussy from behind, I can do nothing but grasp the sheets and hold on tightly. I rock my hips back against his face as he hums in pleasure. I melt into the mattress as he pushes two fingers into me to finger fuck me.

I scream his name as I come. Just when I think I might be spent, he lifts my ass and straddles my hips. Reaching for his length, he pushes into me and begins to stroke slowly.

Then he wraps his arm around my shoulders and takes one of my hands in his. He laces his fingers with mine as he continues to rock his big body into mine. I am consumed by him, covered in him like I'm wrapped in a blanket.

I cry out and pant as I take him. His strokes are perfect. He nips my shoulder then kisses the side of my face. I melt down into the mattress again.

This time, he begins to increase his pace. His body has me pinned down as he alternates between fast strokes and deep, long ones where he presses deep into me and holds it. My eyes cross as my heart pounds.

"Is this what you wanted, baby? Am I fucking you how you want?"

"Yes, more please."

He lifts up and pulls both my arms behind me to loop one of his around them. Then he lifts my upper body up off the bed as he fucks me harder, making my teeth chatter.

I'm so wet; the sound fills the room. Everything in me sings for him. I'm a coming mess.

By the time Michael is done with my body, I'm exhausted and sated all at once. I love this side of him. I want him to dominate my body more often.

As hard as he remained throughout the night, I think this is something he liked as well. I make a note of that to remember for the future. I fall asleep in his arms with a smile on my face.

CHAPTER FORTY-THREE

New Friend

Symphony

Our date is tonight, and I have no idea what I should wear. I went to Valentina to ask for help. I didn't think she would take me shopping, not when she has the responsibility of Vita and the newborn twins.

It's been so long since I've done this with a friend. I think we are becoming friends. I am older than Val by two or three years, but she still has a maternal aura about her.

She's watchful and protective when it comes to me. She doesn't treat me as if I don't understand or like I need more help than I do. She's more like a whisper. Suggesting things I should do, like the oil and panty display I put on for Michael the first night I arrived.

"That's it. That's the one," Val sings when I step out of the dressing room.

I look down at the outfit I have on and question my own sanity. Why on earth did I even try this one? I'm not wearing this on my first date.

"You have lost some part of your mind. I cannot wear this," I say.

"Why not? You look sexy and Michael won't be able to keep his hands off you. It's perfect.

"Those long legs were meant to be shown off. We'll take the outfit and the shoes," she says to the salesclerk.

"I would like to find something else."

"Okay, fine. We're still taking this one though," Val huffs.

"I think we're doing too much. I don't even know where he's taking me. I think something casual is in order."

"You asked me for help, and I happen to know where he's taking you. You should listen to your sister. I'll never lead you astray. I've got your back."

Her words fill me with so much joy. I want to be close with her like sisters. I've been so happy here in New York so far.

I've been invited to meet all of Val's friends. I can't wait for our outing. Although I have to say I'm a bit nervous about that.

"Okay, fine. If you know where we are going and you really think this will be appropriate, I will wear it."

"That's my girl. Now come on so we can find the right undergarments for when he tears you out of that little number."

My mouth falls open and I begin to blush as I glance around at the staff members who have been helping us. They are all smiling with knowing looks. I drop my gaze to the red heels on my feet and turn to rush back into the dressing room.

Maybe I don't want to be friends with Val. Why would she say those things in front of strangers? I don't want people to know that I have sex with my husband.

You're an adult, Symphony. Everyone knows you have sex with your husband. He's your husband.

"Oh, shut up," I chide my thoughts.

Michael

Sim spent the entire day out shopping with Val. When they returned Sim had a huge smile on her face. I love seeing her so happy.

I am grateful to Val for taking Sim in so quickly. I can see they are fond of each other and have a fast-building bond. This will be good for Sim, I think.

Her first few days here, she popped that wristband a lot. I've come to notice she does it when she is anxious or having difficulty finding what she wants to express. I try to give her time to gather her thoughts when I feel it's the latter.

"You look like a nervous teen on the way to prom. You have been on dates before. Why are your knickers wound so tight?" Uri says as he walks into the kitchen where I've been standing, lost in thought.

"I have never taken Sim on a proper date. I don't want anything to go wrong."

"It is good to see you like this. I can see how much she means to you. You're happier with her around."

"I should have found another way," I grumble.

"Don't beat yourself up. You did what you felt was right for her and look how accomplished she has become. Besides, think about all Leonardo has done trying to get to you both.

"I would have had to bathe Italy in blood and burn it to ash if anything happened to either of you. Her distance gave you focus. You have gone from my baby brother, my shadow, to a man of your own.

"I don't think you made any mistakes. Don Trovati doesn't either. He has watched you both. When you are not with him, he still knows of your actions."

"Thanks, Uri. I needed to hear that. I have big shoes to fill. I don't think I thought of how enormous this undertaking would be.

"I just saw a kid in need. All I could think about was losing Papa and how we had to live after. How you had to live.

"No one ever stepped in for us. I didn't want her to have to go through something like that. Not when ... you know.

"Someone else would have taken advantage if we didn't step up. I could see you didn't want to do it. Seeing you with Val now, I'm glad you didn't.

"Sim wasn't the one who needed me. You were right for the job and still are. You were never meant to be in my shadow. I believe we are both on the paths meant for us," he says.

"Speaking of which, did you know Don Trovati planned to have Don Alfanzo offer me a seat at the table?"

"No, I didn't know he would be involved. I've always been under the impression that this is LaSalle's thing."

"It is, but apparently Don Locatelli has a few seats he plans to fill. I have been given one. If you don't want me to take it or if you would rather I do so you don't have to—"

"I am a Donati. We are men of our word. I have already accepted my role.

"Do as you wish, Michael. You are a grown man. I have trained you as much as I can.

"What you do from here, you do as your own man. These are your decisions. Yours and Sim's," he interrupts me to say.

"There you are. Come, she's ready. You need to watch her come down for the full effect," Annabella says excitedly.

I grin and grab the bouquet of red roses from the countertop where I placed them, then I follow my sister to the foyer. Her excitement is infectious. I pull out my pocket watch to check the time.

My grin grows as "Für Elise" begins to play. I never leave home without this watch. I have cherished it since Sim gave it to me. It has been a reminder that, in time, all things fall into sync.

Uri clears his throat beside me, causing me to lift my head. I close my watch in my palm and grasp it tightly. Sim has a nervous smile on her lips, but that's not what grabs my attention.

It's her long, silky legs that are on display that have my mouth watering and my slacks growing tight. She has on a pair of red fuck me heels that scream she's my naughty girl. I have to bite back my reaction when my gaze rises to the garment she's wearing.

I want to demand she turn around and go change, but I don't want to hurt her feelings. However, she may get someone hurt before the night is over. She's wearing what looks like a black sleeveless tux jacket—nothing else.

From this distance, I'm left to wonder if anything is underneath. It molds over her breasts and stops mid-thigh. She has done something different with her hair. Her locs seem to be twisted together in twos and then pulled back away from her face in a high ponytail that hangs down her back.

The elegance and grace of Sim's walk only enhance the visual of her coming to me. Her full lips are painted red with a glossy shine to them.

The look is tightly skating the line of classy but sexy. My wife could have had a career as a supermodel if she wanted. She is a head-turner, for sure.

"I am ready for our date," she says as she stops in front of me.

I place a hand on her hip and pull her to me to kiss her soft lips. I don't take it too far, just a peck. When I pull away, I hand her the flowers in my other hand.

Her eyes light up with excitement and she claps her hands together. I will have to bring her flowers more often. She takes them in her hands and gives them a sniff.

"I am used to getting flowers in my dressing room, but this is so much different," she says excitedly. "Thank you, Michael."

"You are welcome."

"Annabella, will you please put my flowers in some water for me? I don't want to damage them on our date."

"I've got you."

Symphony's eyes light up as Annabella takes the roses from her. I can tell something has come to mind to make her happy and excited. It's as if I can see her downloading information in her head.

"Oh, I don't want them to die too quickly. Do you know to make sure you use a clean vase? You have to trim the stems at a sharp angle underwater and remove any leaves that could be submerged in the water. Michael, can we stop for some flower food to add to the water when we return?"

I kiss her cheek. "We might not find anything open by then. I will buy you another dozen tomorrow."

"It's okay. I want to save these. I will order online and have it delivered."

"In that case, we should go."

CHAPTER FORTY-FOUR

Born Diva

Symphony

"No matter what happens, hold your head high." Valentina's words continue to play in my head from when she whispered them to me as she hugged me before I left for my date.

My first date has been amazing so far. I've done all that Val and Annabella told me to do. Up until this point their advice has paid off.

First, Michael took me to dinner at a lovely restaurant. I'm a picky eater, so I was a bit nervous when we first arrived. I'm glad I didn't allow my nerves to get the best of me.

Once I looked at the menu, I was able to find something I would like, and it was divine. Michael kept the conversation going smoothly and shared bites of his food with me to try.

When I got too excited to find my words to express myself, he didn't get annoyed with me. He allowed me time to calm and figure it out. I appreciate that.

This has all been so exciting and overwhelming for me at times. I can dance and perform before hundreds of people, but sitting across from Michael and wanting to impress him has been a bit daunting. However, Michael has made it worth the effort.

It is only now, as we sit in our box seats at the opera that I'm conflicted on whether or not I should follow Val and Annabella's advice. As the beautiful performance continues below us and I begin to realize this is the part of the date the ladies were hinting about, I don't know what I should do.

"Are you okay?" Michael leans to whisper in my ear as I pop the band on my wrist and bounce my knee.

I nod my head and lick my lips. Suddenly, I'm hyperaware of his nearness. His large hand on my bare thigh, his warm breath tickling my neck.

Maybe my sisters are right. Val and Annabella have only ever looked out for me. I haven't known Val for long, but she has been genuine with me.

She confirmed the things I already knew about Julissa and made sure to let me know this was the reason she wanted me to come back to Michael. She wanted the woman gone.

"I have trusted them this far," I whisper to myself.

"What was that?" Michael replies.

Instead of answering him, I place my hand behind his head and join our lips. Michael quickly takes over the kiss and deepens it as he groans into my mouth.

He breaks the kiss with so much lust in his eyes as he looks back at me; the war I'm having with myself is broken. I reach beneath my dress and hook my fingers into my panties as the ladies told me to. Then I lock my gaze with Michael's and pull the tiny fabric from under the dress.

Once I have them in my grasp, I reach for Michael's hand and press the tiny scrap into his palm. He looks at me with so much want I shiver. However, I remain focused on my instructions.

I straighten in my seat and cross my legs as if nothing just happened. Michael reaches to place his fingertips beneath my chin and turns my face to his. His blue eyes are blazing as he looks back at me.

"Does this mean you are ready to go home?" he asks huskily.

"If you have the restraint to wait that long, it is up to you," I reply.

"*Symphony*," he growls in warning.

"Yes?"

"Don't try to play innocent with me. I will fuck you right in this booth. I have wanted you since you came down those steps in that tiny thing you think is a dress," he says as he slides his hand up my thigh.

"Oh, how exciting. You will fuck me here in public? Will you shove those in my mouth so I don't scream?

"I am wet already. The decision is yours. I have had an amazing time. This will only make the night unforgettable for me."

He palms the back of my neck and tugs me forward for a passionate kiss. All apprehension has melted away. I want this more than anything.

Val was right, Michael is totally turned on by the thought of taking me in this box while people are all around us. My belly drops as he smoothly moves his hand along my skin, up under my dress.

Grasping my thigh, he uncrosses my legs and begins to finger me. I whimper into his mouth as he continues to kiss me passionately.

In no time, the sound of his fingers moving in and out of my juices fills the air. I reach for his tux jacket and hold on tightly. He moves his lips to my neck and begins to press kisses there.

Without a word, he stands from his seat and takes me with him. Swiftly, he moves us into the shadows of the box. In the next motion, he shoves my panties into my mouth and lifts me onto his waist.

"I'm going to fuck you hard and fast. Hold on tight, baby. Breathe through your nose and take me," he breathes in my ear as he fumbles with his pants.

I whimper around my panties as he thrusts into me. I am thankful he stuffed them into my mouth because I'm sure I would have screamed had he not.

Wrapping my arms around his neck, I hold on tight as he fucks me up against the wall. I dig my heels into his ass. He grunts into my ear as he thrusts deeply, filling me up.

"You like that, baby? Is that hard cock what you wanted? Was this what you were looking for?"

I nod my head as my eyes roll back. I will have to thank Val and Annabella later. This is amazing and I don't want it to stop.

I lose count of how many times I come before the lights come on and Michael slips from my body, placing me on my feet. My legs are shaky, and I can feel his semen running down my inner thigh, but I've never been more satisfied.

With my head held high, I leave the opera with my husband after what has been the best first date ever. Michael wraps his long coat around me and holds me closely as we return to our car to head home.

I'm happier than I thought I could ever be. My life finally feels complete. Michael kisses my forehead then leans into my ear.

"*Ti amo*, Symphony."

I look up into his eyes. "I love you too."

CHAPTER FORTY-FIVE

Killer Vacation

Michael

Two weeks later ...

We are here in Greece for work, but I wanted to make it a romantic getaway as well. So many years, so many lost vacations and time to spend together. I plan to make up for it all.

I have always been able to find the calm within the storm. In the last week, I believe I have created that for Symphony as we have been here on this island. Tonight, we will leave for the island where our target is—in and out—but for now, it's the two of us.

I look up as Sim walks out of the house in black shades and a black two-piece. Her body calls to me as the little scraps of fabric barely cover anything. Her curves are on display and her brown skin is glowing. Her locs are shining in the sunlight, the honey-brown strands turning to gold.

"Will I ever get enough?" I murmur to myself as I begin to grow hard.

We have fucked almost everywhere on this property since we've been here. My wife is nearly as insatiable as I am. I say nearly because I still dream of having sex with her even though she sleeps beside me.

Those dreams are so vivid I wake up needing to take her. She is always so ready and willing. Our sex life has become intoxicating.

"Will you get in the water with me?" Sim asks as she climbs onto my lap and lies against my chest.

"If that's what you want."

The pool here is amazing. I have grown accustomed to swimming laps in the evenings. Everything about this place is soothing.

"I do, but now I am comfortable. We will get in in a bit. What are you thinking about?"

"Are you happy?"

"Yes, very much so. I had fun going to the club last night and the Jet Skis this morning were thrilling."

"Have you put any thought into what you would like to do for our next anniversary?"

"I would like for you to surprise me. I think you will come up with something acceptable."

I chuckle and kiss her forehead. "I will come up with something. I'm just happy we will be together this time."

"Me too."

I smile as I feel her body growing heavy on top of mine. She has fallen asleep. Thankfully, my lounge chair is under the umbrella.

I tighten my hold around her and allow her to rest. While she sleeps, I stare down at her gorgeous face. She looks so peaceful and innocent.

If you told me I had an assassin lying on top of me, I would tell you that you lie. Symphony looks more like a princess who spreads light around the world. She has brought light back into my life with her return.

I don't know what I would do if I had to be away from her again. One thing I know is that I never plan to find out. I'm never letting her go.

"You were just what I needed," I murmur and brush my fingers along her temple.

***

We slip onto the island under the cover of night. Thick clouds are rolling in, noting a storm is brewing. We need to handle this quickly.

Symphony and I make it to Damian Balaska's vacation home undetected. This one is a favor to Uncle Nicholas. Balaska fucked up when he stole from a Donati.

It's not about the money he took. It's the principal and the fact that this guy has done so with his chest poked out and his tongue wagging. That can't go unanswered.

Not when Luca is about to take over the family. Uri wants all old grievances cleaned up before the transitions of the families. Valentine Caprisi has ensured Uri won't have any issues taking over the Caprisi family.

I have nearly cleared the board of Trovati problems outside of Leonardo and here we are to handle the last of the Donati issues. I have met Balaska once, I didn't like him then. He was arrogant and dismissive of the woman I would later come to learn was his wife.

I guess it's not strange that he's here with his mistress on this island. The funny part is he would be nothing without his wife and her family. If you ask me, I think it was his wife who snitched him out to Uncle Nic.

"I have neutralized the girl," Sim says through the comm.

We are here for Balaska. Sim and I both agreed we didn't want to kill his young mistress. Symphony's task was to slip by the guards undetected to sedate the mistress.

"Meet me in his office," I reply.

Swiftly, I begin to make my way toward the office doors from the outside of the house. There are two guards standing outside. I wait until they are standing, lined up side by side, and take the shot, sending a bullet through both their skulls in one blow.

Once they are down, I move quickly into the open double doors of Balaska's study he has been held up in. I slip into the office through the shadows and lock my gaze on my target. The asshole is so busy watching porn on a laptop on his desk as he jerks off he hasn't noticed a thing.

I guess a mistress half his age isn't enough, or maybe he needs to prime the pump before he gets to the main show. Either way, it doesn't matter. He's not going to get to finish.

I flip my watch open, and "Für Elise" fills the air. I laugh as Balaska nearly jumps out of his skin. The door to the office opens and the sound of three sharp pops is all that's heard before Balaska falls back lifelessly in his chair.

I close my watch and hold my hand out for Sim. She takes it, and I turn to leave out the way I came in. I mumble to myself as we make our way back to the waiting boat.

"I thought we agreed I would take the kill shot," I say once we are back on the boat.

"You were playing with your food. I like to eat and be done with it. You can have the next one. Why play the music?"

I smile at her assumption that this will continue. However, the thought of working together like this doesn't bother me as much as it once did. We feel like a team. I would rather be with her to watch her back than have her work alone.

"Think of it as a parting gift. A grace of sorts. Something beautiful before they meet their end.

"Besides, it makes me think of you. A light to lead me back from the darkness," I say and peck her lips as I hold her to my side while I drive us away from the island in the speed boat.

"At this speed, we will beat the storm. Can we go a little faster?"

I give her waist a squeeze as I increase our speed. We reach our destination right as the sky opens up. Our driver is waiting to take us to the airport for our flight home. Our work is done here.

CHAPTER FORTY-SIX

Russian Friends

Symphony

Two weeks later ...

"Are you okay?" Michael asks as he walks up behind me and wraps his arms around my waist.

We are in Russia. We've just finished assisting Uri and Val in an extraction. A small child.

The girl is only four. I cannot imagine how scared she must have been. When I looked at the girl's face, I thought of Vita.

My niece and nephews have come to mean so much to me. I would wipe out Vita's kidnapper and his entire family if something like this were ever to happen to her. Uri and Val wouldn't even have to ask.

"What if that were Vita? I can't get her face out of my head. I remember how frightened I was when you rescued me. She's so much smaller than I was."

"No one is crazy enough to try something like that with Uri's daughter," Michael says through clenched teeth.

"Isn't her father some Russian mob boss? Someone dared to take her."

"Not someone. This was Misha's own family. They're"—he shakes his head—"they are all crazy enough to have a death wish in doing this. I am sure he has already murdered at least one person for this."

"Why would someone do this to their own family?"

"I have kept you hidden from your uncle for years."

"That's not the same. Leonardo Trovati isn't my blood. I am no more important to him than a piece of pooh on the bottom of his shoe."

"People are complicated and will go to extremes when power and greed are involved. It will take some time, but Milanie will be fine, just like you were," Michael says softly.

"I don't like what this world does to children. I would never want our children to have to go through something like we have. Losing our parents, being kidnapped—"

Before I can finish my thought, Michael spins me around and crushes his lips to mine. I'm taken by surprise as he kisses me passionately. I wrap my arms around his neck and return the kiss.

He breaks the connection and looks me deeply in the eyes. I cling to the front of his shirt as he has made me weak in the knees. He smiles back at me and cups the side of my face.

"You would like to have children? You want to have babies?"

"Yes. Is it something you don't want? Not with me?"

"Of course I want them with you. You are my wife."

"Why did you sound so surprised?"

I search his gaze, wondering what I am reading in his voice. Disappointment begins to set in. This is something adults get to talk about before they get married. We weren't afforded that luxury or opportunity, and Michael may not want to pair his genes with mine.

"You are a dancer. You have never mentioned wanting to start a family of our own. I never thought to ask.

"We haven't been using protection, but I didn't think to ask. Yes, Symphony. I would like a family of our own."

"I would like to be a mother. I only have a few more years left of my dance career. I would be okay if I had to retire sooner.

"I am on birth control for now. I can discontinue whenever you think we are ready. I very much would like to have babies with you. Please."

He captures my lips again. This time more passionately. I moan into his mouth and lift on my toes to get closer to him.

"We are about to enter a war. It might not be time to start now, but we will revisit this. For now, practice always makes perfect," he says against my lips while squeezing my butt.

"Shouldn't we check on Val? We should see if she needs help with Milanie."

"I've just come from their room. Milanie is fine. She's fast asleep and I believe my brother and his wife are about to do the same thing we are. Come to bed, Symphony. We have done our part," he croons as he tugs my hand for me to follow him.

Michael

If Misha Krupin decides he doesn't want his own family's blood on his hands, I'll be happy to erase them all before we head back to America. I'd return to do the job if I had to. What they have done is unforgivable.

When Uri asked for me and Sim to join him and Val on this trip, I did so without question. Once I found out what we were needed here for, my blood began to boil. I was more than happy to be here to help.

Once again, I learned firsthand that Sim and I are a well-oiled machine together. We entered that hotel and cleared it as if we were breathing one breath. I knew then we were made to do this life together.

However, when Sim said she wanted to have a family, I began to think about how much I wanted that too. There is a lot of work I will need to do to make sure my children never have a life like the one I did. I'm ready for that.

"What are you thinking about?" Sim yawns.

"You really have never driven a car?" I say, not wanting to tell her all the thoughts I'm having about murdering people and starting a family.

Two things that shouldn't be thought of in the same cycle of thoughts. We've just finished making love for hours. I want to keep the serene vibe we have going.

"No, Michael. I haven't. You have provided me with a driver since I was fourteen. Adriano has never allowed me to go anywhere alone. I've never had the opportunity to learn to drive, although I would love to."

I begin to work my jaw. Adriano hasn't returned to Italy. He has been in our home working as one of the family guards. I haven't told Uri I want him sent back yet.

Symphony seems to be attached to him. While I don't like it, I am grateful to him for being there for her. I want to send him away without her being pissed off at me. I just haven't figured out how yet.

"We will have to change that. I will give you your first lessons when we return home," I murmur and kiss the top of her head.

"Thank you. I am most excited to go home now."

I chuckle. "The company will begin rehearsals soon, won't it?"

"Yes, I'm excited to start with them. New York has some of the best companies. I didn't think I would make one."

"I knew you would. They would have to be crazy not to extend an invitation to you."

She releases a sweet giggle. "You do know that I am aware that you and your friends pulled strings."

I roll her onto her back and begin to kiss my way down her body. She is right. LaSalle called in a few favors for her to get an audition, but her name spoke for itself. She earned the job.

"I have no idea what you mean," I croon against her silky-smooth skin as I make my way down to her sweet pussy.

"Yes, you do," she pants as I settle between her legs.

"No, baby. I don't."

I begin to feast on her and all else is forgotten as she begins to ride my face. I devour her until she comes in my mouth and then I take her body once more. We get lost in each other until she's fast asleep in my arms and I'm lost in my thoughts again.

***

"Hello," I whisper into the phone as I leave from the bedroom where Sim is fast asleep.

"Hey, Michael. How are you?"

"Julissa?"

"Yes, why do you sound so surprised?" she snickers.

"I wasn't sure I'd hear from you again after our last conversation."

"I'm sorry about that. I wanted to check in and see how you are doing."

"I'm fine. I'm great actually. Everything has changed."

"You sound happy. Did … did you and your wife talk things out?"

"We did. This is probably the last time you and I will talk."

"Oh," she says, sounding surprised. "Um, I'm happy for you. I'm glad things worked out. She's very lucky to have you."

"I'm sorry I dragged you into this—"

"No, don't you apologize. You were the only one who was truly kind to me. You were honest with me.

"I knew you loved someone else. I knew you were married. You also told me how much she meant to you and why we couldn't be more.

"I had hoped … It doesn't matter. Thank you, Michael. I will respect your wife and your marriage," she says with a shaky voice.

"Julissa, I'm so very sorry. I thought ... I didn't know we could work things out. I always knew if I could, I would."

"No, Michael, you don't owe me anything. I saw how much you love her from the moment you told me about her. I'm glad I could be there when you needed a friend."

"Thank you. I ... if you ever need me. You know, if your life is in danger, call me. However, I do love my wife, and I know speaking to you will upset her, so I'm going to go."

"Goodbye, Michael."

"Goodbye."

I hang up, but not before I catch her sobs on the other end. I feel like shit. I did care for her.

However, I'm crazy about my wife. I love Symphony in a way I could never explain. Maybe someday Julissa will find what she's looking for in someone who can return her feelings.

CHAPTER FORTY-SEVEN

I Can Help Him

Symphony

Five months later …

I am having a bad day. The last four months have been difficult since Ellen Mairettie was murdered. I told her she could come to me. If she could see things, why didn't she come to me?

I would have protected her. Everyone wouldn't be so sad if she would have allowed me to help. I have been trying to understand how she could help me keep Michael alive but not ask for help for her own life.

Her decision has been messing with my head. Today has been especially difficult and I can't figure out why. I have had to put on my weighted vest to try to realign myself.

"Sim, baby, did you hear me?"

I look up to find Michael looking at me expectantly. I notice I'm popping my wristband and I'm chewing on my tongue. I'm so confused.

Why would a woman who could see things not change such a horrible thing? Did she not see that I'm one of the best? I could have helped. I could have done something.

"I'm sorry. What was that?"

"Are you okay?"

"Yes, I'll be fine. I just need a little time today. I'm having a bad day. Did you need something?"

"No. You take all the time you need. Misha is coming by to see me and Uri. He's bringing Sammy along. I'll be with them."

I pop my head up at the mention of Ellen Mairettie's son. I still remember how she said I would be instrumental in his life. I desperately want to do all I can to repay his mother for her words of caution.

Had it not been for his mother, he wouldn't be alive, nor would his father. I like Sam Mairettie. It would have been a mistake to take his life. I am sure of that now.

"I am fine. I would like to see the boy. Will Milanie be with them? Is she well?"

"Uri didn't say, but I don't believe so. Apparently, Sammy is having a bad day too. No one could calm him down at the house.

"Misha and Uri have some business to talk about. He's bringing the kid with him. That's all I know for now. What can I do to help you?"

"I will go play for a little while. Please let me know when they arrive."

Michael closes the distance between us and pulls me into his arms. I relax a bit just from being in his embrace. I inhale deeply, taking in his intoxicating scent.

"I love you. Whatever has you unsettled, if I can do anything about it, let me know. Whatever you need, I am here," he says and kisses my forehead.

I look up at him and smile, making sure to look him in the eyes so he can see I'm already feeling better. Michael likes it when I give him my eyes. I try to when I'm aware and able to.

"Thank you. You have done more than you know already."

He turns to leave, and I go to head to the piano room. Something about knowing Sammy will be here has shifted my mood. If he's having a bad day, maybe I can help.

Michael

I leave the sitting room in our wing of the house, where I'd found Symphony sitting by herself. I knew something was off when I didn't find her with Val and the children. Sim loves spending time with them.

The children love her as well. I expected to find her hanging out with them and Val when I first went in search of her. When I did find her, I was concerned to find her staring into space while popping her wristband and making that chewing sound with her mouth.

I believe she's been struggling with Ellen's death. They didn't know each other for long as friends but I know Ellen was the woman Sim met at the charity event who gave her the warning for my life.

"Hello," I say into my phone after it rings, pulling me out of my concerned thoughts about my wife.

"Michael?"

"Julissa? What's going on?"

"I think I'm being followed. I didn't want to bother you, but I don't know what else to do."

I pause in my tracks. I did tell her to call if she ever needed me. If she were ever in danger.

"For how long?" I bite out.

"I thought I was being paranoid at first, but it's been about three weeks I believe."

I think fast. Symphony is having a bad day. I'm not about to tell her I'm running off to help the same woman she threatened to kill and I'm not going to help Julissa without telling my wife.

I think of a solution that might work in my favor. Adriano has been working my nerves with the way he watches my wife. I want to say he's just doing his job, but I know it's more.

"Listen, I'm going to send someone to look after you for a while. He will keep you safe. Stay inside for now. Adriano will be there in a few hours."

"Thank you, Michael. I thought this was over."

"I will get to the bottom of this and take care of it. Breathe. This could be nothing."

"Okay."

I hang up and go to find Adriano. I sent him on some errands earlier to get him away from Sim while I got some work done. Now, I will get him out of our home, at least for a little while.

Uri

"LaSalle will be promoted soon. Don Trovati is ready for you and Sim to take over as well," I say to Michael as we sit waiting in my office for Misha to arrive.

Michael sighs and pulls a hand down his face. I stare at him closely as he sits across from my desk. He has something on his mind.

"What is it?" I ask.

"Sim has been struggling. The timing just sucks. We'll be ready."

"Uri, Michael, my friends. We have arrived. You have drink for me, da?" Misha croons as he enters my office.

I lift a brow as my gaze lands on Sammy, who walks in with him. Sammy is wearing a holster with two guns. However, he seems more focused than ever.

"Does Sam know about this?" I ask, pointing to the boy.

"He knows I plan to help. Michael, your wife, she is like Sammy, da?"

"She is on the spectrum, but not everyone is the same. Sim was verbal when she came to us. We had to learn what worked for her, what things were best."

"LaSalle's boy likes pressure. Guns have stopped the tantrums and squirming. He talks. We have conversation in car on way here.

"We can help, my friends. Where is wife. She help too," Misha says as he goes to flop in the other seat across from my desk.

As if on cue, Sim enters the office. I notice she has her vest with the blades on. I look to Michael and give him a look.

"The piano wasn't helping today. I decided to train instead. Gino said Misha and the child have arrived," Sim says.

She squats as Sammy stops walking in circles and moves to stand in front of her. Sim places a hand on the top of his head. I swear it seems like they both settle before my eyes.

"These pistols are too heavy. You have the right idea, but there has to be something better. Have his parents tried a vest like mine?"

"This vest you have on, it helps?" Misha asks.

"Yes, it does."

"I will buy. He has small hands. Find small blades, maybe metal stars to throw."

"He doesn't need the weapons. I have a vest without them. I just like to throw blades and adapted my vest to accommodate the skill."

"He is old enough to learn skill. I show him how load gun clip for guns too."

I groan and shake my head. I'll have to check in with LaSalle on my own. Misha isn't going to have my family massacred with him.

CHAPTER FORTY-EIGHT

This One Together

Symphony

I awaken to kisses all over my face. When I open my eyes, sparkling blue ones are looking back at me. I smile at Michael and cup his handsome face.

"Good morning," I say.

"Good morning and happy anniversary, gorgeous. I have a big day planned for us. It's time to get up.

"I just need twenty more minutes," I whine. "Val has been pushing us harder in training. My body hurts. That woman is a tyrant."

"Training? Training for what?"

I gasp and cover my mouth. See? I need more sleep. Michael pulls the covers back and begins to tickle me. I kick my legs and squeal as I lose my breath.

"What have you guys been up to? You and I don't have secrets. Talk, my little brat."

"I am not a brat."

"But you will be in trouble if you don't start talking."

"Bella training. Val calls us bellas. After Ellen's demise, Val thought all the wives should train. When we all get together, we are training," I gasp out as he continues to tickle me.

"Why am I not surprised," Michael grumbles as he finally shows me some mercy.

"I have told you. Now can I go back to sleep? I will be grumpy today if you fail to allow me some more rest."

"Fine. Your gifts can wait."

He lies down in bed next to me and looks up at the ceiling. I go to lie back down but his words settle in, and I become excited.

"Gifts? What gifts?"

"You will see when you wake up."

I blink at him like he's crazy. How am I to sleep now? I get up and rush into the bathroom.

Quickly, I brush my teeth and shower. When I return to the bedroom, Michael is still lying right where I left him. I move into my closet and throw on leggings and a sports bra.

Once I have my trainers on, I head back out to the bedroom. Michael still hasn't moved.

"Well, come on. You have a gift for me. Let's go."

He chuckles and sits up on his elbows. I fold my arms across my chest and glare at him defiantly. He gives me a look I don't understand, confusing me.

"What is this look, Michael? I don't understand. You said you wanted me to wake up," I rant in Italian.

When he does nothing more than purse his lips to stifle his laughter, I continue my rant. Still speaking his mother tongue.

"I have gotten up. Now you sit there with this look. I'm tired and everything aches. Do you know what that woman had to put my body through to get me to hurt like this?

"I will not play these games with you. Nope, not today. You want to be a stupid buttface; you do so by yourself."

Michael roars with laughter as he stands from the bed and comes over to me. He wraps his arms around my waist and hugs me tightly.

"You are so adorable when you're angry. We will talk about this bella training, but first I have something to show you. I love you."

"If you love me, you would have let me rest. I still don't understand this face you make."

"I adore you. It is a look of love and adoration. It hit me in that moment that I can't see my life without you."

"Oh," I say.

He pecks my lips and laces his fingers with mine. My face is flaming. I didn't mean to get so upset.

"Sorry, I've never seen you look at me like that."

"Don't apologize. I love watching you turn into an Italian grandmother. Mama would be proud."

"Speaking of your mother, is she still upset with you?"

"We spoke this morning. She's coming back and would like to spend time with you. I might still have some groveling to do, but she's had secrets of her own that I have been angry about. We will come to a compromise," he says and shrugs.

My mother-in-law, Donatella, was not allowed to know about me. When she did find out Michael had been married for sixteen years, she was angry she wasn't trusted to know about me. She was hurt and, as she expressed to me—wished she had the chance to help.

I love her and wish she had been around more. However, I understand why she couldn't be. Roberto Zuko would have used me against them all.

"I will be happy to see her. Will Adriano be returning soon?"

"Close your eyes," he says as we get out of the bedroom.

"What?"

"Close your eyes and turn around, I'm going to blindfold you."

"Okay." I turn as excitement fills me.

Once the blindfold is in place, he wraps his arms around my shoulders from behind and holds me tightly, kissing the back of my head. I'm super curious now that I can't see. We are on the second floor. I hope we don't have to go down the stairs.

"Trust me," he whispers in my ear.

I nod and begin to step forward as he gives me a gentle nudge. It doesn't take long before he brings me to a stop. I fidget with my fingers in front of me as I wonder where he's taking me.

He releases me, and a few seconds later, there is the sound of a door opening. My heart begins to pound in anticipation. Not able to contain my excitement, I lift onto my toes and lace my fingers together to stretch my arms in front of me and crack my knuckles.

I feel it when Michael steps behind me and places a hand on my hip. He leans in to ghost his face against my neck, his lips slightly brushing my skin. I notice there is an echo around wherever we are.

The blindfold is lifted, and I wait for my eyes to adjust, blinking a few times. Then, my vision comes into focus. I spin around as I take the space in. My mouth falls open. As my brain catches up to what I'm looking at, I fling myself into Michael's arms and kiss him.

"I don't understand, how?"

"I had two of the rooms converted into one. We had the room. Uri was okay with it. You now have all the room you want to dance," Michael says as he smiles back at me.

"But all of this space? Wow, look at the wall of mirrors. It seems to go on for days. The sunlight coming into the space is breathtaking. Look at all the windows. How did you make this happen without me knowing?"

"It took a lot of scheduling and creativity. Val and Uri were a big help, as were Annabella and a few others."

"Is that ..." I race over to the piano sitting in the corner of the room. "This is my piano from Italy. The first one you ever gave me."

"Yes, I thought it belonged here with you."

I can't believe this. I already have a new piano he gifted me. It's downstairs in the music room.

When I asked for a dance studio, this wasn't what I had in mind. I would have been fine with a small room to practice and dance in. However, as I look around this room, I can see all the love that has gone into this studio. From the cool color on the walls to the shiny new hardwood floors and the framed photos of me dancing or playing—it's all breathtaking.

The framed photo Maribel took of me seems like such a lame gift now. Besides, I've had the photo for so long now I'm almost embarrassed to give it to him.

I turn and rush back to him and leap into his arms, wrapping my legs around his waist. I bury my face into his neck and inhale deeply. I didn't think I could fall in love with this man any more than I already am, but … this studio says so much about how Michael gets me.

This space is calming and inspiring. I would love to spend the day here dancing and playing. I think to do just that as Michael holds me tightly in place.

"Happy anniversary, *il mio prezioso amore.*"

"Thank you, Michael. I love it," I sing.

He cups the back of my neck and captures my lips in a searing kiss. It turns heated quickly and I begin to think we are going to christen the studio as he palms my breast over my sports bra while kneading my butt with his other hand.

Michael growls and comes to a halt as his phone rings. Placing me on my feet, he takes out the phone and grunts at it. However, he doesn't look as frustrated as he did when he first put me down.

His eyes are sparkling again. With a huge smile, he holds his hand out for mine. I take his hand and allow him to lead me from the room.

"If I ask, will you tell me where we are going?"

"No."

I pout and squeeze his hand. He returns the squeeze, then lifts my hand to his lips and kisses my fingertips. The gesture puts a pin in my anxiety.

As he leads me downstairs, I can't imagine where we're going. I look back up the stairs longingly, wanting to return to my new studio. However, Michael's excitement rolls off him causing me to focus so I can follow him.

Once in the foyer, I can see lights flashing outside. I turn to look at Michael curiously. He only winks and gives me a blinding smile.

Val and Uri both appear with smiles on their faces. Uri is holding the boys as Vita stands holding onto Val's leg as she looks on as if wondering what's going on with the adults.

I would like to know the same thing as Annabella appears with a face-splitting smile of her own. I notice Salvatore is with her, which makes me wonder where Adriano is once again.

Before I can ask Michael for the second time, he opens the door, and I gasp in shock. There is a flatbed truck in front of the house and it's lowering a brand-new sports car. I look to Michael then look back at the car.

For about two months, he has been teaching me how to drive one of his cars in the garage. He had asked me what kind of car I would like if I had my own. Never in a million years did I think he planned to give me one.

"You bought me a car?"

"Yes, I should have done so years ago. I hope you like it," he replies.

"I don't have a license. It is not legal in New York State for me to drive without a license."

He chuckles as he hands over the key. "I will make sure you are taken to get your license this week. Until then we will continue to practice on the property."

I look at the red car and squeal. This is the best anniversary ever. I bounce in place and clap my hands happily.

"Are you happy?"

"Are you kidding me? Yes, Michael, I am very happy. You will get to fuck me very hard today.

"I will eat breakfast and change into something sexy. I plan to suck your cock too. I am most happy," I say.

Michael's cheeks turn red as Uri, Val, and Annabella laugh. Salvatore is coughing into his hand as he turns away. I cover my mouth as I realize I've brought our dirty talk out in public.

"Oops."

Michael wraps his arms around my head and tugs me into him as he kisses the top of my head. I wrap my arms around his waist and hold him tight.

"Have I ever told you I would change nothing about you? I love you just the way you are, Symphony."

"Good, because I can't change who I am, and I don't want to be anyone else."

"Come, I'm dying to know what's under that tarp," he says.

My cheeks heat. He is speaking of the photo I had shipped in. The one Maribel took for me. I begin to pop my band on my wrist.

"What is the matter?" Michael whispers in my ear.

"I don't think my gift is good enough after all of this."

"I'm sure I will love it."

We go back into the house and move into the drawing room, where I thought I would hide the gift. Too bad he found it last night.

Like a kid, he rushes over to it and flips the tarp off. He steps back and takes in a sharp breath. I wring my hands as I look at the photo of me leaping through the air.

It's funny. In the black and white print—my red slippers being the only pop of color, I'm wearing an all-black costume and red slippers like the tattoo on his forearm. I begin to blink rapidly when I see Michael's eyes mist over.

"I will get you something else," I rush out.

"No, you won't," he chokes out, placing a hand on his hip and lifting his other arm up to his face as if to hold in his emotions.

He looks at me with suspiciously moist eyes and nods a few times. His jaw works and his Adam's apple bobs as he swallows hard once then twice.

"It's perfect. Thank you."

"You are welcome."

Michael

This day has gone better than I could have asked for. When Symphony gave me that breathtaking framed photograph of her, I was floored. It's as if she's leaping from the frame.

It perfectly captures what it's like to watch her on stage. I can't wait to hang it in my office where I can stare at it all the time. I can't believe she didn't think her gift was enough.

As I told her, any chance I get to see her dance is magic, like the very first time all over again. When she said I had never seen her dance, I told her the truth.

I have seen her dance many times. I believe my revelation was the greatest gift I gave her today. The smile on her face after was mine.

It didn't end there. I have taken Sim out for a drive in her new car. Then allowed her to drive around the property for a bit when we returned.

We then returned to the house, where we had a romantic lunch before spending hours in her new dance studio. I have been playing for her while she dances. I'm not nearly as talented as she is, but I've enjoyed her laughter and teasing at my attempt to play for her.

Watching her dance is a gift in itself. This room speaks to her. She has been moving gracefully and happily through it.

The new windows were a perfect touch. Now, as the moonlight spills into the room and bathes her in its light, I'm mesmerized. I play the final notes of the sheet music in front of me and watch as she comes to a graceful pause.

I go to start from the beginning once again, but she stands straight and turns to look at me, shaking her head. "I believe I am done for the night. I didn't mean to get lost in here."

"It's fine. I have been entranced by you. Would you like to go down for dinner?"

"No, I would like to make good on my promise."

"Which promise is that?"

"To let you fuck me. I would like for you to fuck me against the piano, up against the wall and anywhere else you would like."

"Is that so, *bella*?" I ask as I stand and begin to unbutton my shirt.

"Yes, you should have your way with me. You did very good, husband. I am a happy wife."

"Come here," I croon.

Suddenly, she leaps into the air. I catch her in my arms and crush her to my chest. She wraps those powerful legs around my waist.

I take her lips in a deep kiss, devouring her like I've wanted to do all day. When she spoke those words in the courtyard earlier, I wanted to take her inside and fuck her right then and there. Her uncensored words struck me right in my core.

"Did I tell you how sexy it is to see my name on your chest?" she purrs as she traces the tat on my pec.

"No, you haven't."

"I like knowing you are mine and if anyone sees you shirtless, then they know it too. I should get one that says Michael."

I growl and place her on her feet to spin her to face the piano. However, mid-spin, she turns back to me and sinks to her knees. I look down at her as she pulls her arms from her leotard and pushes the fabric down to her waist, revealing her firm, plump breasts.

Her little brown nipples are already erect and begging for my attention. My mouth waters to have them between my lips. However, I am between hers before I can think to make a move.

I groan as she sucks only the tip at first. I grow harder as she continues and begins to add in her hands. My breath hiss through my teeth as I throw my head back and pump my hips.

She hums around me as she really gets into it. Looking down, I find her looking up at me. I suck in a breath as I look into her big, bright eyes with those long lashes framing them.

"Sim, baby, that's so good," I breathe.

Taking my words for encouragement, she begins to take me deeper. Drool begins to drip from the corners of my mouth. I pull out of her mouth and tap the tip on her tongue as she sticks it out.

I love how I don't have to tell her what I like. We have come to know each other so well. I take a step back, knowing what I will find as I look farther down her body.

She has her hand shoved between her legs, playing with her pussy. I stroke myself as I watch for a few beats. When she begins to squeeze and knead her own breast with her free hand, I move back into position and allow her to take me back into her mouth.

She takes me in deep and moans around my length. My toes curl as she sucks me for all I'm worth. I'm growing close, but this isn't how I want to come.

I reach to lift her to her feet. She looks at me with so much lust as I shove her leotard and tights down, then pull them from her legs. I straighten and look over her body as the glow from the moonlight bathes her skin.

Turning her back to my front, I reach over her to close the lid of the piano and press my palm between her shoulder blades to bend her over. I slide into her from behind and grasp her hips. The way she feels as she opens to me and sucks me in pulls a deep growl from me.

She's already so wet. Leaning in, I nip at her ear, then kiss her neck as I rock into her. Wrapping my hand around her neck, I pick up my pace. She lifts on her toes, running from me.

"Michael, shit." She shakes her head as if to clear it.

I can't help kissing all over her skin. I pull out and start a trail of kisses down her spine. Once I reach the base, I lick my way back up slowly.

I grasp her throat again and thrust back into her, capturing her lips and the cry she releases. I kiss her passionately as I drive into her over and over.

I plant my palms on the piano on either side of her and watch as my hips slap against her round, toned ass. Sim throws her upper body across the piano and pounds her fist against it as I pound into her.

"Yes, Michael. You make my body feel so good. I can't stop coming for you. Oh, God, you're so deep."

I chuckle darkly. "That good? My cock has you talking nonsense. *Per chi altro vorresti venire?*"

"You, only you. I have always belonged to you."

"*Fanculo,* Symphony. You make me so fucking hard."

"Good, fuck me harder. I want you so much."

She's so wet the sound mixes with her panting and the sound of our skin slapping together. As I pound into her, I know this is going to be a long night. I've only just begun.

CHAPTER FORTY-NINE

How Could You?

Adriano

Two months later …

"Where the fuck is she?" a guy bellows with a Brazilian accent.

I know the accent well. One of Sim's dance instructors was Brazilian and he loved to flirt with me around campus. I tolerated him as long as he kept his hands to himself.

I place my finger before my lips as I look Julissa in her eyes. I had been in the shower when she came rushing into the bathroom, looking scared. I had just enough time to get us both in the closet to hide, but I didn't have time to grab clothes, only my guns.

We now stand hidden while I have nothing but a towel around my waist. This is my fault. I have been too lax in guarding this woman because of my personal feelings.

Before this, I wanted to kill Michael for sending me here to look after his mistress. I've been with her for two and a half months. I hadn't thought there was any real danger.

I have been making plans to return home to Italy. I no longer have respect for my employer. Now, there are men with guns here and I have to wonder if I have failed in my duties.

"There is no one here. What should we do?" Another heavily accented voice says.

"I will call him. Keep looking. Where could she have gone?"

I strain to hear as the sound of a phone ringing on speaker reaches us. Julissa is shaking like a leaf. If I had to be honest, I can see the attraction.

She is no Symphony, but she is attractive. Both of them have the same Afro-Latina appeal. They are exotic but not in the same way. Julissa's dark eyes and hair cause her to stand out. Symphony's honey-brown hair and big bright brown eyes suck you in, along with her cute nose and perfect full lips.

I shake my thoughts off as the line outside the closet is picked up and a voice comes through the speakerphone. My interest is piqued as an Italian accent flows through the call. My gut tells me this is important.

"Do you have her?"

"No, we have come up empty. She is not in the residence we've been watching. Her and the Cattaneo brother are gone."

I clench my teeth at the mention of my last name. To know who I am, they have been watching us for some time. If they weren't so sloppy, we could both be dead right now.

"How fucking hard is it to kill a retard and her bodyguard? Donati, I can understand. I am handling him on my own for a reason.

"This girl ... she should be dead already. I have run out of time. The Locatellis are setting things in motion.

"If I have to come to America to do this myself, what need do I have of you? If you don't call back in twenty-four hours with confirmation of a kill, consider yourself a victim."

My mind is racing. This is not about Julissa. They are looking for Symphony.

A sharp whistle pierces the air. "Let's go. The wife isn't here. Let's regroup. We need to find her before I have to kill that Italian motherfucker myself. He is getting on my fucking nerves," the guy bellows out.

Julissa and I remain in the closet until they are gone. I give it an extra ten minutes after we hear them leave before I slip out of the closet and make sure they have all gone. I throw on some clothes and find my phone.

Symphony is in danger. I need to make some calls and inform the others of what's going on. I dial Michael's number and get his voicemail immediately.

"*Bastarda*," I growl and bite my fist.

"Adriano, they are after Michael's wife, aren't they?" Julissa asks as she wrings her hands and paces.

"Yes, I believe so."

"We can't just sit here. We have to warn Michael. She means everything to him. Please. We have to do something."

"I am working on that. I have to be honest; I didn't think you cared. If she's out of your way, you can have him to yourself, no?"

"You don't know me," she bites out. "You have had an attitude since you arrived here. Michael is a good friend of mine, and his happiness is important to me. He would be devastated if those men did something to his wife.

"No one knows how much that man loves that woman like I do. You are here because Michael never breaks a promise and he promised me he would make sure I'm safe. That is the only reason you are here.

"I am not his mistress as you have assumed, and he would never choose me over his wife or if something happened to her. Stop trying to judge me and help me help my friend."

I grunt and call Salvatore. Michael's relationship with this woman is none of my business. I need to make sure Sim is safe.

"Brother, *cosa posso fare per lei?*"

"Where is Symphony? I think we have trouble," I reply quickly.

"She and Michael left for Italy. There was an attack on Locatelli's new fiancée and his son. The boss and the family all flew out to the old country for a while.

"The rest of us leave in the evening. What's up?"

"Some guys came here looking for Sim. They think I'm guarding the boss's wife. They want her dead. I wasn't able to reach Micheal."

"This is not good."

"You can say that again. I think we should come with the rest of you. I will be there to join you. For now, I will get us someplace safe."

"I will tell the boss as soon as his plane lands. I will see you later. Be safe, Adriano. I love you."

"*Ti amo, Fratello,*" I say and hang up.

"Pack what you need. We are going to Italy."

Julissa

We have arrived at the safe house. Adriano was adamant that we move here. I have been planning my escape since those men left my apartment.

I will be on my own this time. I can't call Nate and ask for help. Pam and Paige cornered me before Val's outburst and told me not to contact their husbands ever again.

I get it. I totally understand. The pass they gave me the first time was more than gracious.

I was hesitant to call Michael in the first place. Now, I just have this gut feeling like I need to get out of here and away from these people.

Danger finds me when I'm around them. I want to put my past behind me and lay all this to rest. I don't want to cause trouble, and I don't want to find it either.

When those men showed up at my place, I thought it was over. It would have been if not for my noisy neighbor who got himself shot and stuffed back into his apartment, giving me enough time to run and warn Adriano.

"Thank you so much," the woman with the bundle in her arms says with a Russian accent as she steps into the elevator.

Adriano sends me a glare for holding the door for her. He's right; I probably shouldn't have. I look at the woman with her blonde hair and blue eyes.

She smiles back at me as she rocks the little bundle in her arms. She's probably tired and wants to get the baby home. I know I'm exhausted and wish I could sleep for a few days.

We get to our floor and Adriano ushers me out. This isn't as fancy as my apartment building, but it will have to do. We won't be here long.

As soon as I get the chance, I'm taking off. I've seen pictures of Michael's wife. I look nothing like her, so I'm not counting on running into too much trouble getting far away from here.

"Get settled in. I need to make a few calls and then I will go out to get something to eat," Adriano says as we walk into the apartment.

I sigh and nod, moving to find where the bedroom is. I need to lie down. My head is starting to ache.

"Why does it feel like all my shit is catching up to me?" I murmur to myself as I go to face-plant on the bed in the first bedroom I find.

CHAPTER FIFTY

Caught off Guard

Michael

I'm exhausted. For the last week, Sim and I have been on call after call with Don Trovati. It is time. We were scheduled to leave for Italy next week. That was before Sammy and Monique were targeted.

Now, everything is being moved up. Collectively, the dons are making moves and handing over promotions. LaSalle was already in the process. That was the reason for our upcoming trip. We were to follow.

Now it will be simultaneous. The Alliance will be established and revealed to the world. All the planning and chess moves are to be revealed.

"Why do you think Mo was so upset about Sammy's training? He is proficient and it's helping him," Sim says as we ride from the airport to our home in Italy.

Many of the others went to stay at the Mairettie family residence. While I know my brother is there for meetings, I'm tired and need my bed. We can get to business later after I've had some rest.

"He is three. I can understand her concern," I reply.

My phone rings and I groan. The answer is no. I'm not doing anything else at this hour. We are not turning this car around to head anywhere, I'm not taking a life. The only thing I plan on doing at this hour is getting in my bed.

"Hello," I snap into the phone.

"Boss, we have a problem."

"What kind of problem, Adriano?" I huff tiredly.

My brain is barely functioning to allow me to force my eyes to remain open. If the problem doesn't require me to approve someone else doing the work, I'm not going to be of any use.

"Men came here for Julissa, but they weren't here for her. Somehow, they believe she is Symphony. They were here to kill Sim," he says.

"What the fuck did you just say?" I seethe.

"They had Brazilian accents. The man they called was Italian. He mentioned wanting you and your wife dead. He also said something about the Locatellis."

"When did this happen?"

"About six hours ago. I have already moved to the safe house. Her apartment was compromised. We couldn't stay there any longer."

"Thank you, Adriano. I will get back to you with new instructions in a few hours."

"I would like to come to Italy. Symphony is in danger."

"I need you there with Julissa. I will take care of my wife. She is safe with me," I bite out.

"Boss, with all respect. I know Sim better than anyone else. I have been in gunfights with her.

"I know how she thinks. If she were in danger, I would be an asset."

"I will call you with your next instructions."

Without another word, I hang up. Before I turn my gaze on Sim, I can feel the energy has shifted within the vehicle. When I lock eyes with her, hers are burning with anger.

"This is not what you think. Julissa felt like someone was following her. I sent Adriano to stay with her to make sure things were—"

"For two months ... this is where he has been for two months? Do I look stupid to you?" She throws her hands up. "No, do not answer that. Your actions already have. You don't respect me.

"I told you I would not have this. I will not share you with another. You gave her my bodyguard? My friend. What the fuck were you thinking?"

"Symphony," I bark.

I know she's upset, but she's never talked to me like this, and I won't allow it to begin now. The fact of the matter is someone sent killers after who they thought was my wife.

That's the fact that's ringing loudest in my tired brain. Not someone; this was Leonardo. I know that without a doubt. He's the only Italian stupid enough to set something like this in motion.

"You are not and never have had to share me with anyone. She needed help. She's not like you; she can't protect herself and she doesn't have me. I sent Adriano to help her.

"At no point have I been to see her or involved in her life. This is the first time since the first week I sent him to be with her that Adriano has reported anything about her to me. I told him he should only call if there was danger.

"My mind has been on so many other things, on us. I haven't had the time to pull him from watching over her. It slipped my mind."

"Right, it slipped your mind because I haven't been asking after him. Do you love her?"

"No."

"Am I going to have to kill her?"

"Sim, she is nothing for you to worry about. I was messed up after you left without a word. I needed someone to talk to.

"She was a friend. Yes, I tried to date her, but that didn't work out because I was and have always been in love with you. I have always wanted you.

"The only reason I even thought about trying to move on was because I thought I hurt you and we couldn't move forward. I just didn't know what I did or how to fix it—"

"So you give her my bodyguard?"

"Yes," I bellow. "Because I hate him. I hate the way he looks at you. I hate that he has been with you all this time while I have ached to be near you.

"I wanted him out of my face. I was tired of watching him look at you, so I sent him away. Now I'm happy I did. She could be dead, and I wouldn't have known it was because someone was looking for you."

"I don't want to talk to you."

"You don't have to talk, but I need you to listen. You are the most important person in the world to me. Everything I do is for you.

"If I had to choose between you and her, it would be you every time. I'm sorry I have hurt you. I never meant for that to happen.

"I was trying to help a friend who helped me find my way back to you. I was dying without you. Nothing in my world made sense.

"What was the point in all of this if I couldn't have you? It started with me wanting to protect you, but over the years, you began to squirrel your way into my heart. I thought I had hurt you and I ended up in a dark place because of it."

"I hear your words, but they do not fix your actions. You knew how I felt. You should have told me."

"I should have."

Symphony

Right now, I am so mad at myself. I trusted Michael to be honest with me. I thought we had become partners.

If he doesn't care about her, why would he help her and send her my bodyguard? If he is jealous of Adriano, who is my friend, how does he think this makes me feel?

I huff and punch the bed. How can he snore like this when I'm so upset and can't get my thoughts to settle? I want to beat him over his head in his sleep.

Before I do something silly, I get up and climb from the bed. I need some space. My feelings are jumbled and wrapped in anger.

I look at my holster, but I'm too angry to touch it. I can't be sure that I won't pull a pistol and fire it. At the moment, I want to shoot him right in his butt.

"Stupid husband. Stinking liar," I grumble as I turn to leave the room.

I stomp my way through the house. It feels so empty without all the guards that are usually here. Since we left with the family, our men are all coming in tomorrow.

I'm not used to this type of silence. Walking to the sunroom, I decide I want to play to fill in the quiet. It isn't until I get there that I remember my piano is now in New York.

Buttface had it sent there. What does he expect me to play while I'm here? Does he give that woman gifts?

Why did he have to send Adriano to guard her? If something happens to my friend while he's with that woman, I'll never forgive Michael. Adriano should be here—with me.

"Ugh, why can't I stop thinking about this?" I huff as I make my way to the kitchen.

I go to the refrigerator to find something to snack on. Maybe I can eat my feelings away. I think of calling Adriano to ask him about that woman and what's been going on, but I realize I left my phone in the bedroom.

Glancing toward the garage door, I think about going for a drive. I snicker to myself and shake the thought off. I can barely drive in America.

My laughter is cut short as my ponytail is grabbed from behind. The person drags me back a few steps and I'm taken by surprise. I drop the plastic container of fruit to the floor and spin.

When I face my attacker, I grab his wrist with both hands and drop back onto my butt. He still has his hand wrapped around my hair, but not for long. I drive my feet into his hips and push.

When that doesn't free my hair, I take my right foot and kick him in the face with all my might. I keep kicking until he releases my hair and stumbles back. Once I'm free, I leap to my feet and pounce, knocking him to the floor.

Blow after blow, I hit him in the face with my forearm until my body is jolted with blinding pain. I stiffen and begin to convulse. Then everything goes black.

Julissa

I wait for five minutes after Adriano leaves to get us something to eat. As much as I wanted to take a nap, sleep wouldn't come. When Adriano said he was going for food, I realized this was my chance.

If I'm going to make a run for it, it's now or never. This way, I won't be a burden to anyone. I can figure out what's next for me.

The one thing I do know is that I'm done with men until I heal myself. I deserve to find a man who loves me the way Michael loves his wife. Every time he talked about her, there was this look in his eyes.

I should have known I never stood a chance, but I had hoped. Michael is so attractive and has this presence about him. I had wanted to wrap myself in that.

Maybe that's just it. I'm picking the wrong men. Perhaps if I stop looking for powerful men, I'll have more success in a lasting relationship that's healthy and good for me. I sigh and shake my thoughts off.

With my backpack on my back, I open the door to the apartment, ready to restart my life. However, as I open the door, the blonde woman from the elevator is standing on the other side with her bundle of joy in her arms. A nagging feeling settles in the back of my head.

This woman looks familiar in some way. Something about her eyes and coloring. I go to ask her if she needs help with something, but she lifts what I thought was a baby and I'm suddenly staring down the barrel of a gun.

"Oh my—"

CHAPTER FIFTY-ONE

Repercussions

Michael

I wake, inhaling sharply as my phone rings on the nightstand. I bare my teeth and roll over to reach for the device. Why is it so hard to let me sleep?

"Hello."

"Michael, I'm so sorry. All I did was go to get us something to eat. I don't know why she opened the door."

"She knew better than to open the door. Julissa is gone. They killed her."

"They who? Were you followed? Was it the same men? Do they think they have murdered my wife?"

"I don't know. They were gone when I got back. I found her with a close-range wound to the head. I'm so sorry."

Adriano begins to ramble on in Italian, but I'm no longer hearing a thing he's saying. Julissa didn't deserve this. She probably would have been better off without my help.

They were after my Symphony. That bullet was meant for her. Rage fills me as I think of how Adriano could have failed my wife. This could be a very different call.

Suddenly, it dawns on me that Sim is no longer in the bed with me. Something feels off. I know something is wrong.

"I will call you back," I say into the phone as I jump out of bed.

My gaze lands on her holster and my heart drops. She is always armed when she leaves the bedroom. It's something I've come to tease her about.

It's a habit I never realized we all have. What would make her leave this room unarmed? I don't have time to figure it out. I rush through the house, looking for my wife.

When I get to the kitchen and find the refrigerator sitting wide open with a container of fruit spilled across the floor, panic fills me. I rush to the control room to watch the cameras back to see what the fuck happened. This is my fault.

We shouldn't have come here with such a light staff. As I watch the video, I growl at the screens. An animalistic rage rises within me as I watch Sim beat the shit out of one guy until another comes up and tases her.

The asshole who tased her then picked her up and they left out of the garage exit from the kitchen. I slip into a darkness I have never known before. They entered my home and took my wife.

"They are all going to die."

Uri

LaSalle has put his foot into his mouth. I can't say I don't understand his reaction to listening to his woman and son being attacked and feeling helpless. I do, but I know the way he handled things in front of everyone definitely didn't help matters for him.

The problem is things have been set in motion. There is no turning back for any of us. If you have been seated, there is no turning back. This commitment has been sealed.

The bell has rung, and we will all be challenged for our role. From the moment Sam was named Don Locatelli, I could feel the shift in the air. I wasn't surprised by the attack at all.

"I have had enough drama for a week and the day hasn't even started here. I want to get my children in warm beds and find myself in one before I start shooting at people," Val grumbles as I pull her into my arms and kiss her temple.

"I hear you, love. I could use some rest myself. Come, let's get the kids into the car and head to the house."

No sooner than the words leave my mouth, my phone begins to ring. I close my eyes and release a long, slow breath. Nothing good can come from a call at this hour.

I pull the phone from my pocket and see it's Michael. I know he and Sim arrived with Val. However, they seem to have gone to the property rather than come here first.

"Hello."

"He had Sim taken. This ends now. I'm going to kill him. I'm going to kill them all.

"If a single loc on her head is out of place, I'm going to kill every single member of their bloodlines. I am going to soak the soil in their blood, and I don't give a fuck if I have permission to do so," Michael says in a tone so dark I have to wonder if I'm truly talking to my little brother.

"Michael?"

"Julissa is dead. She was killed because they thought she was Symphony. For that fact, I'm going to burn everything they own down. Every family who has helped him. Each one who has been hiding behind his actions, they are going to learn why you don't go after my wife."

With that, Michael ends the call. I stand with my mouth open. There will be no placing a lid on this.

I would do the same if someone tried to harm my Tina. I wouldn't see straight until the problem was hushed. I know that's what Michael is thinking. That's how I trained him.

"Bloody fucking hell," I breathe.

"What? What now?" Val asks.

"Sim has been taken and Julissa was killed. Michael is about to start a war, and I know I can't stop him."

"Wait, I couldn't care less about that trifling ho, but how the hell did her stupid ass get herself killed?"

"From what Michael says, they thought she was Symphony."

"Aw, hell nah. So whoever has her wants her dead? What are we waiting for? Michael needs to set some shit on fire. That means he needs us to have his back.

"We don't fear war. War should fear us. We're getting our girl back. Let's move. Paige, I need you to watch my babies," Val calls out as she starts for the door.

I grin. I should have known I wasn't going to be able to leave her behind. What I'm not expecting is for Annabella to stand and come to my side as I head for the door.

"They are my family, Uri. Michael has called, I will answer. I'm coming with you."

I wrap my arm around her shoulders and give her a squeeze. My family is full of secrets. I have been training killers since they showed up on my doorstep.

Even Nico understands what we do. He froze, this isn't for him. But Annabella, my sister, will be fine.

I sigh. "I guess it's time for the world to meet the Donatis."

CHAPTER FIFTY-TWO

My Family

Symphony

My family will come for me. I will not die here. Nonno and Uri will come to help me.

I am a fighter. My life doesn't end this way. I look around me as I'm chained up, dangling above the ground.

There has to be a way for me to escape. There are many of them, but if I can get free, I can kill them all.

Twenty-three, twenty-four. I have counted twenty-four different men moving in and out since I've become conscious. A smirk comes to my lips.

They know they aren't safe. That's why they keep moving. One way or another, they are going to die. My family will not allow this to go unanswered.

Not counting on when or who will save me, I discretely work my hands free. The challenge will be holding up my weight once

I have gotten my wrists from the restraints. There is already so much pressure on my upper limbs.

Once I get free, I can use the loose chains around me as weapons. I just need to get free. I will kiss Val for pushing me so hard in training. That is the only way I have the strength to do this. Not even dancing could prepare me for this.

"Good, you are awake." The words are crooned in Italian. I lift my head toward the voice and glare. A younger version of my nonno appears on a platform above me.

"You are not what I was expecting. I never thought to look for an American dancer or musician. Morgan made it sound as if you were completely incompetent.

"That is my fault. I should never have trusted the bastard or his word. Especially not after he begged to keep you after he killed your mother for me. I should have known then he was a fucking liar," the man continues.

His words set my blood on fire. My chest is heaving, and my nostrils are flaring. However, I remain silent.

"Imagine my luck to have my men find you now in the home of the man I planned to have killed," he continues and chuckles.

"Looks like you pissed her off, boss," says the man standing in front of me with one arm folded across his chest as he holds a gun in the other.

His face is all bruised and all the blood vessels in one eye are broken. I note that he's holding his arm to cradle it. From the looks of him, he's the one who grabbed me in the kitchen.

"I'd shut your mouth before she kicks your ass again," the man who looks like Nonno snorts in Italian.

"She got lucky, I slipped on the fruit she dropped," the jerkface says.

"Sure," I scoff under my breath.

"So you do understand us, good. My English is so-so," the guy on the platform says as he gestures with his hand. "I can speak, but I don't like it."

"Say whatever you like, however you like, I don't care," I reply in Italian.

"Once I found out you have been in America all this time, I wasn't sure what language you would understand. It is not like you are Italian, you know. This is the main reason I don't know why my brother thinks he can do what he has planned.

"I wasn't even sure you could speak at all from what Morgan told me. A woman, a *ritardare*, and what do they call them in America? Ah, *sì, a moulinyan*. Alessio must be out of his mind to think you are more deserving of our family than I am."

"I'm sorry you are so misinformed. Allow me to tell you who I really am. I'm a woman, a killer, and the Afro-Latina who's going to take your life right before I take my place at the head of the Trovati family. Call me a retard again and I'm going to make your death painfully slower than I already plan to," I bite out in Italian to make sure he understands me.

He roars with laughter as if I told some joke. I can assure him I meant every word. He is going to die.

"Do you know who I am?" he scoffs. "What do these words you speak mean to me?"

I shrug my aching shoulders. "I don't care who you are. No one will mourn you. They won't even recognize you to bury your body.

"Don't worry. I will make sure you have a headstone. It will read Leonardo Trovati, the murderer who earned his death."

"Ah, so you do know who I am. Good, I wanted you to know who killed you. I also want you to know why I'm going to take your life mercilessly," he says with a smile.

"You talk too much."

"Men who have things to say speak as they need to."

"I don't care for your voice, and I don't need to hear your words. Keep talking and I will cut your tongue out and have it made into the platforms of my slippers for me to dance on your filthy words."

"Oh, I think I like you. What a pity. Your impostor husband murdered two people who were important to me.

"Now I plan to return the favor and record it so he can watch it over and over again. You understand this, no? You are going to die because they couldn't keep you safe. And because my brother tried to give you something that never should have been yours." He seethes, spit flying from his mouth.

I laugh from deep in my belly. The only one here who's going to die will be him and his men. I don't make promises I don't keep.

Just as I get my other wrist free, I drop my eyes to the ground as a thought fills my head. I was so angry with Michael, but I know one thing for sure. He will always protect me.

My family has protected me since the day they came to rescue me from that bad man. Michael has told me of his dark times and all the things he has done to keep me safe. He has killed for me numerous times and never with kindness or mercy—not like the kills we have done together.

A smirk takes over my lips as I look up through my lashes. While this jerk has been talking, I have been plotting an escape of my own. But my family will be here, my husband will come for me.

"You don't believe your words. I can smell your fear from here. You are trying to decide what your options are from this moment forward. Let me help you.

"You can unchain me, and I will slaughter you with kindness. I will even hum as I do so. Or you can keep me here and allow my family to come for you.

"They will not be so kind. You will learn why no one has ever been able to differentiate between the two. Why you all believe there is only one savage with the name Hush.

"It has always been two. The one who slaughters and the one who gives a peaceful death. You have taken me and now there might as well be one.

"My husband can be gentle, but once you touch me, he becomes as savage as his brother. Only the dead know of this secret. You will join them.

"You want to know why my husband and I are the only option to run such a powerful family? We don't talk about who we are; we show you.

"Für Elise" fills the air right as I finish my words. It's not the classical version, it's the one I danced to my senior year with Ximena. The first time Michael hid in the audience to watch me.

While still holding myself in the air, I coil the loose chain beside me around my ankle as this jerk continues to run his mouth. I shift my leg into a *rond de jambe*, moving it away from my other leg. Then, bringing that same leg back across my body in a *battement*, I swing the chain across my body with all the force I can muster.

The chain smacks the jerk I beat up earlier across the face. He spins with the impact and falls to the floor. I believe a few teeth fly out of his mouth, along with blood.

I whimper as pain shoots through my inner thigh. I knew there was a chance I would injure my groin from the weight of the chain, but I took the risk. As I release my hold on the chains above me, I drop into a crouch.

At the same time, four figures drop from above. I know right away the largest one is Michael. The tails of his dark coat float up through the air as he comes down like an avenging angel.

The dark look on his face says all I need to know. They will all pay for this. For every ache I feel, he will make them pay.

"I've got you," Annabella says as she catches me in her arms as Val covers us.

I pull one of Annabella's guns to help as she lifts me to my feet and helps me move forward. I fight through the tears and pain and hold my arm up the best I can to aim and shoot.

"We can't leave Michael," I whimper as they try to lead me out and away from where Michael and Uri are in the middle of a gunfight.

"There isn't a single Donati not leaving this building. Let Annabella take you to safety. I've got this," Val orders. "I promise, sis."

I close my mouth and swallow my words as she says her last three words. I trust Val. I know she means it.

Annabella shoots our way out. My arms are so tired I barely manage to help. I'm more than relieved when we get to the SUV.

Logan stands by the vehicle with a red-haired man. They both have smoking pistols in their hands as they seem to be standing guard.

"Aye, so this is the wee lass the lad has lost his noodle over," the redhead says while opening the back door of the SUV and narrowing his eyes at me. "Where do I know ya from, lass?"

"You killed a man for me once," I say as I remember his face from when I worked for the O'Sheas.

"Aye, the accountant."

"I am not an accountant. I told you this back then."

He chuckles. "Aye, love. I know. That's not why I gave you the name."

Logan lifts me from my feet then helps to place me into the vehicle as the redhead laughs. Annabella jumps in after me and gets to work checking me for injuries. I'm sore, but I don't think I have any life-threatening wounds.

"Thank God, no open wounds. She's okay," Annabella breathes.

Michael

As my sister's words come through the comm, an ounce of my sanity returns. Not much, but enough for me to see the faces of the men I slaughter as they fall to the ground.

I roll my shoulder and toss my coat away. Then, just as swiftly, I drop the two guns I have emptied and reach for two more. I put a bullet into the head of the bastard running toward me as I make my way for Leonardo.

That motherfucker is mine. This ends now. LaSalle sent Logan O'Brien and Ronan McGowan after Uri to let him know we have his full support in finally ending this bastard's life.

"You can't kill me," Leonardo screams in Italian as Uri shoots his gun from his shaking hand. "They will come for you all now."

He looks between the two of us as if he's going to shit his pants. It seems he's trying to figure out who's who. Sweat begins to pour down his face.

"Which one of you is Uri? I can give you power. Between the fear you bring and my connections, we can take over everything," he says.

I release a sinister laugh. As if my brother would betray me. Our family isn't built from such cowardice.

"You mistake me for a bloody sod like you. I would never betray my brother," Uri snarls.

As Uri replies, Leonardo pulls another gun and aims it at me. Uri goes to take his life, but I hold my hand up as I continue to move forward. I knock the gun away from Leonardo's unsteady hand and grab him by his throat, lifting him from his feet.

"You want to know which one of us is Michael Donati, yes?"

I squeeze his throat so tightly I think I might pop his head from his shoulders. "I am him. I am the new don of the Trovati family.

"I am the husband of the woman you have been trying to find and murder for over sixteen years. Not what you were expecting?" I snarl and tilt my head to the side.

"*Tu sei il diavolo*," he chokes out as he looks me in the eyes.

"No, not the devil. I am something far worse."

"The Trovati family will fall under you," he tries to say as I continue to squeeze while I move closer to the edge of the platform, holding him over the edge.

"Then the Donati family will rise in its place. I'm okay with that, as are your brother and mine. I hope you kept that suit and shoes I left for you."

With that, I place my gun under his chin and pull the trigger before dropping him to the ground below. Uri comes to pat me on the back. I turn from looking down over the platform to look at him.

"I'm proud of you. I thought you would make it much worse," he says.

"I'm not done. He didn't do any of this on his own. *Andiamo. Abbiamo alcuni vecchi Don da visitare.*"

I walk away as Uri's laughter fills the air. He already knows this isn't over for me. I will not rest until every one of them has met silence.

CHAPTER FIFTY-THREE

Done

Symphony

As I turn the Trovati family ring on my thumb, I stand looking in the mirror at the black dress I have on. The stretchy fabric molds over my body with ruching down the center. It stops a few inches below my knees.

"You're killing that dress and those heels," Val says as she and Tasha appear behind me.

I look down at the red-bottom heels Val gave me. She said they were a gift for today. The day my husband and I take over my family.

"Thank you," I say. Then I turn to Tasha. "I'm so sorry you had to cut your honeymoon short for this."

"It's business. He should be here. Besides, they ruined my wedding. I'm going to enjoy this," Tasha says, rubbing her hands together.

"I will enjoy it too. Those men had a hand in my mother's death, be it directly or not."

"I'm counting it as directly. They sent the assassin to silence that Morgan Christoph guy, so they have your mother's blood on their hands," Tasha says.

"That's why they needed to cover their tracks," Val adds.

"I will never be able to repay you for finding out what really happened to my mom. I appreciate all the both of you have done for me."

"You are welcome, honey. You're my family," Val says.

"Our family. We take care of ours," Tasha says as she runs her hand up and down my arm.

"Are you ready?" Val asks.

"No. I need help with one more thing."

I bend and turn so one of them can reach the clasp of my necklace. Val removes it for me. I catch the chain and my rings in my palm and remove the rings from the necklace.

"Now I am ready," I say after taking a calming breath.

Michael

This is it. I am finally putting an end to this threat. This is their end. I have made my point.

I have known who I was looking for since I took that case from the Germans. They had their own research on Leonardo and his backers. The problem with the evidence was the program that erased everything once I hacked the database.

It was there long enough for me to read the information but gone before I could back it up as proof or restore it. I have been waiting somewhat patiently for this day.

They have earned all the ceremonies I have granted them up until today. I slaughtered their families as I made them watch. Do I feel an ounce of remorse? Not one bit.

LaSalle was happy to unleash me on all three of my targets after they sent that ambush to his wedding. Misha Krupin is here for the man he lost.

He insisted he get to see this all firsthand. I felt it only right to make this the grand ceremony of it all. They wanted me and my wife dead to prevent this alliance from forming.

This has always been bigger than the two of us, but the two of us will go down in history for the role we have and will play. I sit here to take my crown, but not alone.

"Are we ready?" Don Alessio says as everyone gathers to watch my promotion and my first order of business.

I lift my hand in the air. We can't begin until everyone is in place. I feel more than see her walk up beside me.

She places her hand on my shoulder. I turn my head slightly to see she's wearing her wedding rings for this occasion. Her wedding rings and the Trovati family ring.

I lift her hand to my lips and kiss her fingers before placing it back on my shoulder and covering it to give it a squeeze. I then look up into the eyes of the woman I love. I wink at her and nod my head.

Sim gives me a blinding smile. She then looks to Don Trovati. "We are ready," she says to everyone.

"I want you all to meet the new heads of the Trovati family. My granddaughter, Symphony Isabella Mansilla-Trovati-Donati and Micheal Angelo Donati," Alessio announces.

Cheers of congratulation erupt from the crowd. I stand and tug Sim into my arms to kiss her deeply. She clings to my shirt as she kisses me back.

"Okay, everyone, let's go celebrate and eat," Alessio croons to the crowd.

Everyone files out of the hall until the four men on their knees and the members of the Alliance who are in attendance are the only ones who remain. As the doors are locked, Uri, Val, Annabella, and Adriano all line up behind the four men.

Adriano asked me to allow him to take part in this in honor of Julissa. He has felt guilty for her death. Salvatore and Uri talked me into allowing Adriano to keep his job and his life.

I wasn't going to kill him over Julissa. My anger stemmed from the fact that she could have been Sim. However, it was Sim who saved his life.

She explained how, for a long time, he was the only friend she had outside of me. I couldn't take that away from her. No matter how much I wanted to.

"The four of you didn't want to see this day come to pass. The Alliance, my wife and I taking over the Trovati family, the end of your old era. I'm so happy that I could give you a front-row seat.

"I hope you have mourned your losses well. I put in extra special work to exterminate your bloodlines. You see the difference between doing and trying.

"I guess I was more effective because I did the work myself. I like to get shit done. I see the suits and shoes I sent for you all fit perfectly. Uri?"

"Done," he replies as all four of my executioners finish the job I started.

EPILOGUE

Work to Do

Michael

Ten years later …

"I am thirteen, not three. I understand what you mean, Sim," Sammy says in exasperation.

I grin. Listening to these two argue is always amusing. They are both brilliant and love to challenge each other. Neither likes to be wrong.

Many times, neither is; they're just saying the same thing differently. Symphony is usually the first to give in because she knows she's not wrong and being right is more rewarding for her than winning the fight.

"If you understand, then do as I say," Sim snaps.

She hasn't been as patient with Sammy and his training today. She's been snapping at him more than anything. That's not like her at all.

I can see why Sammy seems to be flustered. "Mommy," Artemis, our son, squeals in my arms.

"Not now, Artemis, Mommy is working," Sim huffs.

I lift a brow. Okay, so she's going to be testy with everyone today. Maybe we should go for a snack.

"Ugh, you were nicer the first time you were pregnant. I will stop coming to visit you if this is how you are going to behave." Sammy scowls at Sim.

I turn to look at my son in my arms and knit my brows. I then turn to look at Sim as she stands with the same expression. Artemis has just turned four.

We weren't planning to have another baby. I close the distance to stand next to my wife. She takes our son from my arms and hugs him tightly to her chest.

She worried her entire pregnancy about the health of our son. I can already see the worry etching into her face. I glance at Sammy.

His eyes are distant for a minute. Then he nods his head and focuses on me. A little grin forms in the corner of his lips.

"*Non mi alzerò da solo. Sarà con tutta la mia famiglia e i miei amici. I re continueranno, ma anche le regine. Andiamo. Abbiamo del lavoro da fare,*" he says and turns to walk away.

I kiss my wife passionately. It looks like we'll be having a girl. Marrying this woman was one of the best decisions of my life.

Blue Collection Character Tree
Legally Bound 1
Bobby Mairettie and Paige Kemble-Mairettie.
Father and mother of:
      Peyton and James Mairettie (*twin boys*)
      Sydney Mairettie and Maria Lynn Mairettie (*twin girls*)

Legally Bound 2
Marcus Mairettie and Rita Briggs-Mairettie.
Father and mother of:
      Daniel Mairettie
      Hannah Mairettie

Legally Bound 3
Nathaniel (Nate) Briggs and Pamela (Pam) Kemble-Briggs.
Father and mother of:
      Tiffany and Tracey Briggs (*twin girls*)
      Nathaniel Briggs Jr.

Legally Bound 4
Jasper Briggs and Marie Mairetti-Briggs.
Father and mother of:
      Clay Briggs

Legally Bound 5
Sam Mairettie, a.k.a. LaSalle Samuel Locatelli and Monique Natasha Gabriel, a.k.a. Tasha Locatelli.
Father and mother/stepmother of:
      Jessica Mairettie Locatelli (mother, Ellen, *deceased*)
      Megan Mairettie Locatelli (mother, Ellen, *deceased*)
      Sammy Mairettie Locatelli (mother, Ellen, *deceased*)
      Elijah Locatelli
      Paulie Locatelli
      Karen Locatelli
      Sunny Locatelli

The Mairettie Family

Grandpa Marcello Mairettie and Grandma Marie Ann.
Father and mother of:
   Marcello Mairettie Jr.
   Andrew Mairettie
   James Mairettie
   Jessie Mairettie
   Lynn Mairettie
   Gianna Mairettie
James Mairettie and Minnie Mairettie.
Father and mother of:
   Bobby Mairettie
   Sam Mairettie (Ellen Kensington-Mairettie, *wife*)
   Marcus Mairettie
   Marie Mairettie

The Briggs Family

Thomas Briggs and Raquel Marinos-Briggs (***deceased***).
Father and mother of:
   Nathaniel Briggs
   Rita Briggs
Earl Briggs (younger brother of Thomas) and Caitronia Marinos-Briggs (twin sister of Raquel).
Father and mother of:
   Kelly Briggs-Fecteau (Alexie Fecteau, *husband*)
   Jasper Briggs

The Kemble Family

Peyton Kemble and Davina Kemble.
Father and mother of:
   Pamela Kemble
   Paige Kemble

Other Important Legally Bound Characters

Camille (Cam) McWien-Carter (Seth Carter, *soon to be ex-husband*).
   Father and mother of:
   Seth Carter Jr.
   Eddie Carter
   Aiden Carter
Austin Mc Wien (*Camille's father*)
Baroness Olivia Kontos (Baron Kontos' widow. *Ex-lover of Jasper/Thomas Briggs's new love interest*)
Vanessa (Julissa) Smith-Mims (***deceased***) (Patrick Mims, *husband,* ***now deceased***)
Czar Gabriel (Tasha's brother)
Brenda Gabriel (Tasha's sister)
Kurtrina Gregory (Tasha's sister)
Keisha Gregory (Tasha's sister)
Senator Roland Gabriel (Tasha's father)
Yolanda Gabriel (Tasha's mother)
Misha Krupin and Keisha Gregory (now ***deceased***).
      Father and mother of:
         Milanie Krupin
         Faina Krupin
         Pavel Krupin (***deceased***).
Logan O'Brien and Raven Johnson (***deceased*** *girlfriend of Logan*).
      Father and mother of:
         Shauna O'Brien
DJ, a.k.a. Desha
Phoebe Romaine (Ellen's grandmother, **deceased**)
Fifika Romaine (***deceased***)
Salvador Romaine (Ellen's uncle)
Uncle Alfanzo Locatelli
Marco Locatelli
D'Angelo Locatelli
Uncle Carlo Locatelli

Shura
Afanasy

Hush 1
Uri Donati and Valentina Caprisi-Donati.
Father and mother of:
Vita Khayla Donati
Nori Donati
Inzo Donati
Eva Donati

Hush 2
Luca Donati and Shannon Caprisi-Donati.
Father and mother of:
Carlo Donati (Introduced in Ballers 2)

Hush 3
Michael Angelo Donati and Symphony Isabella Mansilla-Trovati-Donati.
Father and mother of:
Artemis Donati
Baby on the way

The Donati Family
Angelo Uri Donati (*deceased*) and Donatella Manzo-Donati~~Zuko~~.
Father and mother of:
Uri Donati
Nico Donati ~~Zuko~~
Annabella Donati ~~Zuko~~ (*Nico's twin sister*).
Michael Donati ~~Zuko~~

Uncle Nicholas Donati (brother of Angelo Donati) and Ava Donati.
Father and mother of:

Luca Donati

The Caprisi Family
Vincent Caprisi and Khayla Grant-Caprisi (*deceased*).
Father and mother of:
    Valentina Caprisi
    Lissette Caprisi (*deceased*)
    **Shannon Caprisi (*Vincent's daughter*)

Other Important Hush Characters
Uncle Valentine Caprisi (*Vincent's Brother, head hitter*)
Iman Grant (*Khayla Sister, **Shannon's mother, **deceased***)
Roberto Donati – Zuko (*Donatella's husband, **now deceased***)
    **Posed as Dale, the accountant from Legally Bound 3*

Cole "Brooklyn" O'Brien
DJ, a.k.a. Desha

Ballers 1
Bradley Monroe and Tamara Hathaway-Monroe.
Father and mother of:
    Brielle Monroe
    Ashley Monroe and Ashton Monroe (twins)
    Corey Monroe (*baby Tam is pregnant with at end of Ballers 1*)

The Monroe Family
Vernon Monroe and Gloria Monroe.
Father and mother of:
    Trevor Monroe (Donna, *soon-to-be ex-wife*)
    Bradley Monroe
    Ann Monroe (Bradley's twin sister) (Tom, husband)
Trevor Monroe and Donna Monroe.
Father and mother of:
    Jessica Monroe
    Toby Monroe and Paige Monroe (*twins*)

Jonathan Monroe
Tom Rivers and Ann Monroe-Rivers.
Father and mother of:
George Rivers and Melissa Rivers (*twins*)
Amy Rivers

The Hathaway Family
Byron Hathaway and Fiona Hathaway.
Father and mother of:
Ellerie Hathaway
Tamara Hathaway

Other Important Ballers Characters
Stacey (Tam's best friend)
Reese (Tam's best friend, Nico's girlfriend in Ballers 1)
Alee (Tam's best friend)
Cyrus Pierson (Tam's boss).
Father of:
Tommy Pierson
Carey Pierson
Stephanie Pierson

Ballers 2
Nico Donati and Reese Bridges-Donati.
Father and mother of:
Nico Jr. Donati
Lanya Donati
Orso Donati
Santo Donati
Stefano Donati

Ballers 3
Cameron Perry and Maribel Amina Jones a.k.a Amina.
Father and mother of:
Cade Perry
Chance Perry

Cecilia Perry

Pieces of Trevor's Heart
Trevor Monroe and Lynn "Cakes" Galveston.
  Father and mother/stepmother of:
    Jessica Monroe (mother, Donna, ***deceased***)
    Toby Monroe a.k.a Scoot and Paige Monroe a.k.a Snacks
(*twins*) (mother, Donna, ***deceased***)
    Jonathan Monroe a.k.a Bam (mother, Donna, ***deceased***)
    Brooklyn Valentina Monique Monroe a.k.a Twinkle
    Brandon Moses Monroe a.k.a Bird
    Clifton Travis Vernon Monroe a.k.a Doc

Other Important Ballers Characters
Tiberius Roman (Reese's ex-husband)
Symphony (Michael's right hand)

Brothers Black 1
Wyatt Black and Lanelle (Nellie) Bryant-Black.
  Father and mother of:
    Nora Black
    Evan Black (*born during Brothers Black 2*)

The Black Family
Joseph Black and Cassidy Black.
  Father and mother of:
  Wyatt Black
  Noah Black
  Johnathan Black
  Felix Black
  Toby Black (Kamara, *baby mother.* TJ and Lulu, *son and daughter, twins.*)
  Braxton Black

Ryan Black

The O'Brien Family

Logan O'Brien
Cole "Brooklyn" O'Brien
Connie O'Brien
Kate O'Brien
Jamie O'Brien
Dylan O'Brien

The Lockhart Family

Lockhart Brothers
Rob Lockhart
Steve Lockhart
Chase Lockhart
Rob Lockhart and Faith Lockhart.
　Father and stepmother of:
　　Heather Lockhart
Steve Lockhart and Nora Bryant-Lockhart (***deceased***).
　Stepfather and mother of:
　　Lanelle (Nellie) Bryant-Black
Chase Lockhart and Jennifer Lockhart.
　Father and mother of:
　　Rebecca (Bean) Lockhart (Noah's best friend and love
interest.)

Other Important Brothers Black 1 Characters

Missy (Johnathan's ex-girlfriend, ***deceased***)
Lucy (*Heather's girlfriend*)
Barry Coleman (***deceased***)
Joshua (***deceased***)
Carmen Nash, a.k.a. Nene (*reporter, Mariah Briggs, from Yours Series, niece, Ryan's new crush*)
Logan O'Brien

Brothers Black 2

Noah Black and Rebecca (Bean) Lockhart-Black.
>   *Father and mother of:*
>> Brodie Black
>> Connor Black
>> *Baby on the way*

Yours Series

Nicholas Lincoln and Sephora (Sophi, a.k.a. Soph, a.k.a. Lilla du) Emilsson.
>   *Father and mother of:*
>> Nicole Lincoln
>> Nadia Lincoln
>> Nicholas Lincoln Jr.

The Lincoln Family

Dean Lincoln and Shelly Lincoln (***both deceased***).
>   *Father and mother of:*
>> Nicholas Lincoln
>> Rick ~~Carbon~~ Lincoln
>> Gavin ~~Carbon~~ Lincoln

The Emilsson Family

Liam Emilsson (*was thought to be deceased*) and Faraz Emilsson.
>   *Father and mother of:*
>> Lucian Emilsson
>> Ettie Emilsson
>> Sephora Emilsson

Lucian Emilsson and Kimberly Ann Clove.
>   *Father and mother of:*
>> Lilla Emilsson

Other Important Yours Characters
Mark Fienberg (Sephora's best friend)
Ivana Graves (Nick's ex-girlfriend, deceased)
Bianca (Liam's mistress, missing)
Winton (Nick's driver and security)
Jillian Carver (Nick's ex-temporary PA, *deceased*)
Harvey Carver (Jillian's father and Nick's family friend, *deceased*)
Bailey Wilder (waitress, Mark's girlfriend)
Dylan O'Brien

Nick's crew
Wyatt Black
Kevin Briggs (*wife* Mariah Briggs, *Nick's PA*)
Craig Hilton
George Ligal
Lucian Emilsson
Andrew Connor (*Ettie's husband*)

ABOUT THE AUTHOR

Blue Saffire, award-winning, bestselling author of over seventy contemporary romance novels and novellas, writes with the intention to touch the heart and the mind. Blue hooks, weaves, and loops multiple series, keeping you engaged in her worlds. Blue writes for her own publishing company, Perceptive Illusions as Blue Saffire, as well as Royal Blue.

Blue and her husband live in a house filled with laughter and creativity in Long Island, NY. Both working hard to build the Blue brand and cultivate their love for the arts. Creative is their family affair.

Blue holds an MBA in Marketing and Project Management, as well as an MED in Instructional Technology and Curriculum Design. She is also an NLP Master Practitioner.

ACKNOWLEDGMENTS

OMG! This book gave me life. All the small details and pulling it all together after not being in this universe for so long. I fist-pumped at the end of this one. Sim turned out to be all I wanted and more. So did Michael. I'm excited to be in this universe again and looking forward to all that's next. I'll be letting off a lot of books that have been living in my head from these worlds.

Thank you for your patience and your time. I appreciate you rolling with me through this journey.

Once again, my dear reader friends, thank you so much for your continued support. We're one more book closer to The Alliance and Sammy's book. Thank you for the encouraging emails, videos, posts, shares, and DMs. Many hugs and much love.

I am so grateful and thankful to God. I give him all the glory. I love you with all my heart and thank you for continuing to bless me and this pen. Thank you for allowing me to grow and giving me a heart to want to. As always, unapologetically blessed and highly favored.

Next! *Ronan: Kings of New York. We're finally opening Brooklyn and Logan's series. Let's go.*

Wait, there is more to come! You can stay updated with my latest releases, learn more about me, the author, and be a part of contests by subscribing to my newsletter at

www.BlueSaffire.com

If you enjoyed *Hush 3*, I'd love to hear

your thoughts and please feel free to leave a

review on my website. And when you do, please let me

know by emailing me TheBlueSaffire@gmail.com

or leave a comment on Facebook https://www.facebook.com/BlueSaffireDiaries or Twitter @TheBlueSaffire

Other books by Blue Saffire

Placed in Best Reading Order

Also available....

Legally Bound

Legally Bound 2: Against the Law

Legally Bound 3: His Law

Perfect for Me

Hush 1: Family Secrets

Ballers: His Game

Brothers Black 1: Wyatt the Heartbreaker

Legally Bound 4: Allegations of Love

Hush 2: Slow Burn

Legally Bound 5.0: Sam

Yours 1: Losing My Innocence

Yours 2: Experience Gained

Yours 3: Life Mastered

Ballers 2: His Final Play

Legally Bound 5.1: Tasha Illegal Dealings

Brothers Black 2: Noah

Legally Bound 5.2: Camille

Legally Bound 5.3 & 5.4 Special Edition

Where the Pieces Fall

Legally Bound 5.5: Legally Unbound

Brothers Black 4: Braxton the Charmer

Broken Soldier

Brothers Black 5: Felix the Watcher

A Home for Christmas

Doctor Feel Good

Brothers Black 6: Ryan the Joker

Brothers Black 7: Johnathan the Fixer

Wild Hearts

Pieces of Trevor's Heart

Ballers 3: His Team

Coming Soon...

King of Gods Book 4: Immortal Iron Brothers Series
King of Past Book 5: Immortal Iron Brothers Series
Ronan Book 1: Kings of New York Series

Other Blue Saffire Series

Hold On To Me Series
My Funny Valentine
Be My Valentine

Hitter Squad Series
Remember Me

Work Husband Series
Unexpected Lovers
My Best Friend's Wish
The Ones Left Behind
The Last Ones Standing

The Lost Souls MC Series
Forever
Never
Always

The Moran Brothers Series
Love Notes
Stay With Me

The A**hole Club Series
Pit Book 1: The A**hole Club
Ox Book 5: The A**hole Club
Kelex Book 6: The A**hole Club

Immortal Iron Brothers Series
King of Knights Book 1
King of Inferno Book 2
King of Tides Book 3

Check out Blue Saffire exclusives on the
BlueSaffire.com website
The Fixer
His Miracle Baby
Razor

Dane
Trip
Professor Jones
Room 112

Other books from Evei Lattimore Collection Books by Blue Saffire
Black Bella 1

Destiny 1: Life Decisions
Destiny 2: Decisions of the Next Generation
Destiny 3 coming soon…

Star

Other books from Royal Blue Gay Romance Collection written by Blue Saffire
Kyle's Reveal
Beau's Redemption

www.ingramcontent.com/pod-product-compliance
Lightning Source LLC
Chambersburg PA
CBHW051517260626
47170CB00003B/655